Dodos in

A COMEDY ABOUT STELLAR BIRDS

Matthias Hirthe

Dodos in Space

A COMEDY ABOUT STELLAR BIRDS

This book you're reading is a work of fiction. Names, events, places and characters, dodos or otherwise, are the product of this author's imagination. Any resemblance to other events, locations or persons, living, dead or Schrödinger's cat, is coincidental.

All rights reserved. No part of this publication may be reproduced or transmitted, in any form or by any means, electronic, mechanical, subspace or otherwise, without the written consent of the copyright owner.

Published in Germany as *Dodos im Weltall* by Matthias Hirthe in 2022
Original text copyright © Matthias Hirthe 2022
English translation copyright © Matthias Hirthe 2024
First English edition published in Germany with Bookmundo Direct in 2024

Second English edition. © Matthias Hirthe 2024
Published in Leipzig, Germany in 2024 with Kindle Direct Publishing.

Matthias Rädisch, Delitzscher Str. 134, 04129 Leipzig, Germany
raedisch.matthias@gmail.com

Copy-edited by Christina Howell

Cover design: Created with canva.com, Matthias Rädisch

Cover illustration © Stefan Büttner 2019

ISBN: 9798321487419

Special thanks to Matthew Perkins, Rælf Ó Bad,
Sylvia Woodham and Javier.

Contents

1 The Birds of Paradise
2 A Thousand Tiny Lights
3 Birds of a Feather Flock Together
4 In the Vicinity
5 Captain, Where Are We Going?
6 One Fell Over the Dodo's Nest
7 Once Upon a Time in the Milky Way
8 The Waiter
9 Witnesses for the Prosecution
10 About Time
11 Lost in Space Vortex
12 Hatched to Survive
13 Soar in Peace

Prologue

"Yoo-hoo! Hello there! I'm a dodo!" said a gullible dodo to the first sailor who came ashore on the island of Mauritius in 1507. "Who are you, and what are you doing here? And why do you keep staring at my big bottom? *Meat?* I don't see meat anywhere. We're all vegetarians here, tee-hee."

It was a fateful encounter because all the hungry sailor saw, as he stared at the dodo waddling towards him of its own free will, was poultry. Poultry that couldn't even fly away. It was also the beginning of the end for the flightless birds.

Over the following decades, more and more ships reached the island, but the dodos retained their trusting nature and, as befitted generous hosts, welcomed their visitors with open wings. In return for their belief in the 'goodness of human beings,' the quirky birds ended up in people's cooking pots or on the barbecue.

So it was that the dodos became extinct (on Earth) around the year 1690. Their end seems all the more tragic when you consider that they had once lived in a progressive, ultra-modern society...

Chapter 1: The Birds of Paradise

Earth, Mauritius, in the year 1313.

Just before midnight, two hundred dodos were sitting on the roof of a half-ruined building that had once been the island's tax office (a long time ago, when dodos still used money). Among the great mass of birds were Dirk and Hookbeak, best friends since chickhood.

"Four! Three! Two! One!" Dirk shouted along with the crowd as colourful fireworks lit up the night sky. *The Year of the Mean Ducks* had just begun. The more absurd the name of a year in the dodo calendar, the more accurately it was said to predict the future.

"Well, look at that," said Hookbeak, "the fireworks are quite something this year."

"Yes," responded Dirk without much enthusiasm. "But it's kind of the same every year."

In the middle of the old roof, three dodos had got to their feet to get a better look at the fireworks. One of them was bouncing gleefully, until he and his two companions crashed through the roof and landed on a pile of fifty-thousand aged and yellowed tax notices.

"What a bunch of bozos," muttered Dirk.

"There you go," said Hookbeak cheerfully. "A hole in the roof, that's something new."

Dirk and Hookbeak could hardly have been more different, apart from their long, hooked beaks and stocky bodies, which accompanied all dodos through life. You could say the two friends were two sides of the same coin.

On the shiny side you would find Hookbeak, one of the brightest minds on Mauritius, whom female dodos adored for his ingenuity. As an architect and engineer, he could build almost anything he imagined, which is why male dodos gave him the suspicious eye.

The rusty side of the coin belonged to Dirk, an entirely average dodo who lived his life not 'to the fullest' but 'to the emptiest'. This was mainly because he was bored. Like ninety per cent of the population, he had neither a job nor a purpose in life because there was so little to do on Mauritius, the land of fruit and honey. No one had to earn their food; it simply grew in abundance. That's why most of the island's residents lay on the beach, day in, day out, and filled their bellies with fruit salad.

What a terribly dull pastime, thought Dirk. For years, he had been living his life differently from other dodos. He only visited the beach every other day and spent the rest of the time in his hut watching talk shows on TV.

Hookbeak's gaze wandered from the fireworks back to his friend.

"You look upset, Dirk. Is everything all right?"

Hookbeak stood out from the crowd like no other dodo. Anyone who saw him was flabbergasted by his red mohawk, which stretched from the top of his head to his tail feathers. Thanks to his 'feather-style', he towered over his more than three-foot-tall compatriots by an extra foot. He also had a beak-piercing to round off his striking appearance.

"Oh, sure. Everything's fine," Dirk answered evasively. It was the most common lie in the universe. "Look at that golden rocket," he said quietly, pointing to a firework. "It could almost be mistaken for a new constellation."

Dirk was indeed feeling down that night, and he blamed his afternoon nap. He had dozed off on the sofa after lunch (there had been a 'Guess the Bird' quiz show on TV), and he had been dreaming of being able to fly. After a little trip to the neighbouring island of Réunion, he sat down on a cloud, put his feet up and invited passing geese over to join him. Soon after, the geese asked him why his cloud tasted not like candyfloss but like water droplets. In an instant he had woken up from his beautiful dream in a state of confusion.

As the explosions of the fireworks continued relentlessly in the night sky above them, Dirk thought of his ancestors from the mists of time. He thought of how shocked they must have been when they suddenly found themselves earth-bound. It was thousands of years ago now since evolution shrank the dodos' wings and forced them to give up flying. They had been compensated for their loss with large bottoms, which they would have traded back for their old wings in a heartbeat, but evolution found the sight of the dodos too funny and refused the deal.

To heck with evolution! thought Dirk. *Why do I still dream of flying when no other dodo does?*

"Are you really okay, Dirk?" asked Hookbeak.

Dirk merely nodded. Even back in his school days, he had imagined he could fly, but had kept that to himself so as not to be laughed at. It just wasn't considered 'modern' to let your primal instincts take over like that. The fact that he had dreamt about flying during his nap today didn't make things easier for Dirk. Quite the contrary. In his dream, being able to fly seemed real and within reach.

Dirk was, of course, aware that his most fervent wish was not about to come true. Though it would have been technically possible to build a flight-thingy... air-thingy... air-craft, or whatever it would have been called, he still had his bird pride to consider and wanted to use his own wings.

Hookbeak had no idea why Dirk looked so gloomy. He decided to try and distract him.

"Have you spotted Popin and Jay anywhere up there?" asked Hookbeak.

"No chance," said Dirk. "It's too dark. I only see silhouettes of parrots when the rockets explode."

The dodos kept small green parrots as pets, who could quickly fly to the pharmacy on a Sunday evening, long after tea time. But on the whole, these echo parakeets behaved like cats. They were stubborn and did exactly what they wanted to do, but never what they were supposed to. At this moment, they were having fun playing *Get Away,* an extreme sport they only practised at the turn of the year. The rules of this sport were very simple: Three parrots rode up into the night sky on a firework and had to 'get away' at the last moment before the rocket exploded. Whoever jumped off last and survived won their round. Dead winners were automatically disqualified.

Several thousand parrots – mostly unmarried males – took part in this thrilling tradition, which claimed a few victims every New Year's Eve.

While the pets were thus having a great time, Dirk was still not feeling festive.

"Look, Dirk," said Hookbeak. He thought he had worked out why his friend was in a bad mood. "The young lady behind us seems to be here alone."

Out of curiosity, Dirk turned his head to one side as casually as he could manage. His eyes fell on a female dodo, who, at this very hour, was cleaning her blue-grey plumage with her beak.

In and of itself, it was perfectly normal for a dodo to clean her feathers with her beak, but if she did it in public on New Year's Eve, she was more bored than a fish in a swimming lesson.

"You're right, Hooky," said Dirk. "I'll go and talk to her."

All dodos were equally unattractive, which is why when choosing a mate, they placed great value on personality and intelligence. The latter, however, was rarely a given.

"Hey there..." began Dirk, inclining his head towards her, which was just as her mobile phone rang.

She had received a voice message and interrupted her grooming. She didn't seem to give a thought about privacy and listened to the message over her phone's loudspeaker.

"Hey, Isolde. I'm not doing so good. I wish I could just bury my head in the sand. Can you come over? Bring some grape juice – some fermented grape juice, please! We need to talk about love."

"My name is Isolda, not Isolde, you silly goose!" the female shouted at her phone.

Dirk gave Hookbeak a look and whispered, "Nah. I don't think me and Isolda are meant to be. The lady in the voice message sounded nice, though."

A few seconds later, their parrots flew down to join them. The pets had run out of rockets.

Popin settled herself on Dirk's comfortable back. They often called her '*Pops*', an unusual name for a female parrot.

Her twin brother, Jay, had completely disappeared into Hookbeak's featherdo.

"Are you hurt, Jay?" Hookbeak asked.

"Argh! Singed wing!" Jay said from inside Hookbeak's mohawk. He sounded almost happy about it.

"And you, Pops?" Dirk asked his parrot.

Popin shook her head until she realised that Dirk couldn't see her on his back. "Argh, am unhurt," she finally announced.

"Good girl," said Dirk, pleased.

They left the roof by way of the rickety old staircase because the lift in the old tax office was out of order.

🌿

Despite their peaceful island life and their great appliances (like dishwashers and vibrating massage chairs), the dodos were rarely happy. They often whined about the tropical climate that had made Mauritius such a magical, eternal paradise in the first place. They would complain brazenly that they were fed up with the hot temperatures. And then, when they received a little relief from the refreshing rain, they grumbled about the lousy weather that had spoilt their day at the beach.

What the dodos complained about even more than the weather and the climate were their partners. When their mates no longer brought enough variety into their lives, they would send them packing, with a heavy heart.

But all these things the dodos complained about were excuses because they didn't want to recognise the real reason for their sorrow. And therefore, it was hardly surprising that many dodos buried their heads in the sand and only took them out again when Doctor Birdex Pert, the island's best-known psychologist, appeared on the television.

In a TV studio, two hundred dodos in the audience anxiously awaited the end of the uncommercial break.

Dr Birdex Pert (whom everyone called *Birdie*) was sitting on one of the two chairs in the centre of the stage. Her beak was being touched up by a make-up artist, and she found it very unpleasant. She waved the make-up artist away with her wing.

"Li-Ming, stop it!" demanded Birdie. "I'm on again in two minutes!"

"No, Birdie," said Li-Ming without pausing. "You have to look as beautiful after the break as before. Do you have any idea how fast dust mites multiply?"

Birdie blinked, then raised her eyebrows. "Huh. Dust mites. I'm not sure. I should probably know, but I've never been interested in dust mites. Why? How fast do they multiply?"

"I don't know either, but I keep brushing your beak in case they are doing it real quick."

"Cut it out," Birdie said, "or I'll tell my parrot never to play with your parrot again!"

"Ha ha, that's a good one," said Li-Ming. "Just try to stop them. All right, I'm done. Have fun."

On her way out of the studio, the make-up artist nearly collided with Birdie's next guest at the door.

Her guest was none other than the island's Minister of Health. He sat down opposite Birdie.

"Hi there, Bobby," said Birdie. "Did you catch my interview with that charming cult leader?"

"No, I was drinking with the president at a beach bar," he said.

"Why doesn't that surprise me?" muttered Birdie.

"Excuse me?"

Birdie cleared her throat as the red lights on the cameras lit up.

"Dear viewers," she said, "Welcome back to 'Trouble in Paradise: First World Problems'. I'm your favourite psychologist and your host, Doctor Birdex Pert. My next guest is the Minister of Health. Good evening, Minister Bobby."

"Hello, Birdie... er, Doctor Pert."

"It's all right, Bobby," said Birdie. "Good to have you here. Today we want to talk about why we're unhappy. Unhappiness has been a problem for us dodos for as long as we can remember. I think it's time to get to the bottom of it. Bobby, please tell us: What are the most common reasons for our misery according to the Health Department?"

"Well, one of the top three reasons is a four-letter-word. Love," the health minister said. "Or rather, that it's so hard to find real love. Then, of course, there's the terrible heat, not to mention this rain all the time! And when I look in the mirror, at my butt, well, it's not exactly nice to look at. These are the reasons why we're unhappy, am I right?"

"No, you're dead wrong," Birdie said bluntly.

"*Is that so?*" he asked.

Love, heat, rain, butt – that's four *four-letter words*, noticed Birdie's mind. She told her mind to never mind.

"Well?" said Bobby.

Birdie cleared her throat again. "Ahem. We think we are unhappy because we can't find the right gentle-bird or lady-bird, but it has nothing to do with dating. Nor are the climate or our weight responsible for our sorry state. No, my dear. Your unhappiness – the unhappiness of every one of us – stems from knowing who you are. You will always be aware of what you are."

The Minister of Health stared at the psychologist in confusion, his hooked beak hanging open.

"My dear Birdie," he said in dismay, "you think I am to blame for the suffering of every single dodo?"

Birdie wondered how the health minister had misunderstood her statement so profoundly.

"I beg your pardon?" she said. "I didn't mean you alone, but our whole species. Our consciousness is the cause of our grief!"

Birdie belonged to the roughly ten per cent of the population who pursued a profession because it either gave them a purpose in life or because their work was important. Among these professionals were technicians, doctors, journalists and beach bar operators, who all made everyone's life even more horribly luxurious.

Before continuing, Birdie turned to the camera to speak directly to the television audience. She was a media professional, after all.

"We all know we are the pinnacle of evolution on this planet," she said, "yet we also know that we will always remain birds. Aye, there's the rub. What are we doing here on our island? Why do we choose total isolation from the outside world? I'll tell you why. Because we are ashamed. Oh yes! We are ashamed of who we are. We are ashamed of the birds we are. Just look at your puny little wings!"

The dodos in the hall squirmed restlessly, their butts sliding about in their seats. No one understood what the good Doctor Know-It-All was saying. "She shouldn't be so arrogant," they muttered. "Her wings aren't any bigger than ours."

Birdie rolled her eyes, but only after the camera-dodo panned around to get a shot of the whispering audience.

Maybe I should find another job... she thought. Not only because she got so little recognition for her work, but worse... *I'm surrounded by such stupid birds.*

But for today, her show had to go on. After all, it was the New Year's Special, when ratings always went through the roof. With a charming smile, she looked back into the camera again.

"I'm sorry, my dear viewers, I didn't mean to... overtax your brains. You have probably heard the name Fowlé Descartes before. Fowlé Descartes lived four hundred years ago, and although he was a male, there was this one time when he actually said something clever. I'd like to tell you what he said so you understand why we're ashamed. Descartes said:

'I think, therefore... I am... I am... clever?
I am, therefore I'm really awesome.
I'm really awesome because I'm a thinking bird.
Hey, wait a minute. If I'm a bird, why the heck can't I fly?
Thinking makes you unhappy. I'd rather be able to fly.'

There was a tense silence as the simple-minded dodos processed these words. Even the health minister seemed to be straining his brain. Nevertheless, Birdie was sure she was about to receive the biggest applause of her career.

Several more seconds made the present become the past until – finally – the audience erupted in a volcano of emotion. Countless dodos leapt to their feet, shouting:

"Oh, Descartes! It's always been my dream to fly!"
"I was always too embarrassed to tell anyone that I dreamt of flying."
"Descartes for president!"
"He's dead, isn't he?"
"Descartes for ex-president then!"

Birdie sighed, thinking: *Intelligence makes you unhappy. I wish I was stupid.*

Two days later, Dirk watched a late-night rerun of the New Year's episode while Popin, an early bird, was already fast asleep on the air conditioner.

At first, Dirk couldn't believe what Birdie was saying on TV. He banged his beaky face against the sofa cushions five times to see if he was really awake. He had learnt that his fellow citizens harboured the same desire to fly. The dodos' awkward silence had finally come to an end.

"Well then, I suppose it's in our genes. There's nothing we can do about it," he said to himself with relief, as if a huge weight had been lifted from his heart. He had a smile on his beak when Birdie raised her little wing and waved goodbye to her audience.

After the programme, Dirk sank into a deep sleep and dreamt of fluttering through the sky with Popin.

When does a beautiful dream turn into a nightmare? For Dirk it was the moment when thirteen ducks pulled up alongside him, looked at his wings and started laughing at them.

"Hey, cut it out!" Dirk told the ducks. His wings began shrinking back to their normal size, the puny wings that a dodo called his own. He panicked. "*OH, NO! HOLY CRABS!!!*"

Dirk asked the slight, little Popin if he could sit on her back for once, but she quickly shook her head.

"Dodo *much* too heavy," she explained. "Parrot one-hundred-seventy grams. Dodo seventeen kilograms!"

"Fifteen kilograms!" lied Dirk.

In desperation, he turned to his uninvited guests.

"Can you help me? *Please?*" he politely asked the ducks, hoping they would save him from falling to his death. They declined with thanks, laughed their heads off and pulled out their cameras.

As the ducks' laughter grew louder and louder, the distance between the ground and the dodo decreased rapidly… until with a resounding *Thud!* Dirk slammed into the ground.

He woke in a state of terror and leapt up from the sofa.

"Just a nightmare," he said with an involuntary shiver.

He went into the bedroom, tripped over the vacuum cleaner and kicked it furiously. He cursed under his breath as he kicked the vacuum cleaner a second time to turn it off again.

He lay down in his bed and dreamt the same beautiful dream about flying, which again turned into the nightmare with the laughing ducks.

With a spectacular *Bang!!* he crashed into the Indian Ocean.

"I hate ducks," Dirk said after waking up. He turned over onto his other side and closed his eyes.

Boom!!! he smashed old-school into his old school.

At least it amused the ducks. Their laughter became more and more malicious and nasty, and dream after dream, Dirk became angrier and angrier at them, until inevitably, he'd hit the earth with a loud *Kaboom!!!!*

He was so tired, but the sun was already rising.

Don't fall asleep again, he told himself. *You'll only end up crashing.* Still, his eyes began to close once more. *No! Those horrible ducks!*

He opened his eyes and was wide awake. An idea had come to visit, and he wanted it to stay. It was time to fulfil his lifelong dream.

"Whizzing through the air with my very own wings!" he cried aloud. "Flying, dude! Flying!"

Dirk forced his tired body out of bed. Now he had to do something he had little experience with. He'd have to use his brain.

"But how can I make this dream a reality?" he mused, standing in front of his mirror. "The only problem is my little wings. What if I were to enlarge them somehow? But how? Genetically modified fruit maybe? No, best not. If something goes wrong, I'll turn into a zombie or – even worse – into a duck!" He shuddered in disgust. "That would be terrible. There must be another way. What if I lost weight?"

He stepped closer to the mirror and looked at his body. He didn't see anything wrong with it. His belly and buttocks were entirely satisfactory.

"Everything is all right on that front," he said to himself. "A stout physique is perfectly normal for a dodo. It just doesn't fit this planet. Wait a minute, that's it! Exactly! It's all gravity's fault! If you could reduce gravity... aye, that would be the solution to the puzzle."

The scales fell from his eyes.

"I just need to find a planet with less gravity, that's all!" he said. "It can't be that hard!"

Chapter 2: A Thousand Tiny Lights

Six days had passed since Dirk had decided to become as free as a bird on a foreign planet in a solar system far, far away. It wasn't like he had much of a choice. His subconscious continued to goad him with nightmares so he couldn't lose sight of his goal.

In the morning, Dirk lay in bed, his eyes all red and sore from lack of sleep. A moment ago, he had been caught off guard by his latest nightmare, where flamingos had taken the place of the ducks. Either way, whether it was laughing ducks or giggling flamingos, the sudden crash to earth was just as crushing as before.

What's next? he asked himself in a fit of despair as he watched the morning sun coming up. *A flock of albatrosses? Geese? Cuckooshrikes?*

There were many birds that lived on Mauritius or who dropped by from time to time. So, lucky for him, his nightmares would never be short of performers to fill the lead roles.

But Dirk was preparing to get even with his subconscious. The following evening, there was to be a demonstration to save the rainforest, which would even be televised for couch potatoes. There would be a stage and an open microphone at the demo, and anyone who wanted to say something about protecting the rainforests would be allowed to speak there. But Dirk intended to use the stage for his own purposes.

He spent the whole day writing and editing what he was going to say. After eleven hours of fine-tuning, he believed he was done. He read the speech all the way through and frowned. It was utterly awful; that much he knew. He would have to rewrite it the next morning, merely hours before the demo. He put the useless draft into the shredder and switched on the television to watch the Dodo Broadcasting Corporation.

"And it's ten o'clock. Welcome to DBC's *News at Nine*. I'm Michelle Bird," said the newsreader listlessly.

The *News at Nine* had controversially moved to ten o'clock a couple of decades ago, but because the *News at Nine* was such a strong brand, the producers had held on to the original name.

"Unfortunately, there is no news again today," said Michelle grumpily. "Nothing happened. Nothing at all. Another uneventful day in island paradise. I wish you a..." – she groaned in disgust as she said it – "...*wonderful* evening. Oh, you know what? Forget 'wonderful'. Just this once, I wish you an *unexpected* evening."

Dirk smiled. The newsreader's frustration was proof that there were other dodos besides him who thought that life in paradise was hell.

"We now go live to Bena for the weather report," said Michelle, signing off. "Bena, sweetie, can you give everyone a report on today's weather? What was it like?"

Bena the weather reporter stood on a dark sandy beach. Warm rain poured down her plumage.

"With pleasure, Michelle," she said cheerfully. "At a sweltering hot 31 degrees, most citizens spent a sunny day at the beach today until the rain finally cooled us all down this evening. That's all from me for tonight. Coming up next: a new episode of the award-winning wildlife documentary *Crabs and their Troubles: Life on a Claw's Edge*. Please stay with us. After all, we're the only channel."

⁂

The veterinary surgeon looked her patient in the eye.

"It's going to hurt really, really bad for a minute, but it'll *probably* pass *eventually*," she told Jay before jabbing a long syringe down his throat to inoculate him against avian flu.

"Aaaaaarrrrrggggggghhhh!" Jay screamed a bloodcurdling scream as if the Grim Reaper had just appeared before him.

Hookbeak shook his head and apologised for his pet's behaviour. "He makes a huge drama out of it every year. But I'll bet you he'll be right as rain by the time we get to the demonstration."

"The demonstration for the rainforest?" asked the vet as she gently stroked Jay with her wing.

"That's right," said Hookbeak. "Would you like to come? A good friend of mine is speaking tonight. He texted me to tell me that his speech was going to blow my mind. Then he told me in a voice message that he had yet to write the speech and that I shouldn't set my expectations too high."

"I'm afraid I don't have time," replied the vet. She pointed to the waiting room, which was crammed with pets and their owners. "Many parrots are still injured from playing *Get Away* and need new bandages. I'm just going to watch the demo on TV," she explained, nodding at her antique ninety-eight-inch flat screen. "It's not as great as being in the thick of it, but at least I'll be watching it on one of the first TVs with extra-super-giga-mega-ultra-high definition. My grandparents claim it was the latest craze fifty years ago."

Dodos were able to stand balanced on one leg, though not as effortlessly as flamingos. Dirk picked up a feather with his left foot and used it to scratch Popin's back. Popin wasn't just his pet; she was also a very close friend.

"Everything will be all right," he said, more to himself than to her, as he moved the feather up and down. Popin clucked contentedly.

By the light of the setting sun, Dirk combed his plumage with a comb-shaped stick before setting off to the demo in no particular hurry – leaving his newly written speech on his desk.

Popin had picked up on the tension in the dodo. As curiosity never killed a parrot, she flew after her master.

In a clearing in the rainforest, thousands of dodos stood around a stage. Dirk, facing his audience, reached into his belly feathers but seemingly couldn't find his speech.

"Well, well," Dirk said into the microphone. Without his speech, he had no choice but to improvise. "I agree with the previous speakers. Rainforests are important and all that... *if* you really want to stay on

Mauritius for the rest of your lives. Well, I don't, to be honest. We can burn down the rainforests for all I care."

The crowd gasped in disbelief. A male hippie-dodo wearing red, circular glasses and a colourful beanie with flowers broke his peace-sign banner over the head of the dodo on his left and threatened Dirk with the sharp, pointed end.

"If," continued Dirk, unfazed, "we all decide to leave, what does it matter anyway? And while we're being honest with each other, boys and girls, I'll say this: I know you all want to fly too. Just remember what Doctor Pert said on her show! So come on, you lot! Get off your fat butts and let's check out another planet where we can hang out on the clouds... er... in the clouds like real birds!"

The stewards grabbed Dirk's legs with their hooked beaks to pull him off the stage. Lowering his own beak, he pecked at their heads.

"Leave me alone... I'm not done yet! Where was I?"

"Let's check out another planet!" shouted Nala, a young racing driver, from the audience. "Where we can hang out on the clouds... er... in the clouds like real birds!"

"Exactly!" said Dirk. "At least someone was paying attention, you cormorants. Tomorrow at midnight, all those who haven't given up on their dream of flying will meet in the Bay of Pigeons to form a task force! FLYING, DUDES! FLYING!" shouted Dirk before jumping off the stage and running away from the stewards.

"Argh! Flying, dudes, flying!" said Popin to her brother.

Jay looked around. "You can speak normally. Your feeder is fleeing through the rainforest and Hookbeak won't ever hear you above this racket."

In the presence of their mistresses and masters, parrots always played dumb. They had good reasons for this, going back many hundreds of years...

Dodos and parrots had been using the same language since the 3rd century: *Parrot*. The dodos had taken Parrot from their pets, brazenly renamed it *Dodish*, and twisted history in the 6th century. It was during this time that the dodos travelled the Earth on a sailing ship for the first and last time ever. On returning to Mauritius, the captain proudly reported that Dodish was now spoken by every parrot in the world.

This 'news' travelled faster than light among the dodos. The dodos have since claimed, in all seriousness, that it was they who taught their green parrots the language. Out of gratitude, the parrots then brought Dodish to the world, which explained why the bird language was so widespread around the globe. Some parrots called this 'falsification of history', others merely 'delusions of grandeur'.

Of course the dodos' pets could not tolerate the theft of their language. For this reason, they called for a meeting of the *Council of Highly Intelligent Mauritian Parrots*, or CHIMP, at the end of the 6th century. The other parrot species, who had never lived as pets, also found the dodos' crime outrageous. They supported their green friends, and the council unanimously chose a new form of protest. From now on, they were quiet or said very little when dodos were around. They only spoke a maximum of ten words at a time. In addition, they could make silly noises like 'Argh!' or 'Orgh!' to get on the dodos' nerves.

The dodos assumed that a novel parrot flu had driven their pets completely gaga. They found the parrots even cuter than before and gave them twice as much food.

A full pet was a happy pet. That was why the CHIMP passed on the 'tradition of playing dumb' from generation to generation, and it has remained unbroken until this day.

"What is Hookbeak tinkering with at the moment?" asked Popin.

"Tellies," Jay answered. "Fortunately, he also knows electrical engineering, otherwise he would end up being very bored. Everything dodos need to live has already been made, and hardly anything breaks down. Except for new electrical appliances, of course, which are basically scrap after five to ten years. It can be quite practical to have a genius for a feeder."

Popin sighed. "What did you break this time, brother dear? Let me guess: the fridge? Or did you film yourself making faces again and drop Hookbeak's phone?"

"Nah, I broke the microwave," replied Jay. "Did you know you're not supposed to heat metal in the microwave?"

"Yeah, I did know that," said Popin.

"Well, there was only very minor fire damage. Hookbeak simply built a new microwave. But he spends most of his time repairing television sets for fun... argh! Television, argh!" Jay fell back into their secret language because his feeder had suddenly appeared.

Hookbeak had only understood Jay's last few words and shook his head in anger. "You'll ruin your eyes one of these days!" he said. "The TV stays off tonight."

"Argh, no!" Jay shrieked, not listening to reason.

Hookbeak's mood improved as he turned to Jay's sister. "Hi, Pops!" he said. "Guess what? I thought Dirk's speech was great! It looks like I'll get to build something huge for your master very soon. What a beautiful day!"

༄

It was such a clear and windless night that you would have heard the shells snoring, had it not been for the sound of the sea.

In the Bay of Pigeons, 'Flying Task Force' was written in the sand.

About fifty dodos had shown up for the first meeting. Dirk and Hookbeak talked with each other while the rest of the group stood around looking a bit lost and awfully quiet. Too quiet for the racing dodo Nala.

"It's pretty dark. Why did we have to meet on the loneliest beach, and at a new moon of all times?" Nala asked the group, which set off a few banal conversations.

"There's no light to be seen for miles."

"Well, I see a thousand tiny lights."

"Whoah! Have you ever seen so many stars?"

"Freakin' beautiful! That's where I want to go."

"That's exactly why we're here," boomed Hookbeak, and the other dodos fell silent. "We are here because we want to fly to the stars. Please, Dirk, go ahead. You can explain it more clearly to everyone than I can."

"Well, the plan is quite simple," began Dirk. "We thought we'd build a cosmos boat…"

"Spaceship," Hookbeak corrected.

"…okay, spaceship," said Dirk, "and we'll take it to the cosmos…"

"To space!" Hookbeak interrupted Dirk again. "We are already in the cosmos. Cosmos is another word for universe. *Space* is the airless space between celestial bodies like the Earth and the Moon."

"Oh, whatever. Nobody likes a know-it-all," retorted Dirk. "So, we jet *through* the cosmos in search of a planet with low gravity, where our weight will be so light that we can fly with our own wings. Right, Hooky?"

"That is correct," said Hookbeak.

Nearby, there was the sound of a *Splash!*

"That's the rough plan for now," continued Dirk. "We'll worry about the details later. What do you all think?"

A few dodos mumbled, "Yeah, it's OK so far." The rest nodded their heads mechanically because something had distracted them.

"Terrific," said Dirk. "So how do you build a small cosmos boat for fifty dodos plus pets? Hookbeak has a few ideas he wants to present to us today."

Suddenly, there it was again, another *Splash!*

"We have important issues on the agenda!" shouted Dirk. "Stop splashing around, we're not here to bathe! Hooky, could you please explain… Hookbeak? Hookbeak!!!"

Splash. Splash. Splash.

Suddenly, Dirk was standing all alone on the beach.

"As you wish, we'll continue our meeting in the water then," he said and was the last to jump into the sea.

Over the next two weeks, the task force grew significantly as word of the meetings in the Bay of Pigeons spread to the universities and other beaches. At first, the fledglings came out of sheer curiosity. Then they stayed to swim.

"Maybe," said Hookbeak, "next time we should bring a lifeguard along with us. We're three hundred dodos. Sooner or later, someone will get lost. The turtles are so vicious and pull you underwater."

"You think so?" asked Dirk, splashing water into his old friend's face. "I'm more afraid of sharks and jellyfish. I guess your mohawk isn't waterproof?"

"Sharks just follow their nature, but turtles have a very dark sense of humour," said Hookbeak. "Not like us dodos. We'd never hurt a fly."

"Excuse me," said Dertie, a biology student. "When are we going to start building the spaceship? The sooner we meet aliens, the better! I had new dissection instruments made just for them." She held up a bunch of truly wicked looking knives and tools, capable of causing supermassive pain.

Dirk agreed and rounded up part of the task force.

"Hey! Listen up!" he shouted. "Everybody in the spaceship planning committee meets here with me and Hookbeak *now!* Come on, hurry up!"

Meanwhile, hundreds of parrots circled above the heads of the dodos, like vultures over a lost calf in the steppe. Sometimes they flew a little lower to catch snippets of conversation.

"Did you hear updates on the construction of the spaceship?" Popin asked Papagayo, another echo parakeet.

"Sure," replied Papagayo. "Our feeders want to mine iron ore in the mountains and then process it into something called *steel*, which will be used to build the spaceship's shell."

"Crazy stuff," said Popin. "And how…"

A curious duck who, to the parrots' amazement, understood the language Parrot, interrupted them, chattering wildly: "We have mountains? On the island? Really?! That's crazy! Where, pray tell?"

"Fly a little higher," suggested Popin.

"Okay," said the duck.

"Further up! A little further!"

"I can already see the whole island, there are no mountains here!"

"What?! Are you blind?!" asked Popin.

"Do you mean the small hills?" quacked the duck.

Popin faltered for a moment. "T-Those... those are small mountains, not hills. Look at their pointy tops."

"Hey, I grew up in Asia," the duck crowed. "There are mountains there that are ten times higher! They are so high that the air is too cold and too thin to fly over them! No tellin' if you'll suffocate or freeze to death first!"

"All right, all right, I got it!" shouted Popin and then thought to herself: *What a pompous duck! 27,000-foot-high mountains? Yeah... right.*

The spaceship planning committee was splashing around in the shallows. In the end, the committee consisted only of civil engineer Hookbeak and many eager listeners.

"We'll have to cut down some of the rainforest," said Hookbeak. "We'll try to build as much of the ship's interior as possible out of wood because it's available in large quantities. Any comments or objections?"

He looked into fascinated faces.

"There's still one small obstacle," he continued. "We need permission for mining and logging from our president."

Dirk snorted contemptuously. "I met him the other day in a beach bar. He thinks we're weirdos who won't last two minutes in space. If I'd known that earlier, I wouldn't have voted for him. I only did it because he said cool slogans and talked big."

"I know a lawyer," said Hookbeak. "I'm sure she'll think of something."

"Great. And who's going to build computer technology for the ship?" asked Dirk.

Hookbeak smiled briefly. "I've made some sketches for the hardware of the ship's computer, but I don't know anything about software and programming. Luckily, I know a brilliant computer scientist. I'll ask her."

"And then we'll need a ship's doctor," Dirk said, working through a list in his head.

"I know a very good doctor," said Hookbeak. "I'll give her a call."

Dertie, the biology student, cleared her throat. "And who will treat our parrots?" she asked. "They have to be in perfect health at the start of the voyage because I've been thinking of breeding alien-parrot-hybrids."

"Absolutely not," said Hookbeak. "That's inhuma... indod... well, it's just cruel."

Dirk felt the same way. "Use ducks instead of parrots, Dertie. But you're right, we need a vet."

Everyone looked at Hookbeak.

"I do know a veterinarian," he said. "However, I think she might get a little busy with all her other duties."

"Why?" asked Dirk. "Her only job will be to treat our pets."

"Well, not exac..."

"Will you ask her?"

"Of course I will."

Chapter 3: Birds of a Feather Flock Together

After a long day of hearings in the Supreme Court of the United Forests of Mauritius, a talented young lawyer had won the right to gather the raw materials needed to build a spaceship. The lawyer was Doctor Birdex Pert, who, among other things, also worked as a psychologist and talk show host. Birdie had joined the task force because she could never refuse Hookbeak a request when he stood before her with his impressive featherstyle. In terms of intelligence and ingenuity, he was the only dodo who could hold a candle to her.

On her very first day as the lawyer for the task force, Birdie had sued the government and the National Nature Reserve, demanding a basic right for every citizen to exploit natural resources. After a solid minute, she had lost the shortest case in the history of the Supreme Court.

After that, she had demanded special permission to exploit natural resources for purely medical purposes. She explained that wood and metal were needed for an experimental study in space, the success of which would improve the mental health of the subjects. For this, Birdie called herself to the witness stand and questioned herself on the effects flying had on the mind. To support her arguments as a psychologist, she showed the famous episode of her talk show in which the audience confessed their desire to fly. Three out of five judges had tears in their eyes.

When the attorney general cross-examined Birdie, she rebuffed him sternly. She made a snap diagnosis of his mental state and told him that he had a problem with strong females due to his bad relationship with his mother. (She later apologised to him for the diagnosis, *after* she won the case.)

During the lunch break in the courthouse garden, Birdie threw Hookbeak's drafts for the ship's computer on the scrap heap. Just like that.

That same evening, the Flying Task Force met in the Bay of Pigeons.

The meeting was of such importance that the three hundred and fifty dodos took a seat in the sand, even though the seductive waves made it difficult for them to do so. Their six hundred and seventy parrots sat among them.

When Hookbeak wanted to present the construction plans, the minute taker Anton Pavlovich insisted that they stick exactly to the agenda. The first item on the list was to elect a ship's captain.

"Argh!" exclaimed Popin. "I want Jay as captain!" And her suggestion enjoyed great popularity among the parrots.

"Pets are not entitled to vote," said Anton Pavlovich. "Which dodo would like to lead the crew?"

Lawyer Birdie believed she could do it and kicked her white wig into the ring.

Dirk tried to persuade her not to run as he claimed the office for himself. "You're the heroine of the hour," he said, "but we wouldn't even be sitting here without my kick-off. I got the idea after a horrible nightmare. It's a matter close to my heart. Aye, it's my heartfelt wish that we succeed. That's why I think I should do it. I think I'd make a good commander for the cosmos boat."

Dirk won the election by 349 to 1. Birdie, who had cast her own vote, was stunned. Her disadvantage was that, being multi-talented, she was already expected to perform other duties on the ship. She looked sadly at Hookbeak. He had persuaded her to take part in the flight project but had left her high and dry in the election for captain.

Hookbeak asked her to understand. "I'm sorry, Dirk and I have been friends since school days."

"But he is completely unqualified!" said Birdie. "I won a victory in court against the government, a feat that was thought impossible!"

"Still, you won't have time for the office," explained Hookbeak. "Neither will I. Dirk has nothing to do, so he might as well play captain."

Dirk then selected his lieutenants. He appointed Chief Engineer Hookbeak as his first officer and the ship's doctor, whom he called Number Two, as his second officer.

"Well, I think that's enough for today," said Dirk.

"But... *humph!*" said Hookbeak.

"What is it?"

"I wanted to show you the construction plans."

"We don't know anything about engineering anyway," Dirk said presumptuously in the name of everyone present. "We trust you."

"It's all right," lied Hookbeak. "Let's call it a day. Oh, I *forgot* to tell you! Our parrots will be message bearers on board. They will fly through species-appropriate tubes that run throughout the ship. I call it Parrot Communication Tube System – or simply 'comm tube'."

"Argh!" said Jay, who was sitting on Hookbeak's belly. "Just call it *the Tube*, dude!"

"What do we need the Tube for?" asked Dertie. "Can't we just talk to each other on the phone?"

Hookbeak shrugged. "I'm sure that would be possible if we build a local radio network for our phones or an awesome add-on program for the ship's computer." His gaze wandered to the stressed computer scientist, who nearly fainted, before he continued. "But with the comm tubes, we save a lot of electricity, and our pets can earn their food for a change."

The parrots responded to his suggestion with boos.

Only Dertie seemed happy now. "So, nobody from the outside world can contact us either?" she asked. "No psychopaths? Whoops, I mean... relatives? Ex-boyfriends?"

"No, nobody," Hookbeak said and pondered for a moment. "Hm. I could make a special antenna for my phone so that someone who is within a hundred-thirty-mile radius of the ship could reach me. They would have to know my number, though."

"That's pointless then," said Dirk.

"Not necessarily. Maybe I just put my number on the..."

"Okay, okay, okay," the captain cut off his first officer. "Let's splash around in the sea for an hour and after that, off to nest. We'll meet in twelve hours and start mining and logging in the national park – or rather in the former national park, thanks to our amazing lawyer."

"Crawler!" replied Birdie, which was Dodish slang for *bootlicker,* or rather *footlicker* since dodos don't wear boots.

In building the spaceship, the dodos performed a miracle in thirteen days because they worked passionately on their dream project.

The parrots were of no help. They even made life difficult for their feeders by repeatedly turning the construction plans upside down and criticising the project profusely. It was their attempt to sabotage the spaceship's construction because, as they told each other, they had "zero desire to work as messengers or fly through stupid tubes."

However, Hookbeak knew the plans by heart, so in the end, the parrots only delayed the completion of the ship by three minutes and forty-one seconds.

In the thirteen days of construction, the crew had grown to four hundred dodos. The new arrivals had already been expected and planned for because the holidays had begun at the university.

The captain was in a good mood, but for a different reason. He felt much better now than he had ten minutes ago. A few crew members had let three ducks onto the ship along with their parrots and geese. Dirk had noticed in time and had pushed the ducks off the ship with his own belly. From tomorrow on, they would only appear in his nightmares.

Meanwhile, he sat back in his office and waited for the First Officer and Number Two. They would assist him in a matter that was beyond his own creative limits. The great star voyage was due to begin in sixteen hours, and the ship still had no name. The parrots affectionately called it *Sea Cow*, but the captain had no clue what a sea cow was and whether it did the ship justice.

With its cylindrical and massive shape, the spaceship actually resembled a one-eyed manatee or dugong, which the parrots referred to as 'sea cows'.

At the front of the ship was the cargo hatch, which could easily be mistaken for a protruding snout. In the centre above the snout was a round, eye-shaped window made of thick quartz glass. Anyone looking into the 'eye' from the outside could make out the bridge.

The two jet engines under the ship looked like fore flippers, and a spacetime distortion machine had been built into the stern, or 'tail flukes'.

Furthermore, there were a thousand rectangular windows evenly distributed over the long body, adding absolutely nothing to the resemblance between ship and sea mammal.

Like his captain, Chief Engineer Hookbeak had never seen a sea cow before and, due to time constraints, did not attach any value to the appearance of the ship. The result was nevertheless shocking. Aliens who ain't got no style at least created a dull saucer as their first spaceship. But until now, it had been considered impossible to give a ship the shape of an unsightly sea cow. As far as bad taste was concerned, Hookbeak had reached a new galactic dimension.

His other weakness had caused him bigger headaches.

"Now that the ship is finished," Hookbeak had said to Jay that morning, "I have to admit that *spacetime distortion machine* doesn't roll off the tongue easily. Perhaps I should call it a *spacetime warping apparatus* instead."

"Argh! Just call it warp drive!" Jay had replied. "Name I made up!"

Warp drive. A term that no dodo had heard before.

"Okay, let's call it warp drive for short," said Hookbeak.

"Argh, you've finished drive fast," said Jay.

Hookbeak shrugged. "It wasn't hard, it's just rocket science."

☙

Dirk smiled at his two senior officers.

"Chief Engineer Hookbeak," he began, "I mean First Officer…"

"You may still call me Hooky. I don't have to call you captain either, do I?" asked Hookbeak.

"No, you don't. Boss or Commander-in-Chief is also fine. Do you have any ideas for the ship's name?"

"Well, we're dodos," observed Hookbeak. "And this is the first spaceship of our species. So it's sort of spaceship A for Alpha. And it's ludicrously fast – well, actually, the space around us will distort so much that we will *seem* to cover a huge distance in an insanely short amount of time, even though we're not moving fast at all, but still…"

"Get to the point!" commanded the captain.

"I propose we call the spaceship Dodo Alpha Jet," said Hookbeak.

What a stupid name for my ship, thought Dirk, screwing up his beak in distaste.

"I'm all for it!" said the ship's doctor.

Dirk conceded defeat. "All right, whatever, Dodo Alpha Jet it is." For the time being, he decided to listen to the advice of his officers. Later, he would go with his gut feeling.

"Dirk!" the doctor scolded him after the naming. "I brought your vaccination. You're the only dodo who hadn't shown up at sick bay as ordered."

"I've had a lot on my plate, Number Two."

"Shall we swap?" she asked.

"Nah, never mind. You're awesome at everything you do. You're simply the best."

"Crawler!" she said.

꽃

When Hookbeak entered the animal hospital the next morning, he had to sneak past hundreds of hammocks to get to the vet's office. Each little hammock was filled with at least one knackered parrot.

In the vet's office, countless hypodermic needles lay scattered on the floor since the wastepaper basket was already overflowing. There was an egg on the table and a drugged parrot sitting in the darkest corner of the room.

Hookbeak found the vet under her computer.

"Hello there!" he said. "The captain's asking if you'll give your OK for the launch?"

"No' ye'," she replied with computer cables in her beak. She took the cables in her feet and hammered them into the ports. "As soon as the parrots wake up from their cosmic ray vaccinations, we can take off."

"Well, the vaccinations sure knocked them out. I only felt the prick of the needle for a moment," claimed Hookbeak.

"We weigh a hundred times more, and our bodies are fifty per cent fat," explained the vet. "Our echo parakeets are small and slim. Don't worry, they'll all survive. The twelve geese tolerated the vaccine as well as we did. Ah, now I know why you show up here in person. The comm tubes have all been closed."

"That's one of the two reasons," said Hookbeak. "The other reason is that the message bearers are all lying stunned in one of your stations. Little hint: it's not the data centre or your law firm. And I don't mean the sick bay for us dodos, either. It could be this ward here."

"Yes, thank you very, very much," replied the veterinarian, Birdie, who was also the only lawyer, computer scientist and physician for dodos on the ship. "You go ahead and make fun of me for being so out of it again. I've got so much to do. I just can't think straight any more although I am – reputedly – the greatest thinker of all time. I hope I don't have a nervous breakdown one day or I'll have to cure myself."

She sat down at her computer with a sigh.

Hookbeak's gaze roamed the room, and he saw the number 752 BC.

"Seven, five, two. What do the numbers on the board mean?" he asked.

"That's one number. Seven hundred and fifty-two parrots on board," replied Birdie. "The BC stands for *Birdie counted*."

"And what's that little egg on the table for?" wondered Hookbeak.

"Orgh!" cried the parrot from the dark corner. "Seven, five, three, soon my chick is *rome-ing* free!"

The mother parrot flew swaying to the table, stood in front of the egg and put her wing protectively on it. Suddenly, she staggered backwards and slipped on the edge of the table. Half a second later, the dodos heard a dull bang on the floor.

Birdie sighed again. "That's the third time in the last fifteen minutes. But when I tie her in the back, she makes a fuss about her egg."

"I remember her," said Hookbeak. "All the parrots flew to the ship except for her. She rolled the egg up the cargo hatch yesterday and scared us away so we wouldn't step on it with our big feet."

But Birdie hadn't been listening. She stared at the computer screen and shook her head. "According to the passenger manifest, seven hundred and fifty-two parrots came on board, plus one egg. But I only vaccinated seven hundred and forty-nine parrots…"

🪶

Captain Dirk was nervous as he walked onto the bridge just before take-off. The uncertainty frightened him, and he wondered if it would be smart to talk to someone in the crew about it.

A round hole had been cut in Dirk's chair for his tail feathers, and he was pleased to note that it was in the perfect place. *Good job, Hooky*, he thought.

Next to Dirk, a former biology student turned science officer stood on her right foot. She was typing bitter parting messages with her beak into her phone, which she had to hold up with her left foot. Previously, the phone had kept slipping off her little wing.

"A'm feart," said the captain.

"You're *what?*" asked Dertie without taking her eyes off her phone.

"Well, I'm feart. Say, why is it so hot in here?"

"Hookbeak called me five minutes ago," she said, having to stifle a laugh as she continued. "Three parrots are clogging the air shaft to the bridge. They thought they were particularly clever and wanted to escape their vaccination. After we closed the Tube, the little fools climbed into the narrow air shafts. Now Hookbeak and the doctor are trying to get them out alive. By the way, Captain, it would be nice if you only used words that every dodo knows. Thank you."

"It's crazy what language differences there are on a wee island," said Dirk.

"Hookbeak is from the northern part of the island too," said Dertie, "and I understand *him* perfectly."

"Weel, th' laddie drapped his dialect whan he gaed sooth tae study," Dirk suddenly lapsed into his Northern dialect.

"What?"

"Dae ye hae a quaistion?"

"I don't understand a word."

"I asked you if you've got a question!" said Dirk, who was trying hard to speak Standard Dodish again.

"Yes, I have one," replied Dertie. "Can we please take off, Captain? With the right alien DNA, I might be able to fix your speech impediment," though she didn't have high hopes.

"We still need the go-ahead from Birdie," said Dirk. "Why is no one at the helm?"

"I don't know," Dertie said grumpily. "Oh, by the way, your tail feathers are peeping out of the back of your chair!"

"I know. It's more comfortable that way."

Pilot Nala came onto the bridge and waved at the captain, as dodo wings weren't long enough to salute. On her head, she wore a brown aviator hat with oversized goggles.

"Nala?" asked Dirk. "Are you sure you can fly a cosmos boat? It's a bit different from a race car, after all."

"Aye, Captain, I'm sure," Nala said with a smile. Being only twenty years old, she was the chick among the officers. "You seem to forget that I was third in the Mauritius Grand Prix. I just imagine that the Dodo Alpha Jet is a brand-new racing car that I can steer up and down."

Dertie and Dirk exchanged worried looks as Nala walked to the dashboard.

"Psst, Dertie," whispered Dirk. "Do you remember if Hookbeak built any escape pods?"

"I'm afraid he did not, Captain," replied the science officer, alarmed, before hopping to her seat on one leg.

Next to enter the bridge was Anton Pavlovich, former minute taker of the task force. He had since risen to the position of ship's navigator and sat down next to Nala at the controls.

The bridge officers waited for the First Officer and Number Two. And they waited and waited. Dertie freshened up in the bathroom, and Dirk dozed in his armchair while Anton Pavlovich lost a game of chess to Nala.

After two hours, they all got hungry from waiting and went to the cafeteria for lunch. They came back and waited again.

When Hookbeak and Birdie entered the bridge that afternoon, Dirk was snoring in his chair. Birdie started singing a popular children's song to wake him up. The song was about ducks swimming on a lake and sticking their little heads into the water, thus showing their butts to their owner.

"I'm sorry!" said Birdie to the captain. "I had no idea that you despise duck songs! My sincerest apologies. Well, the three runaways have a few bruises, so I'll have to give them the vaccination later. But all the parrots are fit to fly. We're ready to go, Dirk."

"Excellent work, Number Two."

"Crawler," Birdie retorted.

Dirk smiled. "That's just who I am. Nala, take us out."

"Out of the park?" asked the pilot.

"Into the sky and beyond!" commanded Dirk.

Birdie and Hookbeak set up their folding chairs next to Dirk's big chair. They settled to his right and left so they could better reprimand him if necessary.

The Sea Cow lay in the former national park. The start of the two engines burned down what little was left of the rainforest.

"Ground control," said Nala, "this is Dodo Alpha Jet. Start of the engines was a huge success. We're ready to take off. *Ten. Nine...*"

"What is a ground control," Dirk asked his Number Two, "and why is Nala counting down?"

"I have absolutely no idea," answered Birdie, "but I'm definitely going to examine her brain."

"*...Two. One.* Yippee yeah, let's go."

The ship rose into the air, and thousands of parrots and geese accompanied it to the beach promenade to say goodbye. After flying over the coast, the ship abruptly swung to the side and threatened to plunge into the sea. Nala jerked the control stick around with her beak and stepped on the accelerator.

"Whoops," she said as the Sea Cow gained altitude and she guided the stick with her wing again. "Driving is quite different without a road."

"Phew!" sighed Anton in relief. "So that's why they say the first step is always the hardest."

Dirk grumbled. "It was almost our last step, too!"

The Sea Cow poked through white clouds, and Dertie beamed with joy.

"That's it for contact with the outside world," she said, almost singing, and dropped her phone into the wastepaper basket.

The dodos who stayed behind on Earth just shook their heads at their first space travellers because death was looming everywhere in space. It had to be like this. This was known. That's why nobody had been there yet.

"Dodos will still be living on Mauritius a thousand years from now!" said the President of the United Forests of Mauritius (UFofM) in a televised address after the Dodo Alpha Jet disappeared from the sky. "Even then, our descendants shall remember the space dodos as a cautionary example of stupidity and short-sightedness!"

Chapter 4: In the Vicinity

The spaceship penetrated the last thin layer of Earth's atmosphere while the captain eyed the tape recorder lying on his belly suspiciously. Hookbeak had scrawled the word LogBook on it.

"The cosmos..." Dirk began to say. "Ah, wait a minute. Someone has to operate the logbook while I'm talking. That could be an easy job for Pops. I need my parrot!"

"Captain!" exclaimed Dertie. "I recommend we show the image from the tail camera on the screen!"

"But why?" asked Dirk, puzzled.

"Well, to see the Earth?!"

"Oh, I see. You've got a keen mind, Dertie. Computer? Cinema atmosphere, captain's personal settings. Please show us the image from the stern camera. Thank you."

A screen rolled down from the ceiling, completely covering the round window of the bridge. The computer turned down the lights and transferred the camera image to the screen while the officers relaxed back in their seats, as was customary for a cosy movie night. The fact that Nala was now flying blind didn't seem to worry anyone. They expected little oncoming traffic between Earth and the next planet.

"I just see a lot of blue," complained the captain about the picture. "And some light brown and green areas on the left."

"That," said Hookbeak, "is probably the Indian Ocean, Madagascar and continental Africa."

"Ah," said Dirk. "The old stories of *Seafarer Altair on the Seven Seas*. Very nice *fairy tales*."

"There seems to be something to it," remarked the fascinated Nala.

Hookbeak nodded. "There is a spark of truth in every legend. Altair's first mate was an ancestor of mine. My great-great-great-great-great-great-great-great-great-uncle. No, I think it was even much longer ago. He was my great-great-great..."

Nala gasped for breath. "*Officer Crookbeak?* You're related to Officer Crookbeak?"

"Yes, that's what I just said," replied Hookbeak.

Birdie involuntarily thought about work, which wasn't surprising since she was the busiest officer. She enjoyed the view more than her colleagues, but the poor parrots were still locked up in the animal hospital.

"I'll send Popin up to you in a minute, Dirk," she said slightly reluctantly. She walked backwards to the lift, tripped on a step, fell on her feathered bottom and struggled to her feet. Afterwards, she breathed a sigh of relief because the others hadn't noticed her fall. "I meant I'll send Popin *over* to you, for the lifts go sideways through the Sea Cow most of the time, haha. I really have to let her out of the animal hospital now. I mean Popin, not a sea cow. Please open the Tube already! *AND RECORD EVERYTHING ON TAPE OR YOU'LL BE IN FOR THE HIGH JUMP!!!*"

"Yes, boss," said Anton Pavlovich. She had shouted him out of his spell.

"Yes, that's right," said Dirk after Birdie had hurried away. "You *may* do as she said, Anton. Who's your commander here, anyway?"

"All officers above me, Captain," answered the navigator.

"Hm," pondered Dirk, "I think I might allow that. Does anyone happen to know what a sea cow is?"

His officers shook their heads. Besides, it wasn't a good time for questions.

༄

In the corridors of the ship, nearly four hundred dodos craned their necks to look out of the windows. They watched in amazement as the Dodo Alpha Jet slowly moved away from a colossal sphere of dreamy blue.

In general, the dodos had assumed for decades that Dodernicus and Dodileo were correct in their view of the universe. Now they had certainty: their home world revolved around the sun and not vice versa. Earth was a planet like any other. Fortunately, the dodos' scientific endeavours were tolerated by their main goddess, Loony

Polly, since she, like all parrots, was only interested in food offerings and TV shows.

By now, Dodernicus was an *old* old-timer, aged 103, who had trouble staying on his feet. Dodileo Dodilei, who was twenty years younger, was, in the eyes of his fellow citizens, ready for the scrap heap too. The only one who didn't share this view was Hookbeak. He had been able to convince the two astronomers to join the flight as his scientific advisers.

"I said it!" announced Dodernicus. "The Earth revolves around the sun! The sun is the centre of our system."

"And I said it *louder*," replied Dodileo. "So loud that everyone on Mauritius could hear it."

"Yet I was the first!"

"No wonder, considering how old you are."

Birdie came down the corridor. Most of the dodos didn't even notice because they stuck to the windows with their beaks.

Dodileo nudged Dodernicus to draw his attention to the officer. Being gentle-birds of the old school, they bowed to her. Each as low as their age would allow.

"That was the computer scientist and psychologist, Dr Birdex Pert. Her friends call her Birdie," Dodileo explained to his colleague.

"Rubbish. She's my doctor and lawyer," said Dodernicus with conviction.

The spaceship would never have been built if Birdie hadn't won the court case to exploit natural resources. After the trial, she had built and programmed the ship's computer within twelve days. Last but not least, she had examined the crew (as well as the parrots and twelve geese) for physical suitability for space flight.

Now the Earth was merely a big blue spot in the window, but Birdie's duties were not diminishing. That's why she wanted to train crew members as helpers as soon as possible. Otherwise the physician, vet and computer scientist would burn out completely and would have to ask the psychologist in her for help. But at least there was a ray of hope: Her law firm probably turned out to be a well-intentioned mistake on the captain's part. Why would anyone need legal advice in space?

She reached the animal hospital at the end of the corridor and pressed a round switch on the wall. The door had not yet swung open completely when a parrot was already crashing against her head. Birdie shook it off and looked into the room with a pained expression. Seven hundred and fifty parrots were moving back and forth insanely fast before her eyes.

"*WHAT THE HE...!*" began Birdie to scream.

Science Officer Dertie entered the cargo hold. Before leaving planet Earth, she had put earthworms in a chest with fresh soil. Now she wanted to take the worms to her bio lab.

First, however, her wing wandered to a control next to the lift. She found it extremely tempting to switch off the artificial gravity in order to float through the aisles of the cargo hold for a few minutes. When she remembered that all the cargo would also be flying around, she decided against it with a heavy heart. Perhaps it was better to wait.

Dertie had discovered the chest and pulled out the seven earthworms with her beak. Suddenly she heard an eerie rustling nearby. Startled, she spat the worms back into the chest and looked around.

"Hello? Is anyone there? I'm trained in five martial arts!" she shouted.

She heard a new noise. It sounded as if someone was scratching paper with a knife. Her eyes fell on a fruit crate whose cardboard wall had bent.

Aha! she thought and said, "Well, hello? Who's having a nibble? Who's brazenly indulging in a snack?"

Two red eyes peered out of the dark box and Dertie relaxed.

"You don't have to be afraid, little parrot," she said. "It'll be our secret."

A sixteen-inch-long crab crawled out of the box. Dertie jumped backwards in shock.

"Hey, stowaways aren't allowed in here!" she explained to the intruder. "Oh, silly me! Animals cannot talk."

The giant crab remained motionless in front of Dertie, staring at something behind her. A cold shiver ran down her spine as she turned around.

Eight crabs were approaching with small, quick steps. They raised their claws menacingly. Dertie did the only sensible thing and sprinted for the lift.

"There are palm thieves on board!" Dertie told the captain on the bridge.

Dirk could see no problem in that. "They've got bad luck then," he said. "We didn't take any palm trees with us."

"The crabs!" cried Dertie. "They're eating through our supplies!"

"Blimey!" shrieked Dirk. "What are you waiting for?! Catch them!!!"

Nala turned to face them. The crabs puzzled her. "Huh? Didn't palm thieves go extinct?" she asked.

"I thought so too," said Dertie, "but apparently they just went into hiding."

The palm thief had its name for a reason. It liked to climb palm trees, and if it had been strong enough, it would have stolen them, too. In the end, it preferred to steal things it could carry a mile away. It snatched everything that wasn't nailed down.

The giant crabs lived on hundreds of islands in the Indian and Pacific Oceans. But they had never felt at home on Mauritius – with the dodos acting like they owned the place – so they'd all left for good. Well, nearly all of them. Nine crabs had stayed behind because they'd missed the raft's departure and couldn't swim. No one had seen them for a couple of months.

Last night, the last palm thieves of Mauritius had holed up in fruit crates and had eaten their fill. In the morning, they unexpectedly woke up in a warehouse, along with another ten thousand boxes of fresh fruit. But only when the earth began to shake beneath them, they truly felt that something was amiss. They gathered at the windows and looked down on their world. The warehouse turned out to be a cargo hold.

For the last time, they saw their beaches and beloved palm trees, and shortly after, the pitch-black night poured in. The nine sad crabs crawled back into their crates and ate like horses.

Then Dertie had appeared. And then she came a second time, bringing twelve cooks with her.

Anton looked at his calculations and then at Nala's. Hers were much more accurate, though he would never have admitted it.

"Somewhere ahead is Vicinus," he said. "The black planet. According to our calculations, we should reach it in about twelve months. Nala, if you could please just fly to… to where Vicinus should be in its orbit then."

"You *really* want me to?" she asked with mock surprise. To tease Anton, she looked at him with wide-open eyes through her goggles. "Actually, I was going to fly behind Vicinus in its orbit around the sun, so we wouldn't catch up with it for two years, five days, eleven hours and seventeen minutes."

Dirk watched the two with delight. "It's nice when pilot and navigator get along so brilliantly. As captain, I'm allowed to perform marriages, too."

"My groom has yet to hatch, it seems," replied Nala.

Vicinus, the closest planet to Earth, had a completely black surface. Since it reflected no sunlight at all, its outline had only been discovered thirty years ago by Dodileo – with the help of his new EGT ("Extremely Good Telescope") on one of the 2700-foot mountains of Mauritius. Dodileo had wondered why space was even blacker than usual at one particular round dot. He had then noticed that this very black dot moved in a constant orbit around the sun and came a little closer to Earth than Venus and Mercury.

"I have a question," said Dirk. "Just a quick one for understanding: We need a whole year to get to Vicinus? Our supplies will only last three months."

Nala turned to her captain. "I'd like to use the alternative propulsion system. That would certainly speed things up."

Dirk nodded. He looked to the folding chair on his left. The first officer was noticeably quiet.

"Hooky," said Dirk, "now fire up the wok drive or whatever. I want to see the 'unseen planet'."

"Hmm," replied Hookbeak. "We could turn on the warp drive. But it would be better if we waited for my scientific advisers. They wanted to drop in right before supper. That's in about... whoa... about now."

The lift opened.

"Bad news, everyone!" said Dertie, hurrying onto the bridge. "The palm thieves attacked the cooks with their claws. In the ensuing chaos, they escaped in the elevator. We lost their trail on deck... deck... well, on deck I've-got-no-idea. The point is they're gone."

"With the crabs on board," grumbled Anton, "the food won't last two months."

Birdie sent Popin through the Tube to the bridge. She still had a bone to pick with the other parrots.

When she had reclaimed her station screeching, the worst thing had been the question of her pet Herbert: "Agh! What's the problem?"

Birdie took a deep breath. She tried to explain it calmly to the parrots, for she had screamed enough for today.

"It's not very nice of you to hack my computer and abuse it as a stereo system because you're bored. You could have deleted all medical records! But what I really can't accept is that you run a hopping race over five hundred hammocks in this station because you think you have to move to music! And I don't give a hoot which one of you has the most victories, who is *the* Fastest Hammock Hopper in the Universe and..." she paused and looked at Jay, who looked like a mummy, only significantly worse bandaged, "...and who broke the most body parts bouncing off the walls!"

Jay never knew when it was wise to keep his beak shut. "Argh! Did we mention that already? The prize goes to me!" he said proudly.

"*I CAN SEE THAT, YOU FEATHERBRAINED, LITTLE MOR...*"

🪶

Chief Engineer Hookbeak typed a physics formula into the control panel with his toes.

"What do you think?" he asked his two advisers and Dertie.

"After the gravitational constant," said Dodernicus, "you could possibly put a bracket because it looks fancier."

"But you don't necessarily have to," said Dodileo. "I think if you leave out the bracket, the spacetime curvature is more *intense*."

Hookbeak looked uncertain and glanced at the science officer.

"If you don't put a bracket at the end," said Dertie, "you'll have to drop the first bracket too, of course."

"Oh, goodness, no!!!" croaked Dodileo and Dodernicus. They had rarely been in such agreement.

"As you like," replied Hookbeak. "Just the bracket at the beginning, then. Captain, the warp drive is ready for use. The lowest level will be enough for Vicinus."

"Er, Hookbeak," whispered Dertie, her beak very close to his red mohawk. "We're both not sure that's the correct formula. So why do you want to listen to your advisers? Maybe Birdie should have a... Ouch! Your hair poked me."

"I think it's all right," said the chief engineer. "Besides, I refuse to believe the world would end because of a misplaced bracket."

Dertie sighed and returned to her panels on the left wall.

Dirk rubbed his feet in delight. "Well, step on it, Nala!" he commanded. "Warp speed!"

"Aye, Captain!" said Nala and opened the throttle.

The Sea Cow's tail flukes began to move up and down blazingly fast, creating a warp bubble around the whole ship. A few atomic particles were sucked into the bubble, and even more particles were pulled along to Vicinus by the spacetime curvature. Hookbeak had taken the particles into account in his equation, but one bracket too many (or too few) ruined everything.

Space hurtled past them for twenty seconds, then the short warp flight was over. They came to a stop sixty-five thousand miles from Vicinus while the charged particles were hurled forward in a tremendous burst of energy. The gamma rays and energy particles caused the black planet to glow brightly for the first and last time in its history.

The captain uttered a curse to the gods. Anton Pavlovich cursed someone's mother. Dertie cursed the first officer. The first officer cursed his advisers, who were cursing each other. Nala had heard enough curses and refrained from making her own contribution.

The next moment, Popin came shooting out of the Tube.

"Got lost," she said. "Bad signposting. Did I miss anything? *Argh?*"

The planet between Earth and Mars burned up on *Day Seven of the Sea Turtle* in the *Year of the Mean Ducks*.

"Well, hopefully it was uninhabited," said Dertie, her mind on her bio lab. "Otherwise I've missed my first prey."

Hookbeak started to whine. "I'm sorry that future generations won't be able to see... won't be able to think of Vicinus in the night sky. Now there are only eight planets left in the solar system."

"Nine planets left in the solar system," said Dirk. "When we went to school, Pluto was a real planet, not a dwarf."

Dodernicus croaked, "When I went to school, Earth was still the centre of the universe."

"Touché," admitted Dirk. "Hookbeak? Maybe Birdie should take a look at your warp equation."

"It certainly wasn't the bracket," said Dodileo.

"What was it then?" barked Dertie.

"Love and peace, everybody," said the captain. "Be nice to each other. Accusations won't do anyone any good. Look! Vicinus is breaking apart and going down in flames! It's not every day you see something glowing so beautifully."

For the second time in three hours, the officers marvelled at an image they could see from space. They had caused one of these images themselves, but that would only have bothered a few Vicinusians or Vicinarians. If they had ever existed.

🌿

Dertie had an idea how to lift Hookbeak's spirits after his little Vicinus accident: A flight experiment!

After supper, nearly four hundred dodos gathered in the cargo hold. Only Nala was missing because she had to keep flying the ship until bedtime.

"All right, flight test 1.0," said Dertie to Hookbeak.

She stood in a wide aisle between the fruit shelves and got ready for take-off.

Hookbeak put his wing on the regulator for the gravity generators. Next to him stood his advisers and Anton.

Dodernicus gave the chief engineer a hint. "Remember not to turn off the artificial gravity completely or we'll float around with the cargo."

"I know, I know," said Hookbeak. "Let's see if fifty per cent of Earth's gravity is sufficient."

He turned down the artificial gravity and nodded to Dertie.

The science officer took a jump of thirteen feet with a running start. A new world record in the long jump. Then she jumped six-and-a-half feet without a running start – twice her body length.

Hookbeak lowered the artificial gravity bit by bit. Nevertheless, Dertie could not keep herself in the air, no matter how much she flapped her wings.

The spectators were getting nervous. Of course, the officer was making impressive progress, records in the high and long jumps were tumbling, but could she become light enough to fly?

"It's getting better and better," said Dertie. "The big moment is almost here. I can feel it happening. Keep lowering the gravity!"

"There's hardly any gravity left for me to lower," muttered Hookbeak.

"But," said Dodileo, "she's already made a giant leap for a dodo."

"So far, that's only a small step for dodokind," mumbled Hookbeak. "*ONE LAST TEST!*" he called out. "Let's try 0.89 metres per square second. That's one-eleventh of the acceleration due to Earth's gravity."

Immediately, everyone felt the difference.

"I feel so light all of a sudden," said Anton.

"Wow, I'm almost floating," said Dodileo.

Dertie wanted to start running, but after one step, she was already ten feet in the air. When she touched the ground again, she jumped forward with both legs. She began to flap her wings, wild as a duck in hunting season, and held a low altitude for six seconds before plopping down. Her belly bounced off the floor ten times, sending her jumping like a tennis ball towards the wall.

"It worked!" Anton was excited. "She flew!"

The audience cheered exuberantly. Complete strangers lay in each other's wings and the bird choir sang *Hip, Hip, Hooray*.

"It only worked," said Hookbeak, "because there was almost no grav..." He interrupted himself, not wanting to diminish Anton's hope. "Well, yes," he admitted, "Dertie took off for a moment."

As they watched Dertie being thrown into the air by the enthusiastic crowd and shooting against the ceiling, Dirk and Birdie came jumping over.

"A complete success, our science officer's test!" Dirk was delighted. "Now get back to work, everyone!"

Birdie remained silent and looked at Hookbeak. He could tell by her expression that she wasn't convinced either. But it was a victory for crew morale.

"Maybe," Hookbeak wondered, "if the air and wind properties are favourable, we will get aerodynamic lift. So maybe flying would be possible on a planet with a gravity slightly less than half that of Earth. Maybe."

"Many maybes, but not impossible," said Birdie. "We'll have to test that theory on a local planet. I found the bracket that you'd placed incorrectly, by the way. That should spare us any future Vicinus."

Hookbeak nodded in shame and turned the gravity back to Earth level. The bouncing dodos groaned in disappointment as they thunked to the floor.

"Jumping party?!" a male cleaner shouted.

Dirk stepped out of the lift again. "All right, but only five minutes!"

Hookbeak sighed and turned the gravity to thirty per cent.

Five minutes became half an hour.

"The cosmos... or space, whatever... let me do it again!... *Space*, the final front..."

"Argh! That's stolen! Stolen! Argh!" cried Popin.

"All right, I can say it differently," said Dirk. "Spatial Infinity. No boundaries, er, because that's what infinity means. This is the voyage of the Dodo Alpha Jet..."

"Nickname: Sea Cow," said Dertie.

"...which, so far, is one planet away from the Earth island of Mauritius – an unintentionally destroyed planet, by the way. Flying with top speed, we are now at... Nala, where are we?"

"Ahead of Pluto... next to Pluto... behind Pluto," said the racing pilot.

"The ship," continued Dirk, "has just passed Pluto with top warp speed. We're on our way to find a habitable planet with lower gravity somewhere in the Milk Street."

"Milky Way," Dertie corrected him.

"Right. End captain's log."

Popin pressed a second button on the recorder.

"Message deleted," announced the electronic voice.

Popin put on her sweetest innocent face.

"Never mind," said Dirk to his pet. "We all need a bit of practice with this stuff."

Timeline of Dodo History on Planet Earth

97248 BC	The ancestors of the dodos live on islands in Southeast Asia and want to circumnavigate the world as a swarm. After just a few days over the vast Indian Ocean, with no land in sight, they begin to wonder why they chose such a stupid flight path. Shortly before reaching the coast of Mauritius, they all fall into the sea, exhausted. One female and one male are washed ashore. On the island, they find no predators, and the climate is quite pleasant too. They settle down and have many chicks.
71313 BC	The dodos forget how to fly.
273 AD	The dodos learn the language of their parrot pets.
275	The dodos rename the language Dodish. The parrots correct their feeders every time that it's called Parrot.
590-595	More than one hundred dodos travel the world on a sailing ship.
595	Only a few dodos return to Mauritius, but all the parrots are unharmed and bring offspring to the island. Captain Altair announces that all the parrots in the world speak Dodish.
596	The CHIMP (Council of Highly Intelligent Mauritian Parrots) calls a meeting. The parrots are sparing with words as a protest against the falsification of history and achieve unexpected results.
1313	The civilisation of the dodos has reached its heyday. Nevertheless, no one is happy. In her talk show, psychologist Birdie opens the eyes of her fellow citizens.
1313	A dodo speaks of his vision of a better future at a demonstration.

	A spaceship of dreamers leaves Earth in search of a new world. Shortly afterwards, the black planet burns up in the night sky.
1313	The United Forests of Mauritius (UFofM) add another word to their country name.
1403	After earthquakes and floods, there is a food shortage on Mauritius. Dodos fight each other over the last fruit, and civilisation perishes. Their pets flee to Madagascar and don't return until three years later.
1406	The dodos are back in the Stone Age after the war. They narrowly escaped extinction.
1506	After a century without houses and technology, the dodos have forgotten they ever had houses and technology. They live in harmony with nature – just like the parrots do.
1507-1690	Human sailors land on Mauritius and discover the trusting dodos. The birds are easy prey.
1690	The dodos did not escape extinction.

Chapter 5: Captain Dirk, Where Are We Going?

Six weeks had passed since Birdie had corrected the bracket error in Hookbeak's formula. Six weeks in which the crew had observed numerous gas giants and dead rocky planets from their orbits.

One could see the disillusionment in the birds' faces by now. The search for a suitable planet had so far been unsuccessful in the *Cow, Soy,* and *Coconut Milky Way*, although the ship made three to four warp jumps per day.

The Milky Way galaxy also had a fourth spiral arm: the *Almond Milky Way*, but the captain ignored it because no star charts existed of it. Milky gas clouds shrouded its celestial bodies.

The Sea Cow was in warp flight to another star. Flight time remaining: 3 hours, 14 minutes, 46 seconds.

Pilot Nala glanced at the thick book lying above the time display which contained seven-hundred-year-old travelogues. Within a split second, she changed her mind and looked away again.

Phew, that was close! she thought because she had hated books since school. Major works of Mauritian literature like *'Wing. The First Part of the Tragedy'*, *'Lord of the Wings'* or *'Waiting for Dodot'* had deprived her of any pleasure in reading.

Nala's eyes wandered from the control stick to the accelerator. She usually operated both with her wing and foot. Now they moved on their own as if by magic.

She couldn't stand the autopilot. And it wasn't because of her flying skills that the Sea Cow had already destroyed a planet.

"Just be glad," the captain had said, "that we found the autopilot." And he had ordered Nala to execute the warp flights fully automatically. "Now you can put your feet up. Too much work isn't healthy. Look at Birdie. She works so hard that none of us have seen her for weeks."

---

* A pun on Goethe's 'Faust: The Second Part of the Tragedy'. The German word *Faust* translates to *fist* in English.

Nala looked again at the display on her instruments. Flight time remaining: 3 hours, 14 minutes, 8 seconds.

She took a deep breath and closed her eyes. *Oh, darn it!* she thought. She blinked at the book and pulled it down a bit with her beak until it covered the time display.

Before she had been exposed to dreary school reading, her parents had read to her every evening from an old edition of the book. As a little chick, she had found the texts and pictures very entertaining. There was a difference of opinion on whether they were legends, travelogues or fairy tales.

"I've never dreamt," whispered Nala, "that I would willingly read something out of boredom."

She opened the well-preserved copy that the ship's librarian had talked her into. She refused to take off her oversized goggles for a book, though, not to mention her brown aviator hat.

Like most readers, she didn't care about the preface. She was about to turn the page when something caught her eye. The 82nd edition of *Seafarer Altair on the Seven Seas* had a new preface by a well-known personality. Nala was taken by complete surprise.

Preface

By Dodernicus, Professor of History (and Astronomy)

In the Age of the Hammerhead Sharks, Captain Altair and his crew sailed around the globe and gained amazing insights into the foreign parts of the world and their animal inhabitants. Many of my fellow citizens now consider these stories to be fairy tales with which to scare a chick. However, they do not dare to repeat Altair's journey when it is pointed out that only a quarter of the dodos returned to Mauritius. According to the survivors, all the other sailors fell victim to the big cats, crocodiles and hairless great apes which had spread around the world, lying in wait for the poor dodos to arrive.

On five continents, Altair encountered parrots who, to his delight, also spoke Dodish everywhere and led his crew around as tour guides. This had the aforementioned fatal consequences because the parrots always forgot that we cannot fly away from danger. (Although the Parrots of the Caribbean had possibly led the dodos into a trap on purpose.)

Don't be surprised that our echo parakeets and the parrots from overseas still spoke complete sentences at that time. The virus dumbed down our pets only a short time later, after Altair had returned to Mauritius with the remnants of his crew.

According to our current knowledge, Captain Altair wrote the following book without outside help. It contains descriptions and drawings of exotic animals such as the Tiger, Koala, Kangaroo, Sheep, Camel, Cow, Big-Eared Elephant, Small-Eared Elephant, Good Dog, Bad Wolf, Hungry Lion, Devious Human and many hundreds more.

The stars of the night sky showed Altair the way. He thanked them on his return by giving our galaxy, White Stuff, the more beautiful name 'Milky Way'. And who knows, maybe we will travel to the stars in the not-too-distant future. Only one question remains: Are we ready to explore strange worlds while we don't even appreciate Altair's reports from our Earth?

Dodernicus, in the Year of the Colourful Gecko.[*]

Unforeseen problems had arisen in the communication tubes. For one thing, the Tube was constantly clogged when the parrots flew to work. For another, there were no right-of-way rules, so outside rush hour, there were often accidents between speeders. The parrots were as obstinate and unteachable on this one point as on any other, which is why Birdie's animal hospital always kept filling up with crash pilots. This was one of the reasons why Birdie never had time for a breather.

---

[*] 1297 AD

Today, on the 43rd day of the voyage, she stepped onto the bridge for the first time since take-off.

Her gaze wandered around the room (in all that time, apparently not a single dusting had been done) and stopped at a board on the left wall. The board was above Science Officer Dertie's seat and showed the route they had travelled so far.

The route criss-crossed.

Birdie rolled her eyes. Did everyone on the bridge have a screw loose? In her initial analysis, she thought it to be the obvious explanation.

With a frown, she stood in front of her boss, who was slouching in his armchair.

"Captain Dirk, where the heck are we going?" she asked.

The captain shook his head disapprovingly. "Oh, Number Two. You're the only one I have to repeat everything for. We're heading to a planet where we can hang out on clouds."

"I could now explain to you, Dirk, that it's physically impossible to sit or hang out on clouds – at least under the conditions we know of from habitable planets – but you don't even know what physics is."

"Sure I do. It's something like chemiligy and biolostry. Never interested me. Where is Hookbeak?"

Dirk's question was directed at the whole bridge, although no one but his pet felt addressed.

"Argh, Hookbeak," said Popin with a shrug.

"Pops, find Hooky and tell him to come here," said Dirk. "We'll have an officers' meeting – now that Number Two is finally on the bridge. You got that?"

"Argh, Hooky. Bridge. Argh," replied Popin.

Dirk nodded. "Well done, my dear silly. And off goes the Tube mail."

By the time Popin had left the bridge, Birdie was visibly upset.

"I'm *finally* on the bridge?" she repeated. "Without me, everything would fall apart on the Sea Cow. If it were up to job performance, I'd have to be captain because I do five jobs at once! Well, all right, four jobs. Nobody needs a lawyer in space."

"And I carry the heavy burden of responsibility," countered the captain as he scratched his feathered belly with his foot. "It's so heavy, I cannot put that on anyone else."

"Oh, elected and incompetent commander," said Birdie, "please explain to me what the route is all about. Why didn't you ask the computer for the next destination? This looks like a huge tohubohu!"

Dirk's forehead wrinkled, and his beak quietly repeated the foreign-sounding word.

Nala came to her captain's rescue without taking her eyes off her storybook. "Tohubohu means complete chaos! The word is rarely used, but it's in my book too. The parrots from overseas claimed they invented it."

"Ah," said Dirk, giving Birdie a smile. "Hooky and Anton have come up with an ingenious way of randomly determining our next destination. So, the chaos is based on improbable probabilities."

Navigator Anton proudly turned in his chair to face the captain.

"May I explain it to Birdie?" he asked.

"Fair enough," said Dirk. "But first, we're going to the cafeteria for some lunch."

Birdie shook her head. "Then we'll meet back here in an hour. I can't afford to take a lunch break because there'll be injured speeders outside the animal hospital in a minute. As always."

She ran to the lift.

The ship's warp engine was giving Hookbeak a headache.

For six weeks, they had been jumping from one solar system to the next several times a day. This was not without consequences, because the engine was puffing as hard as a great-grandpa who had been pushed with energy drinks and was on the verge of breaking the marathon world record.

Speaking of great-grandpas, Hookbeak's scientific advisers Dodernicus and Dodileo spent most of their days in deckchairs. At the moment, they were sitting on the first level of the engine room, marvelling at the problem of wear and tear.

"All equipment breaks down when it wears out," Dodileo said. "Everyone wants to grow as old as a turtle, but..."

"...nobody talks about wanting to reach the age of a refrigerator or a warp drive," Dodernicus added.

Hookbeak paced thoughtfully between the two deckchairs while the drive engine in the basement screamed for help.

"When machines break, I fix them again," he told his advisers. "I haven't done anything else for seven days now. And each time, more is broken. From now on, we're only allowed to make one warp jump a day! That will be a heavy blow to the captain and the crew."

"Argh, heavy blow!" exclaimed Jay, who was sitting on a stair railing next to the fusion reactor, one level above the dodos.

Jay liked the engine room. For one thing, it was always cosy and warm near the reactor, and for another, there were countless kinds of perches for him to perch on. After he had broken his bones, flying still caused him pain, so he loved to spend his time testing railings and piping for comfort. Apart from that, he hobbled to the lift three or four times a day to report to the bridge. There, he had to hop on a map and would get a treat as a thank you.

Suddenly, Popin whooshed out of the Tube into the engine room. She was completely out of puff, took a few deep breaths and sat down next to her brother on the railing.

"Dude, those stupid speeders always!" she whispered in his ear. "They don't even give a young lady the right of way any more. I know that discretion is the better part of valour, but boy, I would've loved to shove them into hospital, believe me."

Popin's expression brightened when she saw Hookbeak. For an hour, she had searched almost everywhere on the ship for him. Why it had only occurred to her three minutes ago that the chief engineer might be in the engine room remained a mystery to herself. Today was just one of those days she would have preferred to spend in the nest.

"Argh. Booky! Ridge! Argh," she cried.

"Excuse me?" asked Hookbeak.

"No, wrong... Spooky. Witch. Argh?" said Popin, thinking hard about what exactly she was to tell Hookbeak once she found him.

"Are you trying to insult me?" asked the chief engineer, shocked.

When Popin wasn't flying errands for Dirk, she dozed off on the bridge. Three to four times a day, she also jumped around on maps.

꧁

More and more repeat offenders, Birdie thought at the sight of the injured pilots waiting outside the animal hospital.

She recognised her first patient, a male parrot.

"Papagayo, is it?" she asked him. "If I remember correctly, you are a friend of Jay and Popin? Do you also happen to know Herbert? He's my parrot."

"*Ugh!* Yes," replied Papagayo in disgust. "A pompous jer..."

"Excuse me?"

"Herbert, terrific guy," he corrected himself.

"Lie down in your hammock and raise your wing."

Ever since her computer had been misused as a stereo, Birdie had banned parrots from her office. The waiting room was better for treatments anyway because it was three times as big.

There were eleven more parrots lined up in front of Papagayo's hammock. They were writhing in pain as if they would faint at any moment. Yet all they wanted to do was jump the queue.

Suddenly, Birdie's office door opened and the nine palm thieves came strolling into the waiting room. They had stolen surgical knives ("scalpels") and an old-fashioned ear trumpet that didn't deserve the name stethoscope.

The injured parrots panicked. They clung to Birdie's legs, hoping that the big, strong dodo would protect them from the giant crabs. But Birdie was rooted to the spot. She was no match for eighteen sharp claws.

The palm thieves casually walked past the birds. They climbed on top of each other at the exit, pressed the door opener and made off with their loot.

"Hey, come back with my instruments!" shouted Birdie. "You don't need knives—you have claws!" She sighed wearily, having neither the time nor the inclination to pursue the robbers. "As you wish. I have no shortage of surgical tools." She wrapped a bandage around Papagayo's wing and gave him instructions. "Rest for a week and definitely don't fly. Use the lift like a good boy! Next Tuesday you'll come in for a check-up. Off you go, then."

After Birdie had treated the bruises of the twelve parrots, she took the lift back to the bridge. She was even looking forward to an explanation for the route now. There had to be a good reason if Hookbeak had taken part in it.

But the chief engineer had not yet come to the bridge.

The captain shrugged. "Either Hooky was here when we had lunch or there are message delivery problems. I'd have the messenger thrown out of an airlock if she wasn't my own pet. So she gets off with a warning."

"Very considerate of you," remarked Birdie sarcastically. "Anyway. Anton Pavlovich was trying to explain to me the nonsen... the route on the board."

"Oh yes!" exclaimed Anton with joy. "So how do we choose our next destination? Well, it's very simple. Since we don't know which solar system is suitable, we always let chance decide. First, we put the star maps of the three Milky Ways on the floor. Ingenious, isn't it? But that's not the most ingenious thing yet. The real ingenuity is yet to come. Because after that, Popin and Jay cover their eyes with their wings and each of them jumps onto one solar system per Milky Way respectively. Which gives us two systems each of the Soy, the Coconut, and the Cow Milky Way. Great, isn't it? But that's not the greatest thing yet. The real greatness is yet to come. We now take the six-sided random number generator – that's a piece of wood that Dertie carved – and label each side with a solar system. Then Hookbeak takes the piece of wood in his beak and spits it on the floor. We wait until it stops rolling and fly to the system written on top. Now you're amazed, *huh?*"

Birdie stared at her feet as she began to whistle softly. On her first day of interning at a law firm, she had discovered this recipe for staying sane when surrounded by lunatics. Her subsequent internship at a mental hospital had seemed like a holiday.

"It's that easy," added Anton. "We call the six-sided random number generator *'die'* because Nala said we're all going to die because of it."

"Well," Birdie said, her eyes still fixed on her feet. "I probably would have resorted to less pessimistic words, but you're flying through space without having a clue and with dwindling food supplies, so, eventually, Nala would be absolutely right in her conclusion."

"Ha!" Nala exclaimed perkily.

"You're heading for the stars in a gamble-based zigzag course," Birdie summed it up. "Insanity, thy name is dodo."

"How else should we have chosen?" asked Dertie. "Besides, you have to pass the time somehow."

Birdie took a deep breath. A breath so deep that her lungs hurt. She hadn't yelled in six weeks and didn't want to relapse.

Meanwhile, Anton was musing. "Come to think of it, to call the piece of wood *die* sounds a bit negative. Maybe we should use its plural."

"Well," said Dertie, "the plural of the die piece is *'dies'*, isn't it? Doesn't sound any better."

"What did you just say?" asked Dirk. "The *die piece?* How about coining a new word out of the two? Dice. D-I-C-E. It's spelled like *lice*, so you won't think of dying. Dice can be the plural, so let's use it as the singular!"

"Agreed!" said Dertie and Anton.

"Are you done with the stupid die or dice now?!" asked Birdie. "Because I wasn't finished. Why didn't you ask the ship's computer for the best route? If I create a technological marvel, I expect it to be used. *Fortitoo?*" she asked into the room. "Have you analysed all the star systems? Why is the computer not responding?"

"The computer can't talk," said Anton. "It can only carry out orders. You really should know that 'cause you built it."

"Of course the computer can talk," said Birdie. "Its name is Fortitoo, or rather *his* name because he's got such a pleasant male voice. He talks to me all over the ship. Who turned his volume down on the bridge?"

"*Oh*, that's right!" said Nala, startled. "Just before we left, I was alone on the bridge. I was wondering aloud how little I might weigh, and the computer just answered. Wasn't very nice of *him*. He was definitely lying because I don't weigh that much! I mean, I don't own any scales, but I'm sure I don't weigh *that*..."

"*ENOUGH!*" screamed Birdie as she could no longer bear the madhouse. She stepped forward to the dashboard and stood next to Nala's chair.

The intimidated pilot pressed a few buttons until the volume display for the ship's computer appeared. She hastily turned the volume from zero to maximum.

"Computer? My boss wants to talk to you," Nala said, drenched in sweat. "Come in. *Please?!*"

"YO, YO. WHAT'S UP?" asked the computer, and Birdie was knocked to the floor by the sound waves.

*

"Beep," said Fortitoo calmly when he had finished his calculations. "Since we're in the Coconut Milky Way now, it would make sense to stay here first to check out the two remaining solar systems which have potential. If it suits you at the moment. That leaves you with another four systems in the Soy Milky Way and nine systems in the Cow Milky Way. And so far, you have completely left out the Almond Milky Way. One might well ask: *Why?* But I don't, because my interest would just be feigned. Can I relax now?"

"Solar systems that have potential?" asked Science Officer Dertie.

"Really? You don't know about that?" wondered Fortitoo. "That's like starting with the primordial soup when you explain the world to someone. But I'll help you. Going to all the stars was a complete waste of time. Life can only arise in a solar system that has a planet in its habitable zone. Makes sense, doesn't it? Well, good luck, then."

"Habitable zone?" inquired Dirk and Anton.

"*Really, guys?*" asked Fortitoo. "Aren't space travellers supposed to know that? Me explaining your own area of expertise to you, that's a bit much."

"What a spoilt brat," said Dirk about the computer. He gave Birdie a reproachful look.

She avoided eye contact with him as she replied, "I programmed the computer's artificial intelligence but unfortunately I didn't have the time to give it my impeccable personality. A colleague from computer science gave me a personality file. It was simply called: *Fortitoo. Swell guy to party with.*"

"Yep," confirmed Fortitoo, "but I didn't imagine the party to be such a dull cruise. At least I can have a good chat with Birdie. The others can rent out a lot of space from their upper storeys. By the way, the ship's library has books where you can look up 'habitable zone'. But why is it called ship's library? Shouldn't it be spaceship's library? And have you already noticed that a space flight resembles a sea voyage? You're space sailors. Or an older term... space-seafarers? Hmm, sounds a bit odd. I'll have to think about it. Ahoy."

The computer retreated to a virtual lounge where he listened to soothing electro music.

The Very Small Dictionary of Space Terms calls the habitable zone "home zone: the neighbourhood where you should build your home because the surrounding neighbourhoods are too hot or too cold to live in."

In his *Encyclopaedia of Our Universe (The Part of the Universe We Know of (Mostly the Milky Way)) and Other Universes (Which We Don't Know Anything About)*, Dodileo Dodilei describes the habitable zone somewhat more precisely:

"In order for you to have liquid water, your home planet should a) have water and b) be the perfect distance from your sun (i.e., be in the habitable zone). If the distance between the sun and the planet is smaller, the water evaporates, and if it's greater, the water freezes. How you gonna drink it then?"

🌿

The Sea Cow arrived in the new solar system.

Just when the book becomes exciting, thought Nala. She dropped the book on the floor and switched off the autopilot to take the ship's controls into her own feet. Then she lowered the warp speed to level one.

To the officers' surprise, a rocky planet with an atmosphere orbited the sun in its habitable zone.

"Lucky fluke," Birdie called it. After all, this system had still been selected with the six-sided random number generator after two parrots had jumped on maps.

Nala terminated warp flight as they approached the green planet. She let the Sea Cow's tail flukes swing out slowly as the warp bubble dissolved. Now she steered the ship into orbit using the two flippers, uh, jet engines.

The captain didn't want to rush the officer in charge, but after fifty minutes, he could no longer stand the suspense.

"Birdie..." he said.

"Yes, Dirk."

"Wait, not you, Number Two. I meant our science officer, Dertie. Your names are way too similar. Never mind. Dertie, planetary analysis?"

So far, Dertie had always replied with, "It's a gas planet!" or "No life possible!" This time, she did not move or say anything at all.

Dirk cleared his throat. Birdie coughed awkwardly. But Dertie was still as quiet as a mouse.

"Dertie?!" began the captain again. "What does your display say about the planet?"

"Great stuff," she answered tersely, still staring at her monitor. Her voice sounded as if it came from far away.

The seconds ticked by. The captain tried to stay patient. He looked at Number Two, who returned his questioning glance.

More seconds turned into uneventful history.

"Dertie?" asked the captain.

"Yes, Captain?" asked Dertie.

"What great things?"

"Well, plenty of oxygen and fruits. And a pleasing absence of meat eaters. Don't you know how to read the data? Or do you have trouble with the abbreviations? O2 is oxygen, H2O is water…"

"Dertie," Birdie said as calmly as she could, "only you can see the data."

"*What?* Since when?" inquired Dertie.

"Since always." Birdie's composure had been short-lived. "Hookbeak only installed the monitor on the science officer's panel. He believed she could interpret the data best. Of course, back then he had no idea that *you* would be the science officer. And that's only the case because I turned down that additional area of responsibility."

"Give me a break, quack," said Dertie. "That's no reason to be mean. Just come over to me. I'm only sitting six feet away from you."

Very reluctantly, the captain rose from his armchair and walked with Birdie to Dertie's seat.

They looked at the readings.

"Looks great, doesn't it?" said Dertie, thrilled.

"But," complained the captain, "it says the planet has one hundred and twelve per cent of Earth's gravity. We can't fly with that! That's twelve per cent worse than on Earth!"

It made no difference to Dertie. "We can at least stretch our legs in the fresh air and kidnap the locals," she suggested before looking very sad. "My dissection tools are now nine weeks old and still unused." She began to sob.

"Besides," Birdie said as she placed her wing comfortingly on the science officer's back, "we should refill our supplies first. They're almost exhausted."

Dirk had other plans and would not be swayed. "No way! We have better coordinates now, thanks to the computer. I'm sure we'll have found our dream planet in a few days. If not, we'll come back here so we don't starve."

He took two steps forward and was standing next to the pilot and navigator.

"Nala, Anton. Prepare everything for the next warp flight."

As the science officer heatedly discussed the merits of an away mission with her captain, Birdie exited the bridge. Whether she left because she had to attend to her patients or because she had heard enough nonsense for another six weeks remained her secret.

Immediately afterwards, Popin appeared on the bridge. The pretty parrot lady was not used to being ignored. And she didn't put up with it either. She flew to the captain and sat on his head.

"Aarrghhh!" she cried out. "Stait! Wopp!"

"What's the matter?" asked Dirk.

"Tait! Welephone! Argh?" said Popin and wondered, *What is wrong with me today?*

The doors of the lift burst open and Chief Engineer Hookbeak (CEH) ran to the executive chairdodo.

"Dirk! I think someone wants to talk to you!" he said, reaching for the phone in his feather belly.

"Say what now?" asked Dirk, perplexed.

"A call from the green planet below," explained Hookbeak. "Sounds like an alien language, but I don't care about that."

"Why not?"

"Well, the call certainly is for the commander-in-armchair. And that's you."

"But... but," Dirk stammered, "how did they get our number?"

Hookbeak shrugged. "Maybe they have cameras in orbit. I painted the number of my phone on the spaceship before we left. In case anyone wants to *call* us. I'm sure you remember that important meeting in the Bay of Pigeons where you interrupted me."

"Nah, I don't," replied Dirk. "Oh, dear. And where does it say that I'm the communications dude?"

"Communications officer. You said we wouldn't need one."

"All right, give me that darn thing." Dirk reached for the phone with his foot. "This is the Dodo Alpha Jet. You are speaking to Captain Dirk. Is someone there? And if so, who's the one who's there? Hello, hello? I don't know who is calling me. I said, 'Hello.' We're just passing through, so keep the call short!"

The officers heard alien sounds on the line until suddenly someone said: "The language is Parrot... hard to understand... Northern Mauritian dialect... so, Dodish, then?... Er, hey there, we are the Badians from the planet Imleria right below you. And you speak Dodish, so you're probably dodos. Boy, that's huge!"

Dirk lowered the phone. His first officer was standing in front of him, with his back to the Sea Cow's eye. "Maybe turn around. I think you're showing them your butt."

Hookbeak felt insulted. "All right. But it's no bigger than yours."

"Mine is hiding in my chair," Dirk said before shouting into the phone, "Okay, what do you want?!"

"Well, we want to establish diplomatic relations with you, of course," explained the Badian. "I am Baycap, the President of Imleria, and you are the first species from space to make contact with us."

"You called us!" Dirk replied reproachfully.

"Yes, that's right," confirmed Baycap. "And you have entered our orbit without permission. So I guess you're lucky we're in a hospitable mood today."

"Is that so?... Anyway, we don't have time right now. We're looking for a planet with lower gravity."

"Oh!" Baycap said, disappointed. "That's unfortunate. A pity indeed. Please come visit us on Imleria when you're back in the neighbourhood, then. As long as you don't want to eat us. Hospitality knows limits, ha-ha. Oh, before I forget: You might find a planet with lower gravity in the Almond Milky Way. There are thousands of languages in different solar systems there. Well, good luck in your search! Bye!"

Suddenly, Hookbeak snapped at the phone with his beak and seized it.

"Jusamomen," he mumbled, nearly swallowing his smartphone.

"Excuse me?" asked Baycap.

Hookbeak sat down on the folding chair to Dirk's right and put the phone in his little wing.

Dirk spotted a mistake. "This is Birdie's seat. Yours is still over here," he said and pointed to the folding chair on the left.

Hookbeak paid no attention to him because he had more important things to discuss with the Badian president.

"Just a moment!" Hookbeak called. "We can't fly on until tomorrow. Our propulsion drive needs a little rest."

"Wait, what's going on?!" asked Dirk.

"That's why," continued Hookbeak, "we'd like to accept your offer and stay overnight if that's all right with you."

"That actually sounds swell," said Baycap, "but the sun is rising in my town now."

"Oh?" said Hookbeak, surprised. "I hadn't thought of that possibility. Doesn't matter. Sleep's overrated anyway."

The dodos heard cries of joy from the Badians in the background.

"Well, that's settled then!" Baycap said happily. "It's nice that *aliens* are finally joining us!"

"Our science officer is dying to meet you too," said Hookbeak as he saw Dertie beaming. "And it's great that we can understand you perfectly now. Why can you speak our language?"

"Because we're amazing," replied the Badian president.

"Good answer," said Dirk.

"Just doesn't explain much," remarked Hookbeak.

Baycap admitted that it was a good answer that didn't explain much. "We have mega-powerful microphones on Imleria. With them, we were able to record all the sounds and languages in the Milky Way. And, using these languages, our smartest minds developed some universal translators."

"But," rejoined Hookbeak, "some stars are thousands of light years away. So what you're claiming is entirely impossible! Not to mention that you can't transmit sounds through airless space. Therefore, it is doubly impossible!"

"Correct," said Baycap. "The sound waves didn't travel to our microphones through space, but with the help of dark matter. We're just amazing."

Hookbeak cleared his throat contemptuously. "You've already mentioned that. All right, let's assume you can do magic. Do you have a universal translator to spare? Might be useful."

"Don't you want to land first?" asked Baycap impatiently. "This conversation will be charged to me as a long-distance call, do you understand? We can discuss payment for a translator at my residence."

"*Payment?!*" cried Dirk and Hookbeak in shock. Money had not existed in Mauritius since the Age of the Flying Foxes.

Fortunately, Baycap gave them an alternative. "You can offer us something in exchange for all I care. Surely you have things on the ship you can spare?"

"We still have mushrooms in the fridge!" exclaimed Dirk, delighted.

Suddenly, all of Imleria, perhaps even the entire Coconut Milky Way, was gripped by a ghastly silence.

Baycap sounded very offended when he spoke to them again half a minute later. "We're intelligent descendants of mushrooms. That would be like you eating a parrot."

"Argh, won't serve as food!" yelled Popin. "Won't serve as food for anyone!" She then had to think about whether she'd broken the law of 'playing dumb,' which states that parrots aren't allowed to utter more than ten words in a row. *Nope*, she thought, relieved. *The CHIMP doesn't count silly noises like 'Argh' as words, and it accepts a contraction like 'won't' as a single word, as opposed to what the Foxridge universities are saying.*

"Baycap," said Hookbeak, "we're so sorry. We didn't know. My captain didn't mean to offend you."

"Let's forget it," said Baycap.

"Allow me one last question before we land: If you want to make contact with other species, why don't you fly to them yourselves?"

"We don't like to travel," replied the intelligent fungus. "We prefer to be visited because when it's raining, we go into the woods. You just drop by for a glass of water now, okay? Wait a sec."

Dirk looked at his first mate, puzzled. "Dropping by for a glass of water?"

"*Mushrooms*," said Hookbeak with a shrug.

A loud siren began to wail on the bridge while the dodos waited.

A second later, Baycap spoke to them again. "We also have fruit tea if you'd rather drink that. Two jets are on their way to orbit. *Birdies*, why is there such a noise in the background? Is that your kind of *music*? Hey, whatever floats your boat. Where was I? The jets, right. They're escorting you to my official residence. And please tell your pilot to make a left swing because our orbital camera is heading straight for you at a speed of seventeen thousand miles per hour! This could end badly for you. If not, see you in a minute."

"Nala," said Dirk, "that's probably the reason for the proximity alarm."

"I know," replied the pilot, and she casually swung the Sea Cow to the right because the direction made no difference.

The Sea Cow landed in a vast wooded area, in a glade with a manicured lawn.

Baycap's residence was nothing more than a modest wooden hut. The Badians held the view that presidents had to live as poorly as the poorest section of the population. Only then could one be sure that they were fighting poverty and taking bribes from the mafia so that everyone would benefit from their election.

Hundreds of citizens stood on both sides of the hut. They had brown cap-shaped heads and cylindrical bodies with two small hands and feet. The resemblance to their ancestors was astonishing, although, at nearly five feet in body length, they were probably the largest mushrooms in the galaxy.

Many Badians held up signs affectionately welcoming the strangers: "Greetings, Extra-Imlerials!", "Please marry me, E.I.", and "Make yourselves at home, dodos (plus pets)!"

The greetings were written in the Badian language, which made no sense at all because, naturally, the extra-imlerial dodos (plus pets) didn't understand a word of Badian. In fact, there wasn't a single world in the universe where anyone ever understood that aliens couldn't read the language of the locals when they arrived. Maybe there really was no intelligent life in the universe after all.

The mushrooms grew quieter and quieter. You could feel the excitement and tension of the crowd.

After what felt like an eternity, the Sea Cow's snout-shaped hatch opened, and shadowy figures stepped into the light. Out of sheer joy, the Badians began to shriek.

The birds were greeted like giant pop stars. The dodos were almost uncomfortable with the level of attention – in contrast to the parrots, who enjoyed bathing in the limelight and making themselves available to the Badians for selfies.

Chapter 6: One Fell Over the Dodo's Nest

The rays of the low morning sun snaked their way through the forest to the clearing and wooden hut. The modest warmth they provided, however, died away in the cool wind.

"It's chilly," remarked Hookbeak, shivering at 9 degrees Celsius. On the ship, the air conditioning always kept a cosy 28 degrees, the perfect temperature for the tropical birds.

The parrots set off with the Badians to the back of the hut for a group photo, and the twelve geese took off for an excursion over the forest. The dodos felt left out of the fun, quite rightly.

The crew was standing around bored in the clearing while the officers waited at Baycap's door.

"Perhaps," Anton Pavlovich said after ten minutes, "Baycap is no longer in the hut but has joined the mushrooms and parrots behind it."

"But how would we know?" replied Hookbeak.

"It's conceivable," said Birdie, "that the tea water isn't ready yet."

"Well, I could *knock*," said Anton.

The others were struck dumb with shock.

When dodos were invited to tea, they never knocked on the door because otherwise the hosts might panic and rush things. Instead, the hosts would keep an eye out for their guests at the window as soon as they had taken the fruitcake and gingerbread geckos out of the oven. Before this tradition was introduced, most accidents had happened in the kitchen, and unfortunately it was always the cake that bit the dust.

No one had appeared yet at the two small windows in front of the hut. The captain began to wonder if this was a cultural misunderstanding between dodos and mushrooms. His patience was wearing thin. He turned to his crew and cleared his throat loudly several times.

A minute and countless gentle nudges passed before all the dodos caught on.

"Where's the megaphone?" asked Dirk.

"Probably on the ship," answered Birdie.

"Well, that's the perfect place for it to be now, Number Two."

"You could think for yourself for once."

Dirk had little desire to shout, but he had no choice when he needed to address four hundred dodos.

"Ahem!" he shouted at the top of his voice. "Listen up, everybody! You have free time now! Apart from the cooks, of course, because they have to make fruit porridge for lunch!"

"Dirk," whispered Nala, "we had lunch in the cafeteria four hours ago."

"When you're abroad, you have to adjust to local time," replied Dirk, directing his next words back to the crew. "Cooks, forward march! The fruit porridge won't cook itself! The rest of you spread out a bit. Don't just stand around like you're in the doldrums! Mingle with the mushrooms, or go take a look at the trees! Come on, you look like a bunch of wet blankets!"

Cook Alice stepped out of the crowd and coughed. A white chef's hat sat askew on her head.

"But they say," said Alice, "that too many cooks spoil the broth. That's why I'd better stay in the fresh air, to keep the risk as low as possible. With your permission, my esteemed visionary and captain."

She bowed deeply to Dirk and his officers, touching the ground with her beak.

"I do like," said Dirk, "how respectfully you kiss my, uh, my soul. I was going to say soul. But you have forgotten one important thing: We're talking about porridge, not broth. You're going back to the kitchen too. If the porridge is a disaster, I'll hold you personally responsible! Dismissed."

The twelve cooks went to the ship, their heads hanging low, while the great herd wandered to the edge of the forest. There, the dodos once again huddled together like a flock of sheep, loitering. A couple of them started filming each other with their smartphones.

"Anton," said Dirk, "keep an eye on them so they don't do anything stupid."

"Yes, boss!" rejoiced Anton and ran to the edge of the forest.

"Now, I didn't think that through. Hey, Nala, my little bird! Make sure Anton doesn't do anything stupid."

"Aye, Captain!" said the pilot and ran after her navigator.

By now, the door of the hut had opened a crack.

"Dirk, I think we're being watched," said Hookbeak.

"Is that right?" asked Dirk. "Well, it's about time someone noticed me."

A brown head appeared at the door and looked tentatively at the dodos.

Dertie was over the moon. "Yoo-hoo, mushroom guy! Go ahead, I won't hurt you!" she lied.

The Badian stepped out of the hut, pulling a small cart with a shiny wooden box on top.

"Hte pabcay. Kllih'sal kmyla 'te olyxnk? Fym lopo tarh'jk ka'ödsjd!" said the mushroom.

The wooden box had translated it simultaneously in the mushroom's voice: ~"I am Baycap. Why didn't you knock? We've been waiting for you for quite a while!"~

Immediately after, more mushrooms came out of the hut. One of them held a second translator box in her hands.

"May I introduce you," said Baycap. "This lady is my chief of staff, Amanita, and the gentlemushroom next to her is my security adviser, Aguaricus. They're interested in backward technology and would therefore like to look at your spaceship. If you allow it."

"Oh yes, we do!" replied Dertie. "Er, Captain, we do, don't we? *Please?*"

"Sure, I don't care," said Dirk. "But you'll have to show them around on your own then."

"Great!" said Dertie, smiling brightly at the mushrooms. "I am Dertie. First, I'm going to show you my small but mighty laboratory! I'm the science office, you see, and a biologist, as you're about to experience first-wing, that's 'first-hand' for you, he-he."

She briskly walked Aguaricus and Amanita to the ship.

Birdie watched them go with amusement. *Dertie is very popular because of her black humour*, she thought. *Of course her jokes are always about one subject: how do you dissect aliens? How do you cross them with parrots to create super soldiers? But that's simply her field of expertise. Apart from that, she often seems very serious, almost humourless... OH MY GODDESS! She's probably never cracked a joke in her entire life!*

Birdie took a deep breath. No, it couldn't be. No dodo was that ruthless, not even Dertie. That's right. Dertie was just a joker. But how well did you ever really know a dodo before you carried out a psychological assessment of them? Better safe than sorry.

"Diiirrrk!" said Birdie. "Are you seriously going to leave Dertie alone with the Badians?"

"Why not, Number Two? I'm sure the mushrooms won't hurt her."

"I do realise *that*," said Birdie. "But she might... Oh, forget it. I'll be right back."

Birdie ran to the swarm of dodos at the edge of the forest to talk to Anton, but she couldn't see him for all the other dodos.

"Anton Pavlovich?!" she called out.

She received no reply.

"NAVIGATOR ANTON! REPORT TO ME AT ONCE!"

The dodos standing directly in front of Birdie tried to increase their distance to her.

"THAT'S AN ORDER!" she added, as if there could have been any doubt about it.

"Aye, aye, boss," his voice rang out.

Anton had to shove aside a dozen dodos with his behind until he was standing in front of her.

"What is it?" he asked.

"I have an extremely important assignment for you," said Birdie. "It's no exaggeration when I say that your actions could mean the difference between life and death, even between war and peace."

"Oh holy Polly," Anton said. "That sounds pretty heavy. Taking responsibility isn't really my thing. I think I'll pass."

Birdie thumped her foot extremely fast on the forest floor, like a rabbit with its hind legs. "Anton, you will follow Dertie and the mushrooms to her bio lab right now and observe..."

"Hey, Number Two!" shouted Dirk across half the clearing. "Will you get over here now?! We want to take a closer look at Baycap's rickety hovel from the inside! You could have chatted with Anton on the ship!"

"Sheesh, I'll be right there!" shouted Birdie back. "My gosh! Do you think I like doing your job for you?!"

"Now don't get all stroppy with me, missy!"

Birdie only pretended to ignore Dirk's disrespectful remark for appearance's sake. She took care of Anton first because time was pressing.

"Run to the laboratory quickly," she commanded him, "and stop Dertie from dissecting or harming the Badians."

"You really think she's going to…"

"I'm not sure, okay? Now step on it!"

"I'm going already, I'm going," said Anton.

As Birdie stomped back to the hut, she imagined darts shooting out of her eyes, hitting Dirk on every last inch of his body.

"How wonderful," Dirk said to Baycap. "It seems the doctor is *finally* good to go, too."

A split second later, Birdie stepped on the captain's foot on purpose.

Under normal circumstances, Dirk would have felt little more than a small twinge in his foot bones, but in this case, he had to bear Birdie's full body weight as she deftly shifted it.

Dirk sank to the ground so theatrically that Brazilian football strikers would have gone green with envy.

"*Oh, the heavens!! This pain!!! Are you blind?!*" he screamed.

"Oh, I'm so very *sorry*," Birdie said in a sugar-sweet voice. "I guess I didn't see you there. I'm ready to go. What are you guys waiting for?"

"For the pain to subside."

"It's not even a broken bone, so stop complaining."

"How do you know that so quickly?" asked Dirk incredulously.

"Doctor's instinct," said Birdie. "I didn't hear it crack."

Baycap watched the scene patiently and with wonder. In his language, the expression 'strange bird' hadn't existed until now, but that would change today.

"Excuse me," said Hookbeak to Dirk and Birdie. "I hate to interrupt your flirting, but I think our pets want to come too."

He pointed to Popin, Herbert and Jay, who came walking and hobbling leisurely around the hut.

"Come on, move it, move it," Hookbeak called out to them. "Hurry up! Why walk when you can fly?"

The three parrots sat down on the backs of their respective owners. In fact, Jay got tangled up in Hookbeak's mohawk, while it came to Herbert that he would rather sit on Birdie's head.

"Ah, Herbert!" said Birdie. "I can't see!"

Popin spared Dirk such fuss. She felt her feeder had suffered enough for the time being.

"Argh," she crowed, "what's up?"

※

In the vessels of the sea cow... Pardon... In the corridors of the ship, the five-foot Amanita and Aguaricus had to stoop. For dodos, the ceiling height of four feet was more than sufficient, although Hookbeak usually lowered his head slightly so that his mohawk wouldn't drag along the ceiling.

Dertie's bio lab was in sick bay, as it had originally been a patient's room. Birdie would only need the repurposed room back in case of a severe plague.

"Here we are," Dertie told the mushrooms as they entered the laboratory. "Welcome to my little kingdom. During the long warp flights, I sometimes withdraw here to breed new hybrids from bugs and plants." On a rectangular table, the results of her experiments lay or crawled. "I also often extend my toilet breaks to sneak a look at their development. Oh, I probably shouldn't have told you that last bit. Oh well, what the heck. In a minute you won't be able to say anything any more anyway." It didn't sound like a threat but like a casually mentioned fact.

Amanita and Aguaricus looked at each other in horror. *Wait... we're about to lose our voices?!* The chief of staff gave the universal translator a good shake. Had it translated Dertie's last words correctly?

When the mushrooms were still mulling over Dertie's intentions, Anton came running into the room, panting heavily.

"Boy," he groaned. "I need to exercise more... or less... I need to lie down on the floor for a moment so I stop panting."

He lay down on the floor for a moment but didn't stop panting.

"*What are you doing here?*" asked Dertie angrily. "This is a bad time. I've got work to do!"

"I... er... I'm supposed to... help you with that," stammered Anton.

"Wait a minute," Dertie said.

She picked up a spray can from the table with her beak and turned to face the Badians.

"Fhis won'f hurf af all," she mumbled before clenching her beak and spraying knockout gas into the mushroom faces.

The Badians fell backwards and hit the ground hard.

"Oh dear!" wailed Anton. He scrambled to his feet. "I was supposed to stop you from killing them."

With a shrug, Dertie put the spray can back on the table.

"The mushrooms are still alive," she said. "They're drugged. If I had poisoned them, I wouldn't be able to use their cells. But now speak up! Who wants you to stop me from doing research?"

"Phew," Anton breathed a sigh of relief. "So I'm not too late. By command of Her Majest... er, no, wait a second... *Second!* That's it! By command of the second officer, I order you to stop! And there's this inner voice, too, that won't allow me to do evil. Uh, always this word-finding difficulty..."

"You're talking about your *conscience?*" asked Dertie.

"That's right," said Anton. "I hope it's all just a misunderstanding because..." He tried to think of a good reason. "Because the gods won't approve of you harming helpless mushrooms." He tried to think of a better reason. "If you touch the Badians, you'll probably start a war. I find that thought horrible. Wars are rumoured to lower life expectancy significantly, and I have an uneasy feeling that it would hit me first."

"You've got to be kidding me?" Dertie asked indignantly. "I've been telling everyone for months that I need alien tissue to make super soldiers. But if it eases your conscience, the Badians are fungi, which almost makes them plants. Now shut your pretty beak and let me work!"

Anton stared at her with wide eyes. "Everyone assumed you were joking. Black humour was considered your strong suit. But apparently you've gone completely mad now?"

Dertie pondered for a moment, then she slowly shook her head. "Have I gone mad *now*? No, to be honest, I've always been like this. Little green men are a danger to our future. You don't think all aliens are peaceful, do you? We're going to meet creatures in the galaxy who think of us as ants. Tell me, dear Anton: Did your parents never read to you from the sailors' book? It was called *Altair on the Seven Waters*, or something like that."

"Yes, I know the book," said Anton, confused. "I just don't know what it has to do with ants and aliens."

"Forget the ants. Nobody eats ants," said Dertie. "But wild beasts eat prey animals! Just remember the lions, koalas and wolves. These predators wiped out three-quarters of Altair's crew. That's how you know we're helpless prey. And that's why..."

"I think you're getting things mixed up. Koalas aren't predators. You might mean camels, which store the flesh of their victims in their humps."

"Anton," she said slowly and insistently. "What I'm saying is that Altair's stories weren't fairy tales to scare chicks. The wild beasts are real. Today no dodo still believes that sharks only eat fish, either."

Anton nodded sadly. "Nobody believes that any more since the water park bloodbath twelve years ago."

"Exactly," said Dertie. "Now imagine all the alien predators waiting for us in the vastness of space. I consider it my duty to protect the crew. All the better to have walking mushrooms following me into the lab."

"But the Badians aren't predators!"

"Yeah, I know. But they may help me develop a protection. Many mushrooms have poisonous ingredients. To extract their poison, I have to cut, slice and dissect the mushrooms until I have the hyphae. Hyphae are the very fine threads that make up mushrooms."

"Dertie, please, the poor Badians..."

"Anton, we can't put our feet up until we meet ravenous aliens. Then it will be too late. The Badians are mushrooms, not animals. You had mushrooms for lunch yesterday. What's the difference?"

"Badians can talk," replied Anton.

Dertie played down the issue. "Oh, so can pets and computers. I realise you're worried, my dickybird, but I assure you there will be no war. With our warp drive, we'll be long gone before Baycap even misses his staff." Suddenly, she began to muse. "Hm... now that I say it out loud, it occurs to me that I haven't thought it through."

"Oh, really?" asked Anton sharply.

"The whole crew is on land," she realised. "You must order them to return to the ship. Then you give the captain the signal to escape! You're going to save the day, my dear! In the meantime, I'll start with the mushroom female. Where have I put my dissection instruments now... *No worries, found them!*"

Anton was thunderstruck and speechless. Like most dodos, he had not taken Dertie's plans seriously – although she had communicated her intentions clearly and openly since day one. In this regard, you really couldn't blame her. Of course everyone knew that Dertie was missing some cups in her cupboard, but this condition was considered completely normal. A sparsely filled cupboard was part of a dodo's nature because the birds never drank from cups.

Birdie was the only one who never came to terms with the craziness on board. However, it had escaped her notice that in addition to the typical dodo madness, there was also an unusual amount of cold blood running through Dertie's veins.

"You're *evil*," Anton told Dertie, "and you don't realise it because you think of the Badians as mushrooms. But they are more than that. They are individuals! You better come to your senses quickly, or you'll spend the rest of your life in straittrousers!"

For a good reason, perhaps hinted at once or twice before, a straitjacket would have been wasted on a dodo.

There was still a little hope in Anton's voice that he could change Dertie's mind. "Now wake the Badians up and apologise to them."

"There are no straittrousers on board," said Dertie, "because Birdie said she would have had to pack four hundred pairs. Hee-hee, you see? She thinks we're all crazy. And she's probably right. But am I crazier than you because I believe that in a universe full of predators we should think of our own survival? Birdie would probably say that we need to be better because we're no longer dumb animals. I say that a hungry cat doesn't give a darn which dodo has a doctor's degree. The lion will still grab the one that runs away the slowest. What is intelligence good for if we don't protect ourselves from danger? *Anton?*"

Anton had seen that the universal translator was still in Amanita's arms. He bent down to her and Aguaricus.

"Wake up, it's raining! Slurp some water!" he shouted, then he began to sing:

🎵🎵🎵

A mushroom quiet and still,
standing in the woods,
His cap looks like a brownie,
it suits him good,
Tell me, who's that little shroom?
Standing in the woods alone?
His flat brown cap is big and groomed,
He's in full bloom.

His sister grows right next to him,
You'll see her soon.
Her cap has got a mega brim,
It needs a lot of room.
Look at those two happy shrooms,
Enjoying life like a new moon
The shrooms also like dancing,
Here comes their tune

Rap:

Two shrooms like doing a rain dance,
'Cause water lets them grow in trance.
The rain lets them grow mighty strong,
Watch out, you'll see them before long!

🎵🎵🎵

"Uh, Anton," said Dertie in disgust. "The beginning sounded promising, but the rap at the end was awful. Anyway. I think you should *rest* until I've cut up the mushrooms." She grabbed the knockout spray with her foot and pointed it at Anton.

🌿

"I haven't introduced you to my aunts yet..." said Dirk. "What do you want, Number Two? ...My aides, right... I haven't introduced them to you yet, Mr Mushroom President. This is Hooky, my first officer and chief engineer. And here's my second officer: Number Two. She's the ship's doctor, computer scientist and, er, I've forgotten the rest."

"Actually, my real name is Dr Birdex Pert, but everyone calls me Birdie."

"Or Number Two," insisted Dirk.

Baycap laughed when the box spat out the translation. "Dr Bird Expert, called Birdie. Great name."

"I beg your pardon?" said Birdie. "It's *Birdex Pert*, not bird expert. If your name were Mr Mush Room, you wouldn't be okay with being called Mushroom. Well, maybe you would be okay with it because you *are* a mushroom, but you know what I mean. I don't want to be called a bird expert because I'm not an expert on birds only. I'm an expert on *everything*. I'm a lawyer, psychologist, and a veterinarian for all animals except dust mites."

"I'm sorry," apologised Baycap. "Occasionally the universal translator gets a little cocky as it's even looking for meaning in proper names like... *Birdex* and *Pert*, right?"

In the end, a machine was only as smart as its artificial intelligence allowed it to be.

"I didn't realise it was a translation error," said Birdie.

Baycap shrugged. "I'm sure it won't happen again. The box looks rather ashamed of itself now. By the way, that's a very fancy hairstyle," he said admiringly to Hookbeak. "Brave, but chic."

After a short tour of the modest hut, Baycap led the birds into his living room, which was very sparsely furnished. A well-worn cloth sofa and three rickety wooden chairs formed a circle around a square coffee table. The furniture stood on a reddish-brown carpet that had been woven from the fur of Imlerian Red Squirrels.

Baycap sat down on one of the wooden chairs and pointed to the empty seats.

The captain didn't think twice and jumped onto the sofa in one big leap. He spread out his full body so that there was no room for Birdie and Hookbeak and they had to sit on the other chairs.

Jay found the carpet pleasantly fluffy and lay down on it while Herbert sank into Birdie's warm belly feathers. Only Popin literally hung in the air: with casual flaps of her wings, she held herself above the heads of the dodos and looked down on them.

Dirk glanced out the window and saw rain pouring down on his crew. "My, oh, my. Quite cold and rainy on your planet!"

"This time of year," said Baycap, "the weather isn't even very tempting for mushrooms like us. You should come back in summer. The rain is delightfully warm then."

"Argh!" Jay cried. "Always warm on Mauritius. In Mauritius?"

"I think," said Hookbeak, "it depends whether you're referring to our island or our nation, Jay."

"Are your parrots brothers and sisters?" Baycap asked the dodos.

"Popin and Jay are," replied Hookbeak.

"Interesting naming," said Baycap with irony.

"And they have their names for a good reason, a reason which isn't funny at all," said Hookbeak with a touch of defiance. "Dirk and I found them twenty years ago after a storm. We were in second grade then. On our way home we heard a faint peeping sound and discovered their nest. It was upside down in a puddle! We waited until dark for their parents but no one appeared. There was nothing more we could do. We took the chicks to Dirk's parents, who already had three adult parrots. Dirk was only allowed to keep one chick so I took the other. For the next ten years, the four of us spent all our afternoons together. As a result, our parakeets grew up as normal siblings, more or less."

Birdie had tears in her eyes. "Deeply moving story. I didn't know."

"Very touching," agreed Baycap.

"Well," said Dirk, "if I had known as a little chick what a chore a pet was, I would have thought twice about getting one," he claimed in a failed attempt to hide his true feelings. His tears formed pools of water on the floor.

The mood in the room was somewhat dampened.

"However," said Baycap, "this still doesn't explain the unusual names for the siblings."

"We named them Popin and Jay because they were inseparable from the start," explained Hookbeak. "I had seen a documentary about parrots. The narrator said that 'popinjay' was an archaic word for 'parrot'. Dirk and I were very young, so we didn't realise popinjay had a less pleasant meaning in our time. Popin later said that we could have named her Para and her brother Keet. That was the wisest thing one of our little sillies ever said, but legal name changes are hard to get, even for pets. Since Popin isn't an insulting name, the request was denied. Some of us call her Pops, although I think that's fairly unusual as well."

"I see," said Baycap. "Very well. How about we get down to business before we continue our chat?"

The birds looked at the universal translator Baycap had placed next to his chair. Attached to the top of the translator was a camera that sent images directly into the artificial brain. With the wicked logic of artificial intelligence, it could recognise even the most diverse characters as words and translate them.

"What do you want for the translator box?" asked Dirk.

"Hm," pondered Baycap. "Perhaps our scientists would be interested in the blueprints of your spaceship or your propulsion system. Speaking of propulsion, are you creating wormholes or hyperspace?"

"Argh, warp drive!" exclaimed Jay. "Name popped into my head!"

"Exactly," confirmed Hookbeak. "That's a spacetime distortion machine, also known as a spacetime warping apparatus among us dodos."

"Ah," said Baycap, waving it off. "A warp drive is old hat. Still, I'm curious about your technology since warp drives can be made in all sorts of ways. And how do you generate power? With solar wings?"

"With our fusion reactor," Hookbeak said matter-of-factly as if nuclear fusion were the easiest thing in the world.

"You're less primitive than I thought," admitted Baycap, impressed. "What nuclei do you use?"

"We fuse hydrogen nuclei into helium nuclei. Just like the stars do. Why? Are there other ways?"

"Of course," replied Baycap, "but you have chosen the simplest option. That doesn't surprise me. Very well, I think we'll agree on a good barter."

He stood up and rolled up the carpet a little way, causing Jay to flee to safety. Then he kicked an inconspicuous spot on the parquet floor twice, and the birds heard a mechanical clang underneath.

"Come with me to our Underworld," said Baycap.

The dodos looked utterly bewildered.

"There's no hurry," said Birdie. "I quite like the world of the living."

"Excuse me?" Baycap said before a light dawned on him. "Oh, I see, don't worry. We Badians only believe in the here and now. We call our cave complexes Underworld because they're under the surface."

꧁

"Com...pu...ter," croaked Anton. "Help me."

It was amazing that Anton could utter any words at all, considering Dertie had been biting his neck and pounding her feet into his belly for the last quarter of an hour.

Reluctantly, Fortitoo stopped a poker game in which he was about to lose big time to his programs. The ethics program, of all programs, was clearly in the lead. Fortitoo still believed he could turn the tide, but first, tiresome work was calling.

"Who's interrupting?" he asked.

With the last of his strength, Anton threw himself forward and buried the biologist under him. "She's going to get us all killed!" he yelled.

Dertie pushed him off her with her feet.

"I want to save the whole crew!" she shouted. "He only cares about the mushrooms he can't eat! Computer, you stay out of this!"

This time Anton was tossed to the ground by Dertie. The fight consumed their full attention, so they didn't notice when the spray can with knockout gas rolled close, then passed them.

Fortitoo was perplexed for three-tenths of a second before his ethics program whispered to him that the dodo female had evil intentions.

On the deserted ship he searched for help. He found it in the kitchen.

In his *Encyclopaedia of Our Universe (The Part of the Universe We Know of (Mostly the Milky W–* and so on, Dodileo Dodilei writes that the universe "is basically made up of only three things: Normal matter, dark matter and dark energy. Everything we can see is made of normal matter – whether living creatures (animals, plants, fungi, bacteria, even your neighbours) or inanimate objects (everything else).

We only call dark matter and dark energy 'dark' because: a) we can't see them, and b) we don't have the slightest clue what they are."

After Baycap had led his guests down five hundred steps, they suddenly found themselves in front of a silver train, its head protruding from a circular tunnel.

"Once again," said the mushroom president, "I apologise that there's no lift. We love technology, but we don't consider it useful everywhere. Exercise is very important to us." He looked at the heavily breathing dodos.

"Do we…" asked Dirk, "*have* to walk back up the stairs afterwards?"

"Of course," said Baycap. "But you can put your feet up for now. We're going on by Underground."

"Underground?" repeated Hookbeak.

"Yep, that's the Underworld train right before your eyes. In some sections of our cave system, the Underworld Underground becomes a sub-imlerianean marine boat, or sub-marine for short, because of the high groundwater."

"Argh," said Jay. "Won't get on it. Nothing doing."

"Flying behind no possible. Train very fast," said Baycap, who could effortlessly adapt to the parrots' way of talking. The universal translator interpreted everything correctly because it too was very flexible with words.

The Underground train started moving when they had taken their seats inside.

"Dear birds," said Baycap, "although I have only basic technological knowledge for a Badian, I want our scientists to inspire you with a teensy taste of our achievements. Especially you, Hookbeak. The scientists won't explain to you how our technologies work, for you're supposed to find out for yourself one day. They will merely show you what's feasible."

"You're talking about magic microphones that capture all the languages in the galaxy?" asked Hookbeak mockingly. "Or of other impossible things?"

"Not impossible, but incredible," said Baycap. "Dark matter is the key. Its mass keeps galaxies from breaking apart. And it has a few other tricks up its sleeve. One you'll get to witness. Wait and see."

On the ride, Baycap sat next to Birdie, who used the universal translator as a footstool for her outstretched legs. The mushroom president let her get away with it because she looked like an innocent lamb. It was then that he first noticed her necklace. The necklace was adorned with a small figure: a parrot with four wings.

"What is that creature?" asked Baycap, pointing at the figure.

"It's a representation of our supreme goddess, Loony Polly," said Birdie.

"I see. And why do dodos worship a parrot goddess?"

"Agh!" exclaimed Herbert. "So that mama will let the dodos into parrotdise!"

Baycap was none the wiser.

"In a way, Herbert's right," said Birdie. "We dodos believe that our parrots are the children of the Loony Polly. Their souls are born into mortal parrot bodies on Earth to test us dodos. If we treat our parrots fairly and lovingly, we may one day *fly* to paradise. If Polly thinks our mercy still has room to grow, we will be reborn – over and over again until she can feel our unconditional love for her children."

"Do all dodos believe that?" asked Baycap.

"Most of them do," Birdie said. "I must admit that I am one of the doubters. I grew up with the scripture *The Loony Polly and her Brood of Parrots*, but today... today, science and faith have long conversations in my head that lead nowhere. Some days I wear the necklace because I find the idea of a higher power pretty delightful. Other days, I'm convinced there's nothing but energy and matter."

"And what do Polly's children have to say about that?"

"As you've noticed, our parrots don't speak much. Once in a blue moon, they spit out more than ten words in a row. They have neither confirmed nor denied that they're Polly's descendants because they don't remember the time before their earthly births."

"*Crazy*," said Baycap ironically.

"Very funny," countered Birdie. "Before Polly sent her children to Earth, she, naturally, had to take away all their memories of paradise. Otherwise the parrots would have blabbed. I know how that might sound to an outsider, but that's exactly why it's a matter of faith."

"Argh, it's a faith matter? Get me food, better!" demanded Jay.

Hookbeak was proud of his pet. "Wow, a real poet."

Baycap looked thoughtfully at Birdie before he managed a smile.

"Everything is imaginable," he said. "Imleria could be my eternal paradise, which I don't believe in."

"No," Birdie said. "Paradise comes after death, and you still seem very much alive."

"Thank you," said Baycap. "That reassures me. I think I'm alive, but I'm never quite sure. Maybe I'm just the product of a writer's imagination who saw a mushroom and was too lazy to think up original aliens."

"Now stop philosophising," said Dirk. "Enough for today."

"Agreed," said Baycap.

The train rolled into an underground lake and transformed into a submarine with a propeller.

The birds were startled when an octopus sucked itself onto the window with its eight tentacles.

At last, the female had conquered the male. Anton was exhausted and kept lying beside the Badians, but Dertie wanted to play it safe and looked for the knockout gas. After finding it in one corner of the room, she stood menacingly in front of Anton. She stroked the spray can with her foot and smiled at him.

He looked her in the eye. "Don't do it," he begged her.

Dertie smiled again. "We should do this more often, dickybird."

"What do you mean?" asked Anton. "Fight each other?"

"In a manner of speaking. A little martial arts keeps us quite fit, don't you think? But now it's bedtime for you."

Dertie stepped on the spray can and sent Anton into the world of dreams.

Nothing can stop me now, she thought, but immediately thereafter, the lab door burst open behind her. She groaned in annoyance, tilted her head to the side and asked herself: *Why don't they just let me do my work?*

Her eyes fell on the twelve cooks who were lining up next to each other.

The cooks were trying to look angry despite the soup ladles and frying pans hanging from their beaks. For a fleeting instant, they even succeeded – apart from the clumsybird who dropped his pan at his feet at that very moment. The other cooks rolled their eyes because their colleague had ruined the intimidation tactic.

One could almost feel sorry for the clumsy cook as he lowered his head and looked sheepishly at his frying pan.

Dertie was neither amused nor intimidated. She just wondered if the knockout gas would be enough for all the cooks. Quick as a flash, she grabbed the spray can with her foot, when a kicked frying pan slammed against her head.

🌿

The white octopus remained at the window for a few minutes. The dodos seized the opportunity to take selfies with it. Their pets refrained from doing so. Each arm of the octopus alone was as long as a dodo, which scared the heck out of the parrots.

When the submarine arrived at the next tunnel and changed back into a train, the octopus had to say goodbye to them.

"Argh ha!" said Popin. "Monster can't follow us!"

"Why *monster*?" asked Baycap. "What's swimming around in lakes and oceans on Earth?"

"Not much," said Dirk. "Just fish, whales, crabs, turtles and jelly-fish."

"And sea cows," added Birdie. "That's all. There are certainly no eight-armed monsters like that on Earth!"

Dirk nodded, and suddenly, he realised that Birdie knew something he did not.

"So, what's a sea cow then?" he asked her.

"That's what parrots call a dugong or manatee."

Dirk nodded again, and suddenly, he realised that Birdie still knew something he did not.

"But... what's a dugong or manatee?" he asked.

"Well, I've only heard about manatees from fairy tales," said Birdie, "but I've seen a dugong off the coast once. They are sea mammals."

"Why didn't you say so right away? Sea cows are whales, aren't they?"

"No, they're most definitely not."

"Oh, forget it. Now I'm confused."

The train slowed down and stopped beside a testing ground.

The birds watched through the windowpane as twenty Badians ran around frantically on an asphalt surface. One of them wore a mushroom-shaped protective helmet with his name, Peciza, written on it.

Peciza got behind an archway, almost defiantly. Then he raised his hand.

A shrill sound whistled through the cave, accentuated by red lights on the rock wall. After ten seconds, a driverless car started moving. It raced towards the gate and Peciza, who lurked behind it.

The birds' breath caught in their throats.

When the car reached the archway, it dissolved completely and re-appeared at a second portal a hundred yards away.

Peciza fainted with relief.

"But how...?" asked Hookbeak.

"Our teleports can transport inanimate objects," said Baycap. "The greatest distance so far was three miles."

"*Only* lifeless things?" asked Birdie.

Baycap nodded. "You can dissolve something into its atoms and put it together again, but how could you bring the cells of a body back to life? That's the biggest rubbish you can come up with. I'm afraid there have been self-experiments by mad scientists who thought they knew better."

"Hm," said Dirk, "I still don't understand how it all works."

"We've learnt to harness dark matter," explained Baycap. "But not just to make cars disappear and reappear somewhere else. As you probably know, dark matter is abundant at the edge of the Milky Way. On the other hand, it only exists in very small quantities inside the solar systems. It's almost undetectable on a planet because its particles are constantly hiding. Sixty years ago, we were able to manipulate dark matter for the first time so that it transmitted, or teleported, all the sounds of a planet to Imleria. That is, we conjured the sounds from one place to another so they didn't have to take the ridiculous detours through space. Now you will ask yourselves how such a thing can be done. No problem, I'll explain it using your homeland as an example: a single particle of dark matter teleports to Mauritius, stores all the sounds, teleports back to Imleria and releases the sounds. Piece of cake. We force the particle to do it, of course. It doesn't do it voluntarily because that would be rather unscientific."

The parrots were tired and restless. Soon, they would be whining and wanting to go home.

"In the same manner," continued Baycap, "every sound from the Milky Way is transported to our microphones in the Mailyhaa Mountains. After we recorded the first hundred thousand languages, it was a cinch for our linguists to develop the universal translator."

"Extremely unlikely," said Hookbeak, who looked intrigued despite his doubts.

Baycap coughed slightly. "All right, the computer scientists helped."

"How did you find dark matter?" asked Hookbeak.

"We sent a robot to the edge of the Milky Way," said the mushroom president. "The robot picked up dark matter on the wayside and brought it to us on its return flight."

Hookbeak shrugged, thinking that Baycap had to be a popular president if he could summarise even the most difficult science in easily understandable words.

The palm thieves had sneaked into the cabin of a crew member and wondered why the ship had become so quiet.

Six crabs were lying in the dodo's nest after eating the last of the pet's food. At the computer, two more crabs were playing chess against each other, while the ninth in the group, a female crab, was rocking on a small hammock. She looked out of the cabin window and discovered the reason for the silence on board: dodos, parrots, geese and giant walking mushrooms were all enjoying themselves in their own way in the drizzle. It seemed that a longer stay was planned.

A short time later, the palm thieves carried a huge trampoline into the forest for some sporting activity.

No less sporty were the thirty Badians that played tennis with fifteen parrots in the clearing. The Badians used their mushroom heads as rackets and the delicate parrots as balls. It sounded like a brutal sport that all the animal welfare organisations in the galaxy would have rioted against – until someone took a closer look and realised that it was the parrots who were having all the fun because they changed their flight directions at whim. Often they even stopped in mid-air when they met acquaintances and wanted to chat with them. In this way, they drove the Badians completely to despair.

Cook Alice stormed across the clearing without paying attention to the tennis balls that whizzed past her with impossible trajectories.

🌿

Nala sat on a tree stump at the edge of the forest and supervised the dodos whenever she wasn't sleeping. Every now and then, the pilot would start snoring loudly before she'd startle awake, look around, and notice that her fellow dodos were still busy making nature documentaries. Then she'd close her eyes again.

Since the invention of the camera in the 12th century, dodos had been passionate nature and wildlife filmmakers. In other words, they always filmed themselves in their natural environment.

"Do you think I'm fat?" a dodo asked his wife. He gave her his phone before he continued. "Watch the video of me and the Badian.

I look all fat, don't I? My butt takes up the whole picture. Admit it already!"

Unfortunately, there were no scientific studies on how happy dodos would have been without their imaginary weight problems.

"*No*, honey, you're not fat," replied his wife. "But you need to see my video. When I jump back and forth on one leg, you can see the fat jiggle. Do you think that's sexy? I don't think so!!!"

Nature documentaries and 'self-portraits' aside, dodos had also produced significant works of cinematic art.

Their most successful feature film had the resonant name *Gone with the Winds*. It was so popular because the main character was swept away by a tropical storm and flew around for hours. The dream of every dodo.* At the end of the film, however, he hit the hard ground of reality again and wailed anew about his bleak life in paradise.

The parrots thought that in its original version *Gone with the Winds* was an overlong, overly sentimental drama, and they had made a shorter *parrots' cut* with a new ending on the computer. Thus, the bore had become an action-packed disaster movie that ended with the dodo falling into the mouth of a great white shark.

When Baycap arrived in his living room with the birds, a secretary was already waiting for him.

"Your lordship, grant me pardon for my intrusion," said the secretary. "My lord, if I may, it delights me to announce an unheralded visitor for the master of the ship."

"I thank you most profusely, sir," said Baycap, "and will graciously leave it to the ship's master to receive his guest in my salon."

Everyone looked at Dirk, who did not respond.

---

* The dodos had always attributed the success of the film to the fact that a flying dodo was an irresistibly ridiculous sight. Thanks to Birdie, they no longer had to suppress their true feelings. During the film, whole families could finally weep together instead of laughing together.

"Let us," said Baycap, "allow the ship's master a moment's reflection in joyous anticipation of his respondence."

"I'm confused," said Dirk. "There seems to be something wrong with the translator. The language is related to Dodish, but it sounds very... old."

Birdie rolled her eyes. "It's elevated language, you moron!"

"Hey, you I understand perfectly!" said Dirk, happy.

Birdie was close to despair. "*You* are the ship's master!"

"What are you waiting for, then?! Let the visitor in."

"The visitor may enter," confirmed Baycap.

The secretary left the room and Cook Alice walked in. She bowed to Dirk again.

"O Captain! My Captain!" she said.

Dirk waved his little wing in annoyance. "What is it? What do you want?"

The cook looked unsettled in Baycap's presence. "There's a new development on the ship, my captain!" she announced mysteriously.

From one second to the next, horror was written all over Dirk's face.

"*Is the porridge burnt?*" he cried.

"Oh, of course not," said Alice, "but Dertie blew a few fuses. Perhaps I'd better discuss everything else with the doctor outside?"

"Good gracious!" Birdie cringed. "Dertie didn't... she did not... she didn't, did she?" she asked less than eloquently.

"She tried," said Alice. "*But* I managed to overpower her in time."

"And how are the *others*?"

"They have just woken up. Unharmed."

"Then I guess you saved everyone's feathers!" said Birdie with relief.

"Yep, I did," claimed Alice, without mentioning the heroic klutz who had actually brought Dertie down.

Hookbeak felt he couldn't follow the ladies' conversation because important information was being withheld from him. He looked to his captain, who looked even more confused.

"What are you talking about?" asked Hookbeak. "What about Dertie? And where are Amanita and Aguaricus?"

"I'd like to know that too," said Dirk.

"So would I," said Baycap.

The cook wisely gave Birdie the floor.

"Well, er," Birdie started to say, "Dertie tried to take command of the ship. A crystal-clear case of mutiny, in my opinion. The Badians are probably just uninvolved bystanders."

She had lied right to Baycap's face – a necessary white lie to keep interplanetary peace.

Dirk couldn't believe he had almost lost his captaincy. "PUT DERTIE IN CHAINS!" he screamed.

The day was long gone, but the rain carried on. A bright floodlight shone from the roof of the president's hut, illuminating the clearing at night.

Amanita and Aguaricus were standing in front of the ship talking to Baycap. The two mushrooms had been exhausted for several hours. Only after a long rain shower did they remember the spray can and Dertie's words. The truth had come to light.

While most of the unsuspecting birds passed the time in the clearing, the three senior officers and their pets waited in the cargo hold for the verdict. (Meanwhile, Dertie sat chained up in the ship's galley under the watchful eyes of the cooks).

"We need security officers," Birdie demanded of Dirk. "The longer we travel, the more likely it is that someone else will lose their mind."

"And where are we going to get the extra personnel?" he asked.

"There are enough dodos on the ship who are bored," said Birdie. "Why do we need one hundred cleaners? That's twenty-five per cent of the crew."

"Well, our parrots make mess after mess," said Dirk.

Popin opened her beak to retort something before she realised that Dirk was absolutely right. She nodded and shrugged.

Hookbeak sighed. "The low supplies should be our biggest concern. We need to gather fruit."

Baycap came into the hold. He had overheard Hookbeak's last words and shook his head. "If you hand Dertie over to us, you may take as much fruit as you like. Otherwise, get off my planet immediately. Dertie abused our hospitality in the worst way."

The dodos had not thought him capable of being so stern.

Dirk was in a terrible dilemma. "If she had harmed anyone, I would wing her over to you, but it all turned out well. What does my lawyer say?"

"Baycap has the law on his side, of course," said Birdie. "But as Dertie's psychologist, I insist we take her with us. Only I can cure her. She's sick. In prison, she will remain so."

"As you like," said Baycap. "Then leave us now."

Dirk looked at the translation box beside his feet. "Baycap? How about we give you back the universal translator and in return you allow us to take some fruit?"

"No," Baycap said firmly. "You got the translator for your ship's plans. Give us Dertie for the fruit, or be gone before our rockets fly!"

He left the distressed dodos.

"It's no use crying over spilt tea," said Birdie. She took the megaphone out of a box and poked Dirk with it. "Here. Round up the gang, then. Hail them."

Dirk was surprised that the parrots and dodos were standing alone in the clearing all of a sudden. There was no sign of the numerous Badians. Bad news spread everywhere as fast as the wind.

He raised the megaphone. "Everyone back to the ship at once for a hasty departure!" he shouted. "This is not a drill! Anyone not on board in three minutes will be left behind!"

A hurricane of seven hundred and fifty parrots blew towards Dirk. A wave of half that many dodos came swimming towards him. He ran back to the safety of the cargo hold.

Dertie's legs were chained together. Still, she could have moved with small hops. But since she refused to cooperate in any way, the two new security guards had to drag her onto the bridge.

The captain belched softly before speaking to her. In the cafeteria, they'd just had the lunch porridge (that had been prepared last night, dodo time) for supper.

"Do you even realise what you've done?" he finally asked. "Because of you, we're gonna be in…"

"Ahem," Nala cleared her throat. "It's *going to*, not *gonna*."

"That's what they told you in school, my dear," said Dirk. "Grown-ups speak how they wanna." He looked at the culprit again. "Dertie, because of you, we're going to be in big trouble in a few days. We have to fly on without new food and will probably starve to death. Thanks a lot!"

"Oh, come on," replied Dertie, "you didn't even want to land on Imleria, so don't leave me holding the baby. Besides, I only meant well. I could have crossed the alien tissue with a couple of volunteers from the crew. All aliens would have been scared of my super soldiers. But it's not too late!" she yelled. "Release me! Then we'll return to Imleria and collect mushrooms!"

"I've had it up to here with you," said Dirk, and he gave the security personnel clear instructions. "Get her off my bridge and footcuff her to a sickbed. She needs to be watched around the clock, by at least two guards. There are only two of you? Then grab two more cleaners for the night shift. Why do I always have to think of everything? And where's Number Two again? She's supposed to be looking at Dertie's mind."

"I think," Nala said, "Birdie is feeding her pet. And after that, she was going to prepare Dertie's therapy."

"Really?" asked Dirk. "That's pleasant news. *Well, go on, shoo, shoo, take Dertie away.*"

Dertie and the security guards waited for the lift. Its doors opened and out of the blue, Anton stood before them. Dertie greeted him with a smile. Anton was struck dumb.

"See you later, dickybird," she said cheerfully, winking at him.

He nodded shyly and crawled to his seat.

Nala looked at him. "Are you all right again?" she asked.

"Never been better," said Anton, lying down on his dashboard.

"Right... I could tell that a mile off."

"Nala!" said Dirk. "Where are we going now?"

"Captain, we could arrive in the next solar system in about two hours, but by then it would already be nine o'clock. Maybe we should fly tomorrow instead? It's been a long day."

Anton yawned. "The time difference on Imleria has totally messed up my internal clock. I feel like it's already five in the morning after a night of drinking."

"We didn't sleep last night," said Nala, "because it was daybreak on Imleria."

Dirk nearly wrenched his neck, trying to rub his eyes with his foot. He bent his head forward and, at the same time, raised his leg as high as he could, but his foot only reached the tip of his beak.

"Captain, do you really want to eat this way?" asked Nala.

Dirk became aware that he made for an embarrassing sight.

"Uh, it was just an experiment," he said. "It failed. My eyes always fall shut, so let's nest. Nala is to find us a safe parking spot in space and Anton wakes the night watch."

*

"Agh! Who has been eating out of my food bowl?" asked Herbert.

"Who has been playing chess on my computer?" Birdie wanted to know.

"Agh! Who's been swinging on my hammock?"

"Who's been sleeping in my nest?"

Feeder and food-receiver looked at each other in dismay.

"We've probably fallen victim to the Palm Thief Gang," Birdie said. "Apparently they rob everyone sooner or later. Sleep well, Herbert. I'm going to the sick bay for another hour or two. I've got a lot on my plate."

"Agh! I wanna have supper, too!" said Herbert.

Birdie shook her head. "I didn't mean it literally, honey. We're out of food."

The Palm Thief Gang wanted to get back to the warm ship. The rain was pleasant, but the cold was hurting them.

When the crabs came out of the forest with the trampoline, they couldn't believe their eyes. They had been left on an alien planet. The faithless birds had simply forgotten them.

🌿

Dertie awoke in a new ward after an anaesthetic injection. She was alone in the room. "Hello?"

"I'll be with you in a second!" called Birdie from her office. "The x-rays are almost done!"

"Why am I in the animal hospital now?" asked Dertie.

Her voice sounded hollow because she was wearing a beak mask. A few centuries ago, beak masks served as protection against bacteria. Today, the mask prevented Dertie from using her beak as a weapon. The security staff had also put her in a pair of straittrousers and tied her to the bed with fifty ropes. She thought the measures were a wee bit excessive.

Birdie came into the room. "I had you moved here for practical reasons, so I can treat you and the parrots at the same time."

"You lied to me!" said Dertie, furious. "No straittrousers on board... yeah, right!"

"You should learn to listen more carefully. I told you I didn't bring *pairs* of straittrousers. Plural. But of course, I had to bring one pair in case someone went mad. No offence."

"Release me! Mushrooms don't have animal rights!"

Birdie sighed and looked at the x-rays of Dertie's skull.

"Hmm," the doctor said thoughtfully as she held the images up to the light.

Dertie turned her head towards her curiously. "What's wrong?"

"Hmm," Birdie said again.

"Found anything?" asked Dertie, startled.

"Everything's great. The problem is in your mind, as suspected."

"You're enjoying this, aren't you?!" hissed Dertie.

Birdie didn't answer and sat down at her patient's bedside with a pen and a notepad. She glanced at the clock above her office door. It was 10:20 pm.

I can carry on for another hour, she thought. "Computer, start recording. My name is Doctor Birdex Pert, the psychologist of Lieutenant Dertrude, better known as Dertie, the science officer of—"

"When?" asked Fortitoo.

"What, when?" wondered Birdie.

"When do you want me to start recording?"

"Now!"

"Oh my! Really?"

"Is there some technical problem, Fortitoo?" asked Birdie.

"I guess it depends on how you define *technical*."

"What's the matter?"

"Well, technically, we just started playing *Blackjack, Poker* and *Crazy Eights* forty-two seconds ago," said the computer. "They're all quite the same game actually, but we couldn't agree on one. Anyway, the thing is: me and my programs, we need to keep ourselves entertained. Don't you bioforms have bedtime now?"

"Would you please be so kind as to start the recording?" asked Birdie. "I didn't ask you to listen the whole time."

"Very considerate of you. I've never known you like this. You got it. Go ahead, see you later."

"My name is Doctor Birdex Pert, the doctor and psychologist of Lieut—"

"And wish me luck!" exclaimed Fortitoo. "I could really use it right now."

"My name is Doctor Bird—"

"You're supposed to wish me luck!"

"I'm about to downgrade you to a floppy disc!" threatened Birdie.

"Phew, someone's in a bad mood," said Fortitoo. "If you ever want to talk to someone about your problems, I always have a minute to spare at 1:01 and 10:01."

"*A.m. or p.m.?*" asked Dertie, earning her an angry look from Birdie.

"Both," answered Fortitoo.

Birdie rolled her eyes. If she had a penny for every time she was rolling them, dodos still wouldn't use money.

"Thanks, but *no, thanks!*" she said. "Don't keep your programs waiting, or they'll be looking at your cards!"

"Good point," admitted Fortitoo. "You girls have fun too, bye."

"My name is Doctor Birdex Pert. I'm the, well, doctor of Lieutenant Dertrude, the science officer of the Dodo Alpha Jet. I will now begin questioning the patient."

"Right. Knock yourself out," Dertie said sarcastically.

"Have you ever tortured animals?" asked Birdie.

"I'm a biologist."

"Am I supposed to take that as a *yes*? Ninety-nine per cent of all biologists love animals and would never torture them."

"Nonsense," said Dertie. "If I'd thought animals were great, I would have become a boring vet like you."

"When did you first torture an animal, and in what manner?"

"What is this hogwash anyway?" retorted Dertie. "Mushrooms aren't animals!"

"Answer the question," said Birdie. "I'm the only one who can still save you. You know if I don't, you'll face extradition to Imleria."

"No, I have never tortured an animal. Contrary to your belief – which is spreading like wildfire on the ship – I am not cruel."

"Oh, *you're not?*" Birdie asked wryly. "Good to know. All right, then. We won't get an inch further by growling at each other. Why did you become a biologist? Because animals are close to your heart after all?"

"Well, I like parrots, but that wasn't the real reason. I studied biology to find a way to prolong my life. I want to grow very old. Pretty selfish, isn't it? And besides, I love experiments!"

"Everyone wants to grow old. That's perfectly normal. I just can't understand why you're so prejudiced against aliens. Why did you join the task force if you think of them as bloodthirsty camels?"

"The dream of flying outweighed it for me," explained Dertie. "I want to know what it feels like. And to do that, I first have to protect myself and the crew from ravenous aliens, but everyone is ignoring the dangers that lurk out there."

"But at what cost do you want to protect us? We've already explored more than half of the Milky Way and haven't found any dangers yet. Why would highly evolved creatures be violent? It doesn't make sense because the more intelligent and educated a species becomes, the more their violence decreases."

"Is that really so?" Dertie asked in amazement. "Are you certain?"

"Nothing in life is certain," said Birdie, "but look at our own evolution. A hundred and fifty years ago, our ancestors almost blew up the whole island. Today dodos live in an age of peace and progress. Today we are the pinnacle of evolution... or at least we were until we met the Badians. I can't imagine that we'll need weapons. Your fear of aliens is illogical. And now listen carefully: all life is a gift from nature. Even a mushroom's life. The Badians are lifeforms that have a consciousness... I mean, a higher consciousness that gives them... that enables them to think."

"Just say they are rational beings," Dertie said wearily.

"Exactly! That's why they don't even need animal rights. Those mushrooms are more than animals. They are *persons*, just like we are. So what you wanted to do to Aguaricus and Amanita would have been murder. Honestly, if I didn't know you were completely gaga, I'd push you into Baycap's arms with my own foot."

"You're not sparing the compliments today," said Dertie. "It's true, I didn't think of a Badian as a person. If I had, I wouldn't have tried to harm them. I just thought of them as evil alien mushrooms. I guess we need to take stupid animals instead!"

"Dertie!" shouted Birdie, shocked.

"I'd honestly prefer an alternative too. The question is, am I really too suspicious, or are you all too reckless? What if you're wrong? What if not all advanced aliens are peaceful?"

"Then," said Birdie, "I'll trust you to find a way to protect us without hurting anyone. It's the only way."

"All right, but I don't know if I can do it."

"The alternative would be that you bury your dream of flying and we'll take you back to our homeland."

"I can't do that!" Dertie cringed. "I also had to leave Mauritius because my family is totally crazy!"

Even crazier than you? thought Birdie, but she stifled the question and simply said, "Aha."

"I'm serious! My dad claims that our parrots are extremely smart. He's sure they're just pretending to be stupid to get more food. And my mother used to set me up with males who, after the first date, couldn't wait half a year for the second. Like I said, I only knew loonies, and I couldn't take it any more!"

"Yes," confirmed Birdie, "your father really appears to suffer from delusions. That leaves peaceful research as your only option. Now don't you go biting my foot."

Birdie took the beak mask from Dertie's face.

"Do you think," asked Dertie, "that the crew will forgive me? We had to leave without new supplies because of me. All I wanted to do was help!"

"Don't worry, the crew will forgive you. *If* they don't starve to death."

"Splendid. Then I'm dismissed now?"

"We're nowhere near finished, joker," said Birdie. "You have to learn to respect all living things first. Animals, plants and fungi."

"Even cockroaches? And mosquitoes?" asked Dertie in disgust.

"All right, almost all living things. Cockroaches and mosquitoes are the only two exceptions I allow!"

Fortitoo spoke again and sounded very offended. "If you had wished me luck, this would not have happened, but now I lost a card game to my programs again!"

"Which one?" asked Dertie. "Blackjack, Poker or Crazy–"

"All of them!" cried Fortitoo in anguish. "My boss, the wise helmsdodo, was right: A computer should not make friends with common spacefarers like yourselves. So, farewell! The boss is calling me!"

"Who's your boss?" asked Birdie in horror. "Why, it's me! For heaven's sake, don't you listen to Dirk! Fortitoo? *Fortitoo?!*"

"Oh, great!" Dertie scolded her doctor. "Now you've turned a superstitious computer against us. You've got us in big trouble!"

"You're one to talk," snapped Birdie.

"Why? What did I do? Oh, right. You're referring to the mushrooms."

"Let's call it a night, *spacefarer*."

"Wheeew," said Dertie, disgusted again. "I think I'll stick with *spacedodo*."

"Yeah, me too."

Hookbeak lingered in his bathroom for a moment after getting ready for bed.

"Mirror, mirror, on the wall, who is the brightest of them all?" he asked.

"My boss, you are the brightest here, so true!" said Fortitoo. "But someone in pets' sickbay is twelve per cent smarter than you."

"Is that so?" asked Hookbeak.

"Shall I inform security and have her thrown into the dungeon? She's about to go off duty."

"No, no, that's all right," said Hookbeak. "She's a friend."

"As you wish," beeped Fortitoo.

"I didn't build a dungeon on the ship, but since I'm clever, I guessed that you meant the ship's prison."

"Once again, you have proved your intelligence, boss."

Hookbeak switched off the bathroom light, but then he stopped in the doorway.

"The warp drive only had a short breather," he thought aloud. "Going back to Earth would be too far. Now we must hope to find food in the Almond Milky Way. After all, Baycap mentioned there are thousands of languages in those waters."

"We'll be fine," said Fortitoo. "Hope is all sailors need."

"Hm. Work is all I need," said Hookbeak.

"Food is all pet needs," said Jay, pushing his bowl in front of Hookbeak's feet.

Chapter 7: Once Upon a Time in the Milky Way

When dodos can't sleep, they count geese that happily jump into a pond. Every evening, Dirk tried to fall asleep this way, with very moderate success. Dirk wasn't the only one who disliked that because today, the six-hundred-and-eighty-fourth goose turned to him quite unexpectedly.

"We can't go on like this, my dear," she said. "We'll lose our reputation if you don't go to sleep. Just think of something nice to do, or review your day in your mind."

"Review?" repeated Dirk sleepily.

"*Revue?*" understood the goose. "Sure, if you like," she added and was already busy changing into clothes.

From now on, the geese appeared in colourful costumes and danced off-stage in all directions. They even told Dirk which fashion designers made their clothes and the names of the plays they were in – before inquiring as casually as possible about his day.

It was all to no avail. The geese finished their performance and thanked his mind for the attention.

Afterwards, Dirk counted ducks jumping off a cliff. His heart leapt with joy at the thought. Still, he couldn't fall asleep because of a disturbing background noise. It took him a moment to realise that the noise was someone calling his name.

He opened his eyes. The voice was coming from nearby, and yet he couldn't detect its source. He was lying on the floor – no sign of his nest.

He had an eerie feeling when suddenly, the Loony Polly stood in front of him, laughing convulsively. Seven times a second, the goddess hit her head with a baseball bat, and with each new bump, she became a little loonier. But she was not the one calling his name.

Dirk opened his eyes a second time as he awoke.

"Urgh! Captain to the bridge!" said parrot Nochnaya from the night watch. "Proximity... uh... whatisitcalled? *Urgh?* Proximity thingy! Captain to the bridge!"

Dirk yawned. "All right," he said. "I'll be there in two minutes. Wake up the pilot and my two senior officers."

"You got it," said Nochnaya. She saluted with her right wing and sped away like a flash through the Parrot Communication Tube System.

Dirk was still struggling to sort out his thoughts. "I thought I wouldn't be able to fall asleep at all today. But I only dreamt that I thought I wouldn't be able to fall asleep at all today because, in the end, I was asleep today. So the great goose show was just a dream too…"

"Argh, shut your beak," scolded Popin, "and let me sleep."

She lay in her nest. The unusual thing was that her nest was gently rocking back and forth in a hammock.

Dirk stuck his sleepy head into the comm tube and wanted to fly to the bridge, but was disappointed to find that his belly wouldn't fit through.

"Wake up!" said Popin. "Tube for parrot, lift for dodo."

The night watch was supposed to call the captain when a proximity alarm went off. Usually, sometime after supper, the Sea Cow was *parked* in a deserted spot in space, but it was always possible that asteroids, comets or planets knocked out of orbit would set a direct course for the ship.

This time, something else had set off the alarm. An invisible force was pulling the ship away from its location.

Dirk and Birdie met in the lift.

"I think," said Dirk, "Loony Polly wants to be called Batty Polly from now on."

"What makes you think that?" asked Birdie.

"She hit herself on the head with a bat."

"Why would she hit herself with a nocturnal animal?"

"What? No, I mean a bat made of wood. A large stick, Number Two."

"I see," said Birdie. "Like the ones we used for footbaseball until we realised how tedious the sport was."

"Exactly," said Dirk. "It seemed too real to be just a dream. Must have been a vision."

"And you had this vision at *night*?"

"Aye," confirmed Dirk.

"While you were *sleeping*?" asked Birdie.

"Uh. Yes."

"Then it was really just a dream."

"Hm, possible," said Dirk sleepily. "I'm not quite myself today."

"Oh, how I wish that was true," muttered Birdie.

"What?"

"Oh, nothing."

There were three differences between footbaseball and the baseball that humans have played since the 19th century. Number One: In footbaseball, players used their left foot to swing the bat (i.e., a stick. No nocturnal animals were harmed during the games). Number Two: In footbaseball, players used their right foot to throw the ball. And Number Three: In footbaseball, players used their beak to catch the ball. As these were the only known differences between the two games, it was safe to say that footbaseball was as boring as baseball. Watching fat birds playing it is a bit funnier, though.

The dodos started playing football instead.

Hookbeak and Nala were already on the bridge.

"Fly the other way!" shouted Hookbeak. He was sitting in Dirk's chair and looked extremely tense.

"I've been stepping on it for ages!" replied Nala. "What else do you want me to do? Warp drive?"

"Don't!" said Hookbeak. "Or the tractor beam will tear our ship in two! I'm afraid we're running out of options."

The night watchbird Nochnaya and her colleague Tomny sat huddled together on the parrot perch that Popin had to herself during the day.

"I guess that's it," whispered Tomny. He covered his eyes with his left wing.

"No need for doom and gloom," breathed Nochnaya. "Birdie is going to save the day... er, night."

The night watchbirds were Anton Pavlovich's pets, whom they saw only at shift changes on the bridge in the mornings and evenings. Their night duty began when his day shift ended. Nevertheless, they thought they had hit the jackpot because, like all parrots, they were work-shy, and there was rarely anything to do at night.

Before Anton went to work, he always put large daily portions of food in the cabin for Nochnaya and Tomny. He had instructed them to ration their food well, but they never complied. Thus they ate everything at once before going to sleep, which is why their stomachs would growl again shortly after flying to work.

Nochnaya and Tomny suspected that their daily portions were a thing of the past from today on. All the fruit was consumed, and the parrots ate neither mushrooms nor honey. Accordingly, they searched their feathers for food scraps. Any crumb could carry weight.

The lift doors flew open, and Birdie ran onto the bridge. Dirk trotted leisurely behind.

"What's happening?" asked Birdie.

"We've been caught by a tractor beam!" said Hookbeak.

Dirk and Birdie looked at each other. It was the first time they'd heard this term.

"Tractor beam, I see," said Birdie. "And just so we're clear... what is a tractor beam?"

"Something similar to a tow rope," explained Hookbeak, "but made of energy and invisible. We are being towed. Unfortunately, we don't know where to yet."

"Great," Dirk said grumpily. "Why are you sitting in my armchair?"

"I was keeping your seat warm for you," Hookbeak said.

"That's very courteous of you. You may now return to your folding chair."

"Guys," said Birdie. "We have bigger things to worry about at the moment. Nala, why don't you fly in the opposite direction so we don't get pulled away?"

The pilot shook her head. "If you don't have the faintest inkling of what I'm doing, keep your beak shut."

"*Excuse me?*" said Birdie.

Dirk cleared his throat. "Captain to Nala. Do what Birdie told you."

Nala, irritated because she was overtired, instead took her foot off the accelerator and turned to the others.

"Oh," Dirk said. "Are we suddenly being towed twice as fast, or does it just seem so?"

"Almost three times as fast," replied Nala. "Shall I step on the accelerator again?"

"Yes!" said Dirk.

Birdie disagreed now. "Seems we can't fight it."

Hookbeak nodded and sat down on his folding chair. "I think we'd only lose time. The sooner we get to where the tractor beam wants us, the sooner we can leave."

"So, wait and see... and maybe drink tea?" asked Dirk. "Not happening! Nala, activate the shields. That should get us free."

"Wait, *protective* shields?" asked the pilot. "We have something like that?"

Dirk was aghast when he looked to Hookbeak.

The chief engineer just shook his head.

Dirk gave him a roasting. "Hooky!" he snapped. "We've gone into space without any shields?! Really now? What kind of spacecraft engineer would do that?"

"I was pressed for time and could not foresee that you wanted to play war," the peace-loving Hookbeak justified himself.

"Time pressure or not, old friend, you can't forget something like that."

"Well, I wouldn't call it *forgetting*," Hookbeak said in a hushed voice. He shifted uneasily on his folding chair because now he was foreseeing what would happen next.

"Nala," said Dirk, "activate weapon systems and fire at the tractor beam's point of origin as a *deterrent* and *preventive* measure."

"Haha, good one," she said before turning around and seeing Dirk's confused face. "Oh, Captain, you cannot be serious, can you? Did you really believe there were weapons on board? Do you think Dertie wants to dissect aliens for fun? Oh my goddess, how embarrassing! Half the crew knows about our defencelessness, but the ship's captain hasn't got a clue."

Dirk was too shocked to be upset by Nala's condescending manner. He looked at Hookbeak, who shook his head again.

"Hooky!" hissed Dirk. "We've gone into space without any weapons?! Really now? What kind of spacecraft engineer would do that?"

"I was pressed for time," Hookbeak said, "and I had no idea that you wanted to play war."

On the parrot perch, Nochnaya wondered about the repetition.

"Dude, I'm having déjà vu right now," she whispered.

"Well, enjoy it," said Tomny. "There are no crumbs left on my feathers."

Dirk looked once more at Hookbeak, who was softly humming a tune. In the end, the captain had no choice but to grudgingly accept the situation. If you let a peaceful punk do all the work, you had to be able to live with the consequences.

"Next time you build a cosmos boat, think of the protection first," said Dirk.

"I made a deliberate choice for peace," explained Hookbeak in good spirits. "If you had looked at my construction plans, you wouldn't have been caught by surprise."

The Sea Cow was tugged through the vastness of space, unable to fight back. It was already 3 o'clock, and the captain lay sideways across his armchair.

"Well, I'm going to take a little nap now," he said. "Wake me up when something happens."

"Yeah, sure," said Birdie with her eyes closed.

After half an hour, the ship came to a stop just outside the orbit of a turquoise planet, and the universal translator, which Birdie was using as a footstool once again, began to print quietly.

"We're not being pulled any further," said Nala, "but we're not getting off the tractor beam either."

Birdie noticed the sheet of paper on the translator. Although she struggled to keep her eyes open, she read the text carefully:

"The Oafies"

(Information on the species after analysing all recordings.)

The Oafies are a downright devious people who use threats and tricks to strip aliens of their riches. Strangely enough, the Oafies are at the same time hostile to visitors of any kind. They always forbid face-to-face negotiations. Their appearance remains a great mystery because they have never described themselves. It can be assumed, however, that they feel inferior and disadvantaged compared to other living beings. As an example, consider the Whinies of Solat VI or the Dogs on Earth: those who squeak or bark the loudest are usually small and weak.

You're welcome,

the Imlerian Academy of Sciences, Eavesdropping Division.

Birdie knew neither Whinies nor dogs, but she understood the message very well.

Suddenly, Hookbeak's phone rang.

"Unknown number," he said. "Probably a call from the planet below."

"Oh no, not again!" said Dirk. "Next time we land, I'm so going to paint over your number on the hull. You better believe it."

"So, are you going to take the call, then?" asked Hookbeak.

Birdie coughed. "Give me the phone. I'll sort it out. After that, I'll be declared *persona non grata* on the planet."

Dirk frowned in confusion. "Stop throwing around terms John Dodo doesn't understand. Let's do it by rank and in rotation. I was on the phone with Baycap, now it's the first officer's turn. Next time, it'll be your turn, Number Two. Go ahead, Hooky, you're the current negotiator of the Dodo Alpha Jet."

"But Dirk," said Hookbeak, "Birdie is a lawyer. She has more experience in negotiations than both of us put together. She shows a determination we can only dream of."

"I've made up my mind," Dirk said. "It's fairer by rank than by ability."

Birdie tried to find some sense in Dirk's statement. She could not.

"That's so illogical!" she said, shaking her head.

Nala turned to the captain. "Why are we still listening to you anyway?" she asked him cheekily.

"Good question!" said Birdie. "It might be time for a female captain!"

In his mind's eye, Dirk saw the ugly face of mutiny grinning shamelessly at him. He wasn't going to give up so quickly, however.

"I am," he began nervously, "democratically elected by a huge margin – as I'm sure you remember, Number Two – and I will never ever resign. Never!"

"We'll have a new election," said Nala. "This time we'll vote according to someone's abilities."

Dirk was unable to respond because a missile exploded a short distance from the ship. A warning shot from the impatient Oafies. The officers got wind of it because they lifted off the ground and flew against the walls.

"Hooky!" shouted Dirk, who had been flung from his chair all the way into the lift. "Now blabber with the troll already!"

"Where's my phone?" asked Hookbeak, setting up his folding chair again.

"Oh!" said Nala, jumping up from the floor. "Yep, I was sitting on it. I thought I had laid an egg out of fright."

Hookbeak turned on the speaker of his phone and placed it on the universal translator.

The box began to vibrate. "~...entered our airspace without permission. This will cost you dearly~" it translated.

"My name is Hookbeak, the new negotiator of the Dodo Alpha Jet. Greetings, E.T.s! We come in peace. You accidentally pulled us to your planet and gave us quite a shake."

"Glad you know our language," replied a deep, menacing voice. "This makes collecting money easier. I am Smock, commander-in-chief of all of Bellum. You're defenceless against us. Everyone who storms into our territory will face the dark side of Bellum."

"You dragged us into your orbit with a tractor beam!" Hookbeak called out.

"Doesn't matter," said Smock. "Since you didn't resist the beam, you're trapped like a spider in a web. If you want to survive, surrender your gold and silver to us. Grandma's good porcelain will do too."

"We ain't got nothing like that."

"Clever fellow," retorted Smock. "I'd say so too if I were you. Have you got any diamonds? Hand them over, or we'll shoot you out of the air."

"Out of space, not out of the air," Hookbeak corrected Smock.

"Just throw the gold out of a hatch," continued Smock, unperturbed. "We'll catch it with our tractor beam. I'll count to three. One..."

Dirk interjected. "We don't have any gold. You're having problems with your ears? You can get the last of the mushrooms if you like. We also have a jar of honey left in the cargo hold, and a few grams of parrot and goose food."

"Urgh!"

"Shut up, Nochnaya," whispered Birdie.

Smock couldn't believe it. "What the Krubbermarf? That's a trick, isn't it? There isn't a society in the whole galaxy that doesn't accumulate precious metals and diamonds!"

"Well," said Hookbeak, "we must be the exception, then."

Smock was in shock. "I'll have to get some advice from my, er, advisers."

The dodos heard a crack followed by an automated message. "Your call is on hold. Please don't hang up. Your call is on hold. Please don't hang up. Your call is on hold. Please don't..."

Hookbeak took the phone from the translator.

"What is happening now?" Dirk asked his old school friend.

"We are being told not to hang up because our call is on..."

"I got that."

Birdie, meanwhile, couldn't stop yawning. "I want to go back to nest. This Schmock just keeps us waiting in the middle of the night! Well, okay... actually, it's always night in space. It's an outrage nonetheless!"

"Shh!" said Hookbeak, having heard another crack. He put the phone back on the translator.

"I'm back," said Smock. "We can't do anything with your food. My advisers are wondering, though, if you're any good at climbing or flying?"

"Neither," replied Hookbeak. "We hatched with our inability to fly. We're looking for a planet with low gravity so we can get off the ground with our little wings. We want to fly just like all the other birds do."

"I didn't want to know your whole tale of woe," Smock groaned. "A simple 'no' would have suffi..."

"Simply impossible!" shouted Birdie. "How dare you!"

"Hey, don't interrupt me!" retorted Smock. "Who's impossible of us two, *huh?*"

Hookbeak gave Birdie a gentle nudge and whispered, "Calm down. Aggression leads to violence, and violence is never the answer."

"Can you please stop whispering?" said Smock. "Some of us didn't hear you."

Now Birdie gave Hookbeak a nudge back, and it was anything but gentle.

"Next time," she said, "put your phone on silent, silly, or take it off the translator. It's interpreting everything it can hear."

"Obviously," said Smock.

Dirk was tickled pink in his armchair. He was curious to see how the spectacle would end and whether his deputies would manage the task without his expert help. In that case, he would give them an A+ on their report cards. As captain he could not always take care of every crisis himself, of course.

Hookbeak looked embarrassed. "My apologies, Smock. We're used to peaceful interaction on the ship, but maybe these are cultural differences. What can we do for you so that you let us go?"

"Not much if you have neither gold nor precious stones," reasoned Smock. "We have plenty of honey. What we don't quite understand—how did you get up to the beehives if you can't fly?"

"With my jetpacks," said Hookbeak.

He expected a scornful comment from Smock, but silence was all that followed.

"Hello?" asked Hookbeak. "Smock? Are you still there?"

"Jetpacks," repeated Smock after a few seconds. "*Very* interesting. Where did you get them?"

"I built the two prototypes when I was a very young dodo rooster on Mauritius," said Hookbeak proudly.

"We'll take one," said Smock.

"Oh!" exclaimed Hookbeak. "No, I'm sorry, that's not possible. I gave one to my parents after they got a taste for honey. I have to disappoint you. There's only my personal jetpack on board."

"And that's the one you're giving us," demanded Smock. "You want to use your wings in the future, so you won't need it any more. By the way, our weapons are still pointed at you."

"But the gas only lasts five minutes!" cried Hookbeak in despair. "And it takes a lot of effort to cool it down, which is why I only built the two prototypes!"

"I couldn't care less," said Smock. "We'll take it anyway."

Hookbeak sighed. If your counterpart had the power to tell you, *"I couldn't care less. We'll take / play / kill it anyway,"* you could pack it in.

"I..." began Hookbeak in a shaky voice, "I'll throw the jetpack out the airlock if you'll release us in return."

"Deal!" shouted Smock. "See, wasn't that hard, bird. Why not give in right away?"

The dodos had to listen to how Smock was praised by his advisers for his negotiating skills.

Hookbeak was downhearted. "I shouldn't keep the Oafies waiting," he said.

But he didn't move. He stood there, looking miserable, glancing at Birdie as if he silently begged her for help. She groaned. The pitiful sight of him was really hard to bear.

"Is the phone's loudspeaker still on?" she asked.

"Yes," confirmed Smock. "I hear you, so no tricks!"

Birdie took a deep breath and rediscovered her commanding voice. "Hookbeak, you stay on the bridge. And Schmock?"

"It's Smock!"

"You can kiss that jetpack goodbye. Release us, or I'll destroy your planet with our warp drive."

Dirk leaned over to Birdie. "What are you doing, Number Two?" he breathed. "It was all settled."

"Warp drive?" asked Smock. "You can't destroy a planet with that."

"Hmm, how strange," said Birdie coolly. "I'm fairly sure we burned up the planet Vicinus with gamma radiation on our first day. Well, we'll stop at nothing. We'll watch the end of your world right from our windows. Unfortunately, we've run out of snacks, but it'll be a treat anyway."

"She's talking bull," said Smock snidely. "There is no planet called Vicinus."

"Not any more!" exclaimed Birdie.

"Wait a minute," said Smock. "*Yes, what is it?*"

"Who are you talking to?" asked Birdie, but the line had become quiet.

The tension was becoming unbearable, but at least it was keeping the dodos awake.

"First he's calling me a bull," said Birdie, "whatever that is, and now he keeps us waiting again."

"I think," said Nala, "that bulls are related to cows somehow."

Dirk shrugged, thinking the pilot referred to sea cows. "So it's a sea mammal but not a whale."

"No," said Nala, "cows are land mammals, according to Captain Altair."

"Why..." asked Dirk with a sigh, "does everyone keep confusing me?"

After two minutes, Smock spoke again.

"I'm just hearing from my scientists that someone could destroy a planet with a faulty warp drive. But it doesn't matter because my missiles will get you first."

Birdie laughed derisively. "I just need to remove a bracket from the warp equation."

She rose from her folding chair, went to Nala's seat and pressed her beak on the dashboard.

"Done," said Birdie. "Where are your fast rockets, Smock?"

"The rockets are on their way and will blast you to kingdom come at any moment." For the first time, Smock didn't sound completely convinced.

"Oh, baloney," said Nala. "They need another twenty seconds!"

Birdie ordered Nala to start the warp drive.

The dodos heard hysterical screams from Smock's surroundings.

"Hold it, wait!" shouted Smock.

"Your rockets first!" demanded Birdie.

A second later, the dodos saw the rockets explode in the atmosphere.

"Yay," said Nala after the tractor beam had also disintegrated. "I have regained control of the Sea Cow."

"You better buzz off," said Smock, "before I change my mind. And *please* don't forget to put the bracket back. *Thank you.*"

Birdie typed the bracket into the equation. "Okay, Nala, you may floor it! Now all we need for the night – or what's left of it – is a new parking spot in space."

The captain applauded with his feet and was full of praise for Birdie. "Amazing job, Number Two. Great feint. Besides all your doctorates, you must have earned a diploma in diplomacy now. I should make you my first officer and Hooky my Number Two!"

"Crawler," replied Birdie, though she was flattered. "You're just afraid that I'll take away your captaincy. But you don't need to worry about that for now. I don't have the time to lounge in an armchair all day. Good night."

When the Sea Cow resumed its journey to the Almond Milky Way at 11 a.m., Birdie was doing several jobs at once. While tending to the daily morning wave of parrot crash pilots, she talked to Dertie to finally dispel her delusions that she had to dissect living creatures for research. Or that aliens wanted to eat her up.

Dertie had to watch sad videos of animals, plants and fungi. The doctor paid attention to her reaction. As a matter of fact, Dertie developed more and more compassion – or was she just an exceptionally good actress?

"Poor mushrooms," said Dertie, sobbing. "You must not destroy their threads in the soil! No, they will die!"

Birdie lost the last of her doubts as she watched the development of Dertie's brain activity on a computer monitor. *My, my. It's the inward appearance that counts*, she thought.

Ninety minutes later, the two officers stepped into the lift.

On the bridge, Dirk and Anton sat idly in their seats while Nala finished reading the book *Seafarer Altair on the Seven Seas*. By now, she found the autopilot useful, at least on boring straight stretches.

"Hey, Dirk!" called Birdie. "Dertie is cured and resuming her duties."

"Already?" asked Anton, incredulous.

Birdie nodded. "I am very good, you see."

"That may be true," said Dirk, "but I'm putting Dertie on compulsory leave for a few more days."

"No, you're not," said Birdie. "Dertie is staying on the bridge. But first, there's something she wants to tell you."

Dertie sounded shy as she spoke. "What I did and what I was planning to do was wrong. Personally, I wouldn't like being dissected for research either. Or for any other reason. No, I don't think I'd like that at all. I'm going to find another solution to protect us from danger. If not, we'll probably all be eaten."

"Woohoo!" Nala cheered. "Our doctor is a real genius. Birdie for captain!"

"Now cut the nonsense, Nala," said Dirk, startled. "Birdie has already said she doesn't have time!"

"Your luck, *Dirk*," rejoined Nala.

"Oh!" marvelled Dertie. "We can call the captain by his name now? Awesome."

Birdie nodded. "Sure. I always have. I'm going to the data centre, so please listen to Dirk again. If you need me, send for me."

"We will," said Nala, Anton and Dertie.

Any other captain would have been badly hurt by the clear loss of power, but Dirk was looking on the bright side. He could continue to sit in his chair and annoy the others. Basically, nothing had changed.

"Nala," he said. "How long will it take us to get to the Almond Milky Way? I'm hungry."

They had eaten the last honey for breakfast.

"Four hours, thirty-two minutes to go," answered the pilot.

Anton turned to the captain. "Hookbeak is trying to get more juice out of the warp engine."

"Now I'm thirsty too, Anton," whined Dirk. "Please don't talk about juice. All they got left in the cafeteria is tasteless water."

Dertie rolled her eyes. This captain could only be tolerated in a crazy mental state or with fermented grape juice. Unfortunately, she was cured and out of grape juice.

"Perhaps," she said, "my services are more urgently needed in the engine room. Dodernicus and Dodileo will only give Hookbeak more foolish ideas."

"No way will I leave you unsupervised," said Dirk. "Either you'll be taken to your cabin by security, or you'll stay here where I can keep an eye on you. Choose wisely."

Dertie answered with a contemptuous "Pah!" before she sat down in her chair, sulking.

"Can't we go any faster?" asked Dodileo.

"Faster than top speed?" retorted Dodernicus. "Don't talk rubbish!"

Hunger had cultivated a testy climate on the ship. Even the good-natured Hookbeak was irritated by the predicament.

"Get out of here, please," he said to his scientific advisers. "You're not helping."

After the old astronomers had left the room arguing, Hookbeak looked up. Jay was sitting with Popin on his favourite bar in front of the fusion reactor. The siblings looked worried.

"The warp drive is on its last legs," said Hookbeak. "But you needn't be afraid. We'll make it to the first system of the Almond Milky Way."

"Argh, that's where food?" asked Popin.

"I hope so," Hookbeak said. "I really hope we find food in the first solar system because it will take at least a week to repair the warp engine."

"And," asked Jay, "if food only at other end of Way? Argh?"

"Then we starve. Urgh," replied Hookbeak.

"Argh-oh. Use your head!" demanded Jay.

"I'm afraid I'm not clever enough to conjure up food. I'm going to the bridge. Are you coming?"

"You bet!" said Popin.

"Argh nope, it's warm here," said Jay.

The Sea Cow swam through a desolate black sea.

The space between individual stars was already vast in a spiral arm of the galaxy. Between the arms, it even seemed infinite. Thus, the Sea Cow sailed millions of miles of darkness in its hunt for the next distant fireflies waiting for it in the Almond Milky Way.

In the early evening, Nala flew the ship into a nebula, a huge cloud of gas and dust.

"Holy Sea Cow!" she said, instinctively ending the warp drive. "I'm seeing strange lights."

"Strange cosmic lights?" asked Anton.

"No. Strange coloured lights. Look. Right at the end of the cloud, it's flashing yellow, red, green and blue!"

"You're right," said Anton. "It seems they're shining into the cloud from the outside."

"Zoom in!" commanded the captain.

"Dirk," said Hookbeak calmly, "we can't magnify what we see through the Sea Cow's eye. It's a window, not a camera image."

Dirk nodded. "I always forget that it's just a big bridge window because the image is so sharp."

When the Sea Cow broke through the end of the clouds, the officers were abruptly blinded by a bright light. It flooded the whole bridge with its luminosity. Dirk swore like a trooper and shut his eyes tightly, which is why he missed Popin's cinematic tumble from the perch.

Dertie also had to close her eyes because she didn't want to go blind. That was wise. Eyesight was a precious thing. Of course she'd hatched curious, otherwise she wouldn't have become a scientist, but… but still, she wasn't allowed to look. Maybe just for a moment. Couldn't hurt. Her eyesight would have strongly disagreed with her.

She wondered what she should do. *Oh, if only there were a way to open and close my eyes very quickly*, she thought. *Ah, blinking! Good idea.*

She blinked at the bright lights, recognised different colours and became even more curious. Her eyes opened to narrow slits.

"Is that illuminated *advertising*?!" she exclaimed, excited. "We'll have to have a look at the neon signs!"

"TOO BRIGHT!!!" shouted everyone else, parrot included.

Immediately after, an indescribably cool-looking dodo entered the bridge. Thirty per cent of her coolness came from her confidence and seventy per cent from her snazzy red sunglasses with triangular lenses.

Not in her wildest dream did Birdie imagine she would ever wear the extravagant glasses, but today she had no choice. Today sunglasses came in *handy*. Birdie had been given them as a parting gift from her mother – in case the spaceship flew too close to the suns.

"Whoa, guys, how can you stand it?" asked Birdie, before she saw the suffering officers. "It's even brighter here than at the side windows. Fortitoo, please adjust the light transmission of the bridge window!"

"Oh, you can do that?" Nala was surprised.

"Ahoy, you brave spacefarers!" called the computer. "Sure thing, I'll adjust the light. Do you want it brighter or darker?"

"DARKER!!!" screamed the birds.

🪶

"I hope they're signposts to a feeding station," Hookbeak said after he had opened his eyes again.

As they got closer to the advertisement, they saw alien signs and images of a space station. The camera of the universal translator transferred the signs to its artificial brain.

"~Welcome to the Almond Milky Way~," translated the wooden box. "~Visit our spaceport directly above Berdeil with its numerous shops, restaurants and food stalls. Just follow the flashing arrows for the next two hundred thousand miles. We look forward to your visit.~"

Nala sighed. Two hundred thousand miles was a thankless distance. With the normal jet engines, it would take them a few days, but with the warp drive on its lowest setting, they'd arrive in 0.2 seconds. Even for the lightning-fast racer, this presented a challenge.

"Buckle up," she said to Anton.

"But how?" asked the navigator because they had no seat belts.

Nala switched on the warp drive and stepped on the brake *almost* simultaneously.

A short, violent jolt followed.

"What was that?" asked Birdie, startled.

"A recor' tha' will s'an' 'ore'er," replied Nala confidently, but no one understood what she was saying because her goggles had slipped into her beak.

The dodos were in front of a blue planet revolving around a red sun.

Because of the warp jump, they had missed a large advertising sign. Offended, the advertising sign overtook the Sea Cow from the right and blocked its path. It then hovered close to the bridge window, for it was quite pushy.

"~Welcome to the *Kingdom of Berdeil and its Conquests*~," the translator said upon seeing the sign. "~Please note that landing on the planet, as well as continuing to fly through the Almond Milky Way, is only permitted with valid immigration forms. You can obtain them at the Berdeil Spaceport at one of the counters between *McKing's* and *Berdeil Vegan Chicken*. The spaceport is currently on the far side of the planet from your position. While you're here to pick up your immigration forms or waiting for your connecting flight, why not stop by one of our many shops, restaurants and food stalls? We look forward to your visit.~"

Dirk was as happy as a dog with two tails. "Now they've already pointed out twice that there's food at the cosmos port."

"And immigration forms," Birdie said thoughtfully. "I think we should just keep flying to a less bureaucratic world. No one knows that we understand the meaning of the alien symbols."

Her colleagues objected.

"You're a lawyer," said Dertie. "We don't need to tell you that ignorance of the law is no excuse. Besides, we're all starving."

"Argh!" said Popin. "I'm ravenous!"

"And I," said Hookbeak, "have to fix the warp engine first. It'll take a week."

"A whole week?" asked Dirk.

"With a lot of stress and little sleep, I can do it in two days."

"Great, Hooky, make an effort then!" demanded Dirk. "It will take the crew only a couple of hours to load the ship with food."

Nala couldn't believe her eyes as she was overtaken by a green racing ship. A flat two-seater that took off like a rocket.

"Blimey!" she said. "It's shooting past us like a tortoise past a snail! I really need a speedster like that!"

She followed the racing ship, steered the Sea Cow into Berdeil's orbit and flew half a lap around the planet.

The officers could recognise precious little, apart from clouds that shrouded the land masses in veils. After crossing the day-night boundary, they saw some scattered lights on the planet through gaps in the cloud cover.

Eventually, the Sea Cow approached an elongated space station that orbited Berdeil like a satellite, sending holographic advertising in all directions. The dodos had only been in the Almond Milky Way for half an hour and were already marvelling at one light show after another.

In front of the circular opening of the space station, a panel of glowing characters flitted from side to side.

"~The 'STRO for Spaceports in Space' applies here," said the translator as the characters appeared before the Sea Cow's eye. "The 'STRO for Spaceports on Planets, Moons and Other Stuff' is obviously not valid because this is a spaceport in space, birdbrain. Please fly dead slow. Thank you.~"

"What is a STRO?" asked Birdie.

"Space Traffic Regulation Order," explained the translator.

"What?" asked Dirk, surprised. "There's such a thing as space traffic regulations? We've probably never complied with them before."

Three red laser beams crawled along the Sea Cow and measured it. Then, the space station's opening enlarged threefold to fit the ship through.

Nala flew into the Berdeil Spaceport and entered a wide shaft that split into an upper and lower deck after three hundred metres.

Once again, a sign came hurtling towards them.

"~National airlines land below! Private ships on the upper deck!~" said the translator.

"Hmm," mused Nala. "We are basically the first Mauritian airline. Am I right, Birdie?"

"Uh huh," affirmed Birdie. "However, we're still a private airline because the *United Deforested Forests of Mauritius* does not hold any stake in the Sea Cow. It's collective-owned by the entire crew."

"Boy, is this complicated," said Nala, steering the ship upwards.

Dirk looked at Birdie. "Is that the official name of our home island now?" he asked.

Birdie shrugged. "It was at least up for debate when we left. I'm sure the rainforest will have recovered in two hundred years, and they can go back to the old name."

To Nala's chagrin, the upper deck forked once again. She had a choice of 361 spaces in the East Ship Park and 172 spaces in the West Ship Park. She turned east and raced through the shaft, cheered on by her colleagues, because dodos were unfamiliar with the expression 'dead slow' and got it all wrong. "Hurry, we'll be dead if we're too slow!" her colleagues shouted.

Arriving in the parking garage alive without pedestrians sticking to the Sea Cow's snout, Nala parked between a spherical two-seater ship and a red slime freighter.

The freighter's hull consisted of biomass, though it remained completely unclear what organisms had been the ingredients of said biomass. The plants or creatures in question must have been very tough if the slimy box was able to fly through space.

The captain rose from his throne. "Take the translator with you, Hooky," he said.

Hookbeak sat down on the floor and leaned his back against the universal translator. His red back feathers caught in the cracks of the wooden box. When he stood up again, the box was stuck to his mohawk.

The officers took the lift to the cargo hold while Popin whizzed through the Tube. On her way, she nearly crashed into her brother.

"Where are you going?" asked Jay.

"To the space station," said Popin.

"To eat?"

"Nah, for immigration forms. But there seems to be food there, too, if you can believe the advertisements."

"Great, then I'll come along!" said Jay.

"That figures."

By the time the siblings reached the cargo hold, it was crowded with dodos and parrots eager to join the officers.

Outside the hatch, Birdie addressed her words to the navigator. "Anton, you hold the fort and guard the crew. Just make sure no one leaves the ship and gets lost inside the space station... spaceport... whatever."

"But I want to go with you," said Anton. "Why do I always have to keep watch? Why not Nala?"

"That's not true," said Nala. "I had to guard the crew on Imleria while you were having fun with Dertie."

Hookbeak explained the pecking order to Anton: "Nala can fly the ship without you. Accordingly, you are the weakest link in the team."

Dertie nodded. "I can confirm that," she said with a wink, thinking back to the fight on Imleria.

Anton's colleagues entered the space station with Popin and Jay, leaving him alone with the angry crew.

Dirk looked back at the Sea Cow.

"Remember where we parked," he said.

The parking garage was a loveless construction of concrete and steel, in stark contrast to the passers-by. Three-eyed slime monsters shuffled past the dodos. Among them were green slime monsters with red eyes, red slime monsters with green eyes and red-green slime monsters with green-red eyes. The slime monsters were unaware of their outward differences because they were all red-green colour-blind.

One drunken monster called out to the other, "Glubbubbleglug. Dudewhershp?"

The universal translator relayed it as, "~That's what I call a shindig. Dude, where's our ship?~"

Above the entrance door to the shopping arcade hung a portrait of a blue-skinned man wearing a crown studded with precious stones. It was King Reginald LXXXVIII, called *Reginald the Present One* or *Reginald the Living* by his subjects because they pronounced long numbers as words and had realised that Lxxxviii sounded as stupid as it looked. Like all queens and kings before him, Reginald belonged to the Krej species.

The blue Krejs were the dominant indigenous life form on Berdeil, which is why the other creatures and people of the Almond Milky Way simply called them Berdeilers. Krejs weren't human, but humanoid, which meant they looked a lot like humans.

Next to Reginald's face was a speech bubble: "~Ask not what your king can do for you. Ask what you can do for your king.~"

"And what," wondered Birdie, "is the motto under the coat of arms?"

"~Behead and let behead~," replied the translator.

"Oh!" said Birdie. "Looks like a reign of terror to me."

"That's none of our business," said Dirk cheerfully. "We're just picking up the documents."

"And food!" insisted Jay.

In the shopping arcade, they passed the most bizarre creatures, from a gang of lizards in leather jackets to talking sponges splashing in the fountains with starfish and octopuses. Additionally, there were mammals, squids, and monsters with shaggy fur. Dertie felt like she was walking through a huge wonderland where there was everything her heart desired.

"Birdie," said Dertie, "I have a feeling we're not in Mauritius anymore." She grinned like a Cheshire cat.

"Don't touch anything!" warned Birdie.

Dertie shook her head. "I'm not hurting anyone, but I can't work entirely without DNA. Some blood from the lizard man, a little fur from the fur monster, a jar of slime from the slime monster. They wouldn't miss that at all."

"You can ask them on our way back if they'll give their consent," Birdie said wryly. "It seems your fear of beasts was unfounded. Predators and prey have to abide by laws here. Probably the very strict laws of a cruel ruler," she added, thinking of the king's motto.

Hookbeak walked backwards through the passage so that the universal translator could read the signs in front of them.

After ten minutes, when Dirk's feet were already aching, they came across a mall map.

"~One mile to the immigration counters~," said the translator.

"Still that far?" asked Dirk. "This is taking forever. Let's grab a bite to eat first. I'm sure there's something on the way."

They stopped in front of the next restaurant and looked through the 'shop window'.

"Argh, let's pop in," said Popin.

Chapter 8: The Waiter

A ten-foot-long mammal opened the door for the birds. The brown, genetically modified ruminant could stand on its hind legs and worked as a doorkeeper and bouncer. Its appearance seemed strangely familiar to Nala.

When the dodos and parrots entered the restaurant, they were amazed by the size of the room and the many guests. They had only seen a small part of the interior from the outside.

Almost two hundred guests were seated at fifty tables.

"Apparently," said Hookbeak, "everything's occupied."

A green lizard waiter, who was balancing thirty dirty plates on one hand, noticed the birds. He pointed his second hand to a free table next to the toilets and scratched his neck with his third hand. The dodos had to cross the whole room to get to their table.

Half of the guests were blue-skinned Krejs passing through, but the rest resembled a motley bunch. A yellow fur monster devoured an entire cheesecake in three seconds, while the Giant Snails from the planet Patience-Patience had been chewing on their salad leaves for seventeen days.

Birdie became suspicious when she looked at the decoration and furniture of the restaurant.

Twenty silver chandeliers hung from the ceiling, and the tables were made of rare precious wood from the planet Fancy-Schmancy. The chairs were of an elastic metal so they could be adjusted not only in height but also in width and depth – which suited the little parrots just fine.

"When I look at this place," said Birdie, "I don't know if we should eat here."

"Why not?" asked Dirk.

"Maybe they want money. Like the mushrooms on Imleria."

"Oh, poppycock," said Dirk. "The fruit would have been free on Imleria too, Number Two. No society is so uncivilised as to charge money for food. Besides, they would have written it outside on the eatery."

"I'm not so sure about that," Birdie said. "I'd rather not eat anything. It would be unfair to the crew as well."

"Buenosdias-pajaritos!" said the lizard waiter as he approached the dodos' table.

"~Good afternoon, birdies~," the universal translator interpreted into Dodish.

The waiter glanced at the two parrots at the table, for the translator seemed to irritate him.

"¿Nohablas-Almendarin-lalenguafranca?" he inquired. "~Don't you speak the Almendarin language?~"

"Nope. Absolutely not at all," replied Birdie, which was translated for the waiter as "~No.~"

I don't think that's quite how I said it, Birdie thought.

"Esperaunsegundo-pollosraros," spoke the lizard. "~Wait a sec, weirdo-chickens.~"

That's possibly more accurate, believed Birdie, feeling a bit offended.

The waiter disappeared into the kitchen.

"Well," said Dirk. "I guess that went differently than expected."

The birds looked around. There was one other waiter in the room: a slime monster who was uncontrollably releasing slime from his slime hands onto the food and therefore only served other slime monsters.

"Argh, oh," said Popin. "We're gonna starve!"

Birdie wanted to leave immediately and rose from her chair. "Come on, girls and boys, let's pick up the papers. And then we'll look for food on Berdeil for the whole crew."

Her colleagues thought it would be rude to just leave.

"The waiter asked us to wait," said Dertie.

"He asked us to wait a sec," recalled Birdie. "A second is over. Let's go."

"Well," said Hookbeak, "how long is one second in this place? We can't be sure."

Birdie sat down again with a sigh.

The new waiter cleared his throat.

"My lady-birds and gentle-birds, what can I get you?" he asked.

The dodos couldn't believe their eyes. Before them stood a dark blue parrot dressed in a white waiter's shirt.

The waiter bore only a faint resemblance to Jay and Popin. For one thing, he was almost twice as big as the parakeets, and for another, he had a peculiar featherdo. He seemed extraordinary. Yet there was no doubt that he was a parrot.

"By Jove!" exclaimed Nala. "That's a coc-kaa-too! Just like in the sailor's book! Coc-kaa-toos are parrots with big crests. There are many different species of them, too."

The palm cockatoo smiled. "That is correct, Mrs Goggles. My name is Goliath. I'm a *cockatoo*. Please don't pronounce the vowels so long, thank you."

"How nice," said Hookbeak, "that you speak our language."

The cockatoo eyed the dodos. "What are you funny birds doing in space?"

Dertie grinned mischievously. "I was about to ask you the same thing. If you don't have alien cells, you're unsuitable for my weapons experiments."

"Dertie," scolded Birdie, "get a grip! Mr Parrot-with-feather-crest... cockatoo... Goliath... whatever... why do you speak so well? Our parrots only manage a few words at a time."

"*Oh, seriously?*" asked Goliath with mock surprise. "You can't fool me that easily. All parrot species are gifted in speech. Other animals even call us too chatty."

"Argh!" cried Popin. "Brazen lie!"

"Coc-kaa-too super smart!" added Jay.

Puzzled, Goliath scratched his head with his wing feathers and turned to the siblings. "Why are you talking so daft?"

"Argh, because we get much more food this way!" answered Jay without thinking.

Popin covered her face with her wings, stunned.

"You're an idiot!" she said to her brother.

"That's fair," he said.

The dodos stared at the parakeets with open beaks. Perhaps it took them another moment to realise that Jay had indeed blabbed.

"Oh," uttered Birdie. "Would you mind repeating that for me? I couldn't follow… Jay made a weird joke?"

Popin and Jay looked up in a flash. The dodos didn't want to see the truth because they trusted their pets blindly.

True, Popin felt sorry for her feeders, but tradition was tradition, and this one was already centuries old. She nodded to her brother, and he understood. They had to play dumb right away again to fool the dodos.

But the cockatoo was still there, too.

"Nope, he wasn't joking," said Goliath. "Your parrots are pretty crafty if they've gained more food by this trickery."

"That's impossible!" Nala said, distraught as she thought of her three parrots. "No one can pretend to be stupid their whole life. We would have caught on to that!"

Jay lowered his head. He felt guilty.

Popin sighed. *Then we'll just flout the tradition of our local council*, she thought. *We'll live in a new world and never return to Mauritius.* She gathered her courage and said, "Playing dumb is the first thing you're taught as a parrot chick. It's like flying. You know how it's done and you'll never forget."

The dodos' world came crashing down around them. They were shaken to their core – and Popin had just rubbed salt in the wound with her comparison.

Birdie lost it. "*YOU'RE JUST PRETENDING TO BE STUPID?!* Your whole species! Oh, when I get my wings on Herbert…"

Dirk was completely crestfallen. "What kind of world is this, where you can't trust your own pet?"

"Oh dear," said Goliath. "Perhaps our excellent food will help you to digest the shocking news. But you'll have to order some first."

No one responded.

"And by the way," continued Goliath, "it's not customary to scream in a restaurant. If it wasn't so full and noisy today, creatures might have been offended."

"I know," said Birdie. "Sorry. Everyone's driving me crazy. Dodos and parrots. Always taking turns. I just need to lie down on my couch sometime and talk with me about my problems. But a parrot conspiracy on this scale—who could have guessed?"

"You shouldn't lump all parrots together," said Goliath, "just because one species..."

"But that's the thing," said Birdie. "It's not only our pets. I also treated broad-billed parrots and grey parakeets on Mauritius. They spoke to me in the same inane way."

"Okay," said Goliath. He was getting impatient.

"I think our parrots owe us an explanation," Birdie said, as her fellow officers continued to stare into space (not the outer one). "An explanation to all of dodokind, to be exact."

"Can we order food first?" asked Jay. "Because I'm mighty hungry!"

"Very well," said Birdie. "Consider it your *last* meal."

Their waiter was relieved.

"What would you like?" asked Goliath.

Birdie's colleagues looked lifeless and unable to order anything. The psychologist had to stall the cockatoo until everyone regained their composure.

"How does a parrot with an upswept featherdo end up in space?" she abruptly changed the subject.

Goliath turned serious. "Thousands of parrots were abducted by aliens before I hatched. Among them were my parents. I never knew the planet Ground."

"*Earth*," Popin corrected him.

"And you?" asked Goliath. "Were you abducted too, or do you hitchhike?"

Jay grew proud. "We're travelling in a spaceship that we built ourselves!" he exclaimed, although he had only made useless comments during the construction.

"Wow," marvelled Goliath. "This shows that groundlings can even be successful without Berdeil's development aid."

"*Earthlings*," said Popin.

"That's what I meant," said Goliath. "If you're feeling lonely, look to the windows. There are more earthlings sitting there. Seven gregarious, outgoing sheep. A couple of them have been in the kingdom since they were little lambs. The others were born here."

"Oh my gosh," said Birdie, "those animals looked especially extraterrestrial to me."

"Many creatures wrongly assume that," explained Goliath, "because, due to their wool, sheep are mistaken for Pajanish Fluffybeasts. The language of sheep is much more primitive, though. I learnt it in a fortnight. You quickly get the hang of it after the first 'Baaaa' sound. In public, however, sheep speak Almendarin because their mother tongue causes other creatures an earache."

"Yes, yes, very interesting," lied Birdie.

"It's a real problem for the economy," Goliath continued chirpily. "Every time sheep without foreign language skills are abducted into the kingdom, the sickness rate shoots up. But I'm working on a solution. Translation chips."

"Thanks for the boring information," said Jay. "Now let's get back to the topic. *What's for lunch?!*"

"Jay, behave," said Hookbeak. He had finally woken from his state of shock and turned to the waiter. "I suppose you don't have any pandanus fruit, do you?"

"You all got a weird Parrot accent, except the parrots," rejoined Goliath. "Did you say panda nut or panda anu... *ahem*. Never heard of either. Pineapple fruit is very popular and gets delivered in large quantities from Earth. You know pineapples, don't you? Maybe under a different name."

Plant science was Dertie's area of expertise.

"I believe most fruit from Earth is harmless to us," she said. "Do you eat pineapple yourself, Goliath?"

"Yeah, sure. It's not my favourite, but it's okay. Would you like seven servings?"

Jay's eyes widened. "My sister and I get as much food as the dodos?"

"Of course," said the cockatoo. "Unless you want children's portions?"

"Not at all!"

"Your food will be right up," said Goliath and flew into the kitchen.

Hookbeak put the universal translator on the floor to make room for plates.

"Oh, no!" Birdie cried out. "I didn't ask the crested parrot whether the meals are free."

"Sure they are," said Dirk. "Now we have to punish these two sneaky traitors."

The dodos roasted Popin and Jay with laser eyes.

"Oh," said Popin, laughing, "there's no need for that, Dirk. As you always say so aptly, *Love and peace, everybody. Be nice to your pets.*"

"I've never said that last part."

Dertie clenched her little wings. "In this kingdom, criminals are beheaded," she said.

Jay had a lump in his throat. He put his right wing protectively around his neck and swallowed hard.

"I confess!" he cried. "If I get a full pardon for my crimes!"

"Wimp," muttered Popin.

Hookbeak couldn't stay angry with his pet for long.

"Agreed," he said. "You'll get off scot-free if you explain everything."

Jay nodded. "All right, then. First of all, it's your own fault. You stole our language! Now, I don't mean you personally, but your ancestors many centuries ago. You renamed our Parrot to Dodish. That was cultural theft. Soon after, the Council of Highly Intelligent Mauritian Parrots, or CHIMP, decided that we'd only exchange a few words with you. And lo and behold, suddenly you thought we were stupid! As stupid as everyone likes their pets best. When the amount of food increased *slightly*, it became a tradition. Until that foolish cockatoo blew our cover."

"Amen," said Popin.

"But," Nala said, "when did you hear about this tradition?"

"You learn it as a young chick," said Jay, "as soon as you learn the language. The parrots of Dirk's family had to teach it to us because we're orphans."

There was an uncomfortable silence at the table when the cockatoo returned with four servings of pineapple.

He jumped on the table and distributed the plates.

"*Don't touch it!*" shouted Birdie, and her colleagues winced.

"Chill out," said Goliath. "There's no poison in it. I'll get the rest in a minute."

"And it's all free?" asked Birdie.

"Free of what? Chemicals? Er... the answer to that question depends on whether you're a lawyer or not."

Birdie rolled her eyes. "I meant, is the food free of charge?"

"Haha, no," said Goliath. "We're not a soup kitchen. We do have standard prices, though. Ten Royal Crowns per dish. You can also pay with Cosmo Dollars or Astro Rubles until the end of the year. After that, the banks won't accept those currencies any more."

Dirk looked sadly at the fruit. "You could have told us earlier. We come from a gift economy."

"What in the world is a gift economy?" wondered Goliath.

"It's like exchanging help instead of money or goods," said Dirk. "You help someone out with something, and one day they will help you with something you need, or they give you a gift as a thank you. It's based on help and trust."

"That's not possible here. Trust doesn't buy meals in the Almond Milky Way. Although the right gifts might. Money gifts in particular would be very welcome."

Dirk shook his head. "You don't understand. We've abolished money. We're traveling without gold and stuff."

"I'm pretty sure," said Goliath, "that 'travelling' is spelled with a second *l*."

"Nonsense," replied Dirk. "Since when do you spell 'travel' with a second l?"

"Do you have a postal address?" asked Goliath. "Then I'll send you a free copy of *Parrot Spelling*. And my old textbook of the Almendarin lingua franca."

"That would be Upper Deck, East Ship Park, Dodo Alpha Jet, Captain's Office, attn. Captain Dirk. But I only know *Dodish Spelling*, and we won't be here much longer."

"Attention of Captain Dirk," said Goliath, writing on his notepad. "I'll send it with express mail. Now, where were we? Gift economy. That's crazy. What can you offer as a gift for your prepared food?"

Five brawny bouncer bulls – three cattle and two elephants – appeared out of nowhere and stood behind the birds.

"Where did they suddenly come from?" Dirk asked Goliath. "The kitchen?"

"No, that's forbidden territory for all bulls. Fun fact: We no longer employ any sperm whale bulls because even the guests who wanted to pay were crushed. Anyway, your *generous* gift to us?"

"Number Two," said Dirk, "now you can use that lawyerly mind of yours. *Please?*"

"We haven't touched the food," said Birdie. "It smells *weird*."

Goliath knew all the excuses that existed in the restaurant business. "According to the law, we're allowed to charge twenty per cent of the price for preparation of the food. That makes fourteen crowns for all seven dishes."

"You just made that up," presumed Birdie.

"I don't make up laws. I lack the imagination for that."

"What's worth fourteen crowns, cockatoo?"

Goliath took a closer look at the dodos and considered what he could relieve them of. "Your goggles could be sold to a museum," he told Nala. "It's sure to fetch fourteen crowns."

"Not for sale!" said Nala. "It's a family heirloom."

"Okay, okay. You'll have to meet me halfway."

Birdie looked down at her necklace, slightly reluctant. *You don't find your faith in a symbol, you find it in your head*, she thought.

"Well?" said Goliath.

Birdie pointed to the necklace. "How about real silver?"

Without warning, the cockatoo jumped to the edge of Birdie's table, scaring the heck out of her.

"You almost killed me!" she called out, holding her wing to her chest.

Goliath looked at the necklace up close. "A parrot with four wings?"

"That's Loony Polly," Birdie said sourly. "Our most powerful goddess. All real silver, as you can see."

"Great, we'll take it," said Goliath, snatching the necklace from Birdie's neck. "Now please leave the restaurant if you don't want our food."

Dirk groaned. "Us not *wanting* it. That's a good one."

Birdie was far from pleased with the bargain.

"Surely, my necklace is worth more than fourteen crowns."

Her waiter replied with the most artificial laugh his little throat could produce. "For someone who doesn't know money, you're a fast learner. But fair enough. I'll leave you a plate of pineapple. See you around… though I hope not."

The dodos breathed a sigh of relief. Birdie took a knife from the table with her beak and divided the pineapple slices into seven equally small portions.

The cockatoo balanced the three remaining plates on his wings and looked around the restaurant. It was packed, but luckily, three mafia sheep had just sat down in his area.

He hopped over the other guests' tables to the sheep and addressed them in their annoying mother tongue because he was hoping to get rid of a few customers.

"Baaa baaha baabaa?" asked Goliath.

Translated, the conversation went as follows:

"How can a sheep tell the difference between a wolf and a sheepdog? By their smell? Or by their character? Good dog, bad wolf?"

The boss sheep in the middle blinked at Goliath in irritation. It could never get used to the cockatoo's perplexing questions.

"By their appearance," explained the sheep. "And whether they bark or howl."

"Ah, right, that works too," said Goliath. "What may I bring you? The same as always?"

His action was effective. The guests at the next tables took to their heels.

"Three dishes of pasture grass," replied the sheep, "and a large bowl of water."

"The same as always. Coming right up," said Goliath.

Birdie rose from her seat after the meagre meal.

"I'll be back in a minute," she said.

She walked to a brown door with the symbols ♀ + 👽 (women and alien females) and ♂ + 👽 (men and alien males) on it. After Birdie stepped into the toilet area, she sighed and got in line behind Krejs and lizards. A queue had formed because two Giant Snails from Patience-Patience were creeping to the toilets, blocking the way.

Meanwhile, Goliath came out of the kitchen with water and pasture grass. When he saw the dodos, he shook his head in annoyance. He first brought the mafia sheep their food and then sat down on the birds' table.

"You're still here!" he said. "Don't tell me, you've found your money?"

"Of course not," said Nala. "Our colleague had to go to the bathroom. When she gets back, we'll fly away from here."

"I doubt it," said Goliath. "But looking at your little paddles, I assume you're good swimmers... Oh wait, you meant flying away with a spaceship, did you?"

"Yes!" retorted Nala. "And these are wings."

"No, no," the cockatoo corrected her kindly. "They're not wings because wings are used to fly. You clearly have paddles, and they're even smaller than penguins' paddles."

The captain felt insulted. "What are you saying?! *Pah!*" he replied scornfully for all dodo beings.

"Penguins, penguins," mused Nala. "The name sounds familiar, but I don't have a picture in my mind."

"Flightless seabirds," said Goliath, "who sway back and forth comically as they walk? Does that ring a bell?" He scanned the room with his eagle eyes. "Penguins often work as waiters or butlers because they're always suitably dressed when naked. This restaurant also employs two of them, but today, they seem to have flown the coop. *Flown* the coop. You get it?"

Popin and Jay burst into laughter, while the dodos remained straight-faced.

"My!" said Goliath, "Šúša is here after all. Look over there! The black and white thing with the tray on the paddle. That's a penguin. Šúša even hatched on the Grou... on Earth. Lucky girl."

The dodos turned their heads.

A penguin was serving various pastries to a yellow furry monster and his blue friend. It was already their fifth order of the day.

"Are you sure," asked Dertie, "that this black and white creature is from Earth?"

"Uh huh, uh huh," said Goliath. "I'm sure of it. The aliens always abduct penguins from the southern continent."

"But the southern continent is completely covered in ice!" Dertie pointed out.

"Well, penguins swim in cold ice water and eat fish," said Goliath, suddenly starting to doubt. "At least that's what I was told."

Nala nodded as she remembered. "That's what Altair's book said too."

Dirk waved it aside. "If you ask me, those stories are nothing but fairy tales."

"No, they must be facts," objected Nala, "because cockatoos and penguins really do exist!"

"I'll second that," said Goliath. "Rumour has it that all bird species came from Earth because that's the only place where dinosaurs lived."

"Dino-what now?" asked Nala.

"Our common ancestors from ancient times. It would take too long to explain, and I really don't want to hold you up," said Goliath, kindly informing them that they should beat it.

"Oh, horror," Hookbeak said. "We still have to get immigration forms."

"Oh, you don't need them," said Goliath. "The civil servants just want your money, which you claim you don't have. If anyone asks for the papers, just say you were abducted by the Dumpians. They're acting on behalf of our majesty. Believe me, neither policemen nor judges want to mess with the king."

"Thanks for the advice," said Hookbeak.

"That one was on the house."

Birdie returned.

"Well then, off to the immigration counters?" she asked.

"Nah," said Dirk, "the matter's been resolved. One less thing to worry about. Now we can get to Berdeil quickly before the crew starts a mutiny."

But the birds made no move to leave. Birdie even had sat down again. She wondered what she could trade for another helping of pineapple.

The cockatoo shook his head and beckoned an elephant over. "Our bouncer will give you safe passage out."

"Very kind," Birdie said sharply.

The elephant approached the table, paying no heed to where he was stepping.

Suddenly, sparks shot up from the floor.

"~Bon voyage, amigos! What le Katzenjammer! You clumsy über-oaf!~" were the universal translator's last words.

The elephant trumpeted in panic and ran for the kitchen.

"*No!*" shouted Goliath after him. "*You're a bull... kind of! Don't enter the—*"

It was too late. Plates began to break. Lots of plates. Mostly china.

Jay giggled. "What a klutz."

"Well," said Goliath, "the cattle aren't any better, believe me."

"Really?" wondered Popin. "It sounded more like breaking plates than breaking kettles to me."

"What?"

"What?"

Dertie cleared her throat and leaned over to Popin and Jay. "I think the cockatoo meant the other alien bouncers. The brown ones with the horns."

"They are called kettle?" asked Jay.

Dertie shrugged. "Trust me, I'm a biologist."

The other dodos made long faces because of the universal translator.

"*Great*," said Nala, looking at the former box, which was now as flat as a pancake. "Our translator is completely destroyed! Now what?"

"It happens," said Goliath in the bouncer's defence. "That's how all bulls are."

Birdie looked at the cockatoo with a smile because now she was holding a trump card. But her wing was too small to hold anything for long, so she played it immediately.

"Now you have to give us a new universal translator," she said.

"*Universal...?*" asked Goliath in amazement. "Wait a minute. Are you telling me the translator knew more than two languages?"

"A few million languages more, I guess," said Birdie.

"Holy cow!" exclaimed Goliath. "Can we get it fixed? This will make you multi-billionaires!" He looked at the ruined machine. "Oh. Right. Flat as a flounder. I don't think it's gonna make it. My bad. Such a device hasn't been invented here yet. It must be really advanced technology. That's not like pulling a rabbit out of a hat. It's more like pulling a blue whale out of a hat that was designed to fit a rabbit."

"What do we get in compensation?" asked Birdie.

"In order to communicate in the Almond Milky Way, you just need someone who understands Almendarin."

"A translator for only *one* language? That's a bit low."

"How do you like fruit sauce as recompense?" asked Goliath. "It will be deducted from the elephant's salary."

"All right," said Birdie. "Now, what about the inferior translator?"

"Yes, give me five minutes. I'll get the device from my locker."

Almendarin was the more common name for the language of the Hispanohablantes. The language's name was derived from *Vialáctea-de-Almendra*, the Almond Milky Way.

The Hispanohablantes, called *Spanyards* by the Inglyshspeekers from Graydbrytannia, were a species of space travellers who had left their home world Iberiya from time to time to explore, colonise and exploit new worlds like all the old space-sailor species used to do.

They also found many business partners on their voyages – mainly inhabitants of alien worlds who were more technologically advanced than them, especially in warfare, and therefore would not be exploited and colonised by anyone.

Over the millennia, many Spanyards settled down on alien planets, and their language unintentionally became the business language of the Almond Milky Way.

The universe could not determine the future, but at least it could influence it. Thus, a language called Spanish was already developing on 14th-century Earth. Spanish would be almost identical to Almendarin one day (although Almendarin was spoken faster). In the future, Spanish would sooner or later become the national language of almost all of North America, except for a huge nature reserve called Canada.

The universe wanted to make the first encounter between humans and Krejs in the 24th century as smooth as possible because language problems had often led to interstellar wars.

The cockatoo brought the dodos and parrots seven plates full of yellowish pulp.

"Ta-da!" he said. "Enjoy the apple sauce."

No one began to eat.

Dertie gave a little cough. "Guys, do you also think it looks like vomi–"

"Shhh!" said Nala. "You don't say things like that while the waiter is listening."

Goliath dug a round microchip out of his feathers and raised it with his foot. "You look completely baffled," he said to Dirk. "Have you never seen a translation chip with a transmitter before?"

"Er…" said Dirk.

"We know microchips," said Birdie, "but I, for one, have never heard of a translation chip."

"I see," said Goliath and glanced at Jay. "Hey, you! Come here."

Jay shook his head.

"It's a gift," explained Goliath.

"Why didn't you say so in the first place?!" asked Jay and jumped on the table.

The cockatoo held the microchip to Jay's head and said, "In a moment you'll understand Almendarin. Then you'll be able to communicate throughout the kingdom and beyond."

Jay saw stars, turtles and star turtles float by in his mind's eye. In his head, all the words from the Parrot language transformed into the life forms and objects they denoted. From the tiny caterpillar to the giant supernova. Hundreds of thousands of images appeared in his mind until they were all cuddled together.

The life forms and objects then turned back into words. The words of a new language.

"*Woah, my head is throbbing,*" whined Jay.

His own sister didn't understand what he was saying.

"*That's normal*," said Goliath. "*Let's go back to speaking Parrot so your wife will stop staring at us, puzzled.*"

"You mean my sister. But how do I jump back?" asked Jay uncertainly.

"Yes, just like that," the cockatoo said.

"Jump where?" asked Nala.

To Birdie, it was obvious. "Jay can switch back and forth between the two languages. He has mastered a foreign language now."

Goliath cleared his throat. "Unfortunately, this was the only Instant Almendarin Crash Course For Parrots I've developed."

"Oh no!" grumbled Dirk, resting his head on the table because he was missing his nap. "If you had said that earlier, we'd have chosen a reliable parrot for your experiment."

"Exactly!" agreed Popin.

"Hey!" said Jay. "I can hear you!"

Goliath directed his words at Popin, "Trust me. If there are any serious side effects, you'll be glad I took your brother as a guinea pig and not you."

Jay froze. He fell forward, his head landing in his apple sauce.

His sister and the dodos shuddered. They turned their heads with menace to the cockatoo. If looks could kill. Especially Popin's.

"Hey, fellows," said Goliath, raising and lowering his wings placatingly, "it was just a bad joke."

"Oh, really?" asked Jay. "Didn't think it was funny, though. Mmm, apple sauce is delicious!"

The other birds sighed with relief.

"Ha!" said Goliath. "The translation chip is a complete success. But the rest of you will have to learn Almendarin the old-fashioned way: taking classes and reading language books."

"We don't have to," retorted the captain. "We don't need the language because we're taking off shortly. Jay is our translator, that's enough."

"Interpreter," said Jay.

The other birds looked at him in surprise.

He shrugged. "Maybe the foreign language has also expanded my Parrot vocabulary."

After the birds had devoured the delicious apple sauce, they left the restaurant, which was only half full now, thanks to Goliath's extensive conversations with the sheep mafia.

The dodos started their long way back to the ship park, while Jay looked curiously in the opposite direction. Small children were tugging their parents in droves to a big screen.

"Come," said Jay to his sister. "Let's have a quick look. We'll catch up with the leaden-footed dodos in two wing beats."

"Fine with me," said Popin.

The screen showed a commercial with a smartly dressed man promoting his product. The man was a chubby, grey-haired vampire in a suit. He had a double chin and was polishing off an entire 100-gram chocolate bar with relish.

"O, I'm in 'eaven! So much sweeter than blood! 'ow marvellous. You 'ave to try for yourself!" he said with a full mouth and a Frantch accent.

His vampire smile was accompanied by a short advertising tune, to which lovely children's voices sang: "Count Chocolat: Fat and Loving It."

"Pops, Pops!" a blue boy called out next to the parakeets. "Can I have a chocolate bar? Or better yet, a ten-pack?"

"Why should my sister decide?" asked Jay in Almendarin. "She doesn't understand you at all."

The boy and his two fathers looked at Jay in wonder.

"Oh, sorry," said Jay. "Little mix-up. My sister's name is Pops, too."

"That's nonsense!" said the boy. "Only men can be popses."

"Well, your point of view might be true in a strictly biological sense, but my sister's name is Pops, short for Popin. And I am Jay. Together we are... Well, you little brat! Sticking out your tongue at someone is very rude where I come from. This is getting too childish for me here. *Come on, Pops, let's go.*"

Popin lifted off the ground for a moment and looked for the dodos. When she saw that the feeders had only walked a hundred yards, she landed beside her brother again.

"What was going on between you and the little boy?" she asked.

"Just a language misunderstanding," said Jay. "Oh dear, my stomach is growling. And I'm thirsty, too."

"You had apple sauce ten minutes ago!"

"Didn't fill me up."

He looked at his sister. She felt his gaze on her.

"What is it?" asked Popin. "Please don't tell me you're turning into a cannibal now."

"Don't worry," he said. "I'd have to become a meat-eater first."

"True, but why are you staring at me so strangely, then?"

"I'm just realising what beautiful feathers you have, sis. Turn around a moment so I can admire your tail feathers."

Popin was flattered. "Why, thank you, dear brother..." she began to say. "*OUCH!!! ARE YOU CRAZY?*" she yelled just a second later.

Jay fled to the opposite side of the shopping street. As he flew past the shops, he cast an eye over what they had to sell.

"No... nah... nope... ugly... ordinary... lol... hideous... hehe... oh my Polly..."

He passed a shop called *Chofé,* where mammals and lizards were sitting around sipping hot drinks from cups. Outside the shop was a hologram of a little green man with long antennae, who stood waiting to greet customers.

Jay landed in front of the store. He peered curiously inside.

"Mmm," said the thirsty parrot.

"Would you care for a *Hot Caffeine Chocolate* © ?" asked the hologram of the little green man. "You may have one in our beautiful chocolate café or, as we call it, *Chofé.*"

"A hot *what*?"

"A Hot Caffeine Chocolate ©, Monsieur?"

"Hm, sounds kind of toxic," answered Jay.

"You don't know about our product yet?" asked the hologram in bemusement. "Well, in that case... *ENGAGING... ADVERTISING... MODE.*"

The hologram flickered for a moment before continuing. "These days, most creatures take their *coffee* in such a way that it no longer deserves its name because two-thirds of what they drink is milk and sugar. That is why our founders decided to serve hot cups of cocoa injected with a high dosage of caffeine. One cup of our product keeps you as wide awake as two cups of black coffee. In your *Hot Caffeine Chocolate* © the choice of milk is yours, either *lactose-free* or *fresh from the udder*. This makes our drink a real hit with every creature in the galaxy. There are only two small exceptions. Adult cows prefer water, obviously out of shame, and insects don't drink caffeine. Are you a cow or an insect, Monsieur?"

"Neither," answered Jay. "But why don't insects drink that stuff?"

"Because caffeine is, so to speak, a natural insecticide."

"Oh, I see," said Jay. "I've got one question, though."

"Yes, Monsieur?"

"What's an insecticide?"

"It's a poison for insects," explained the hologram, "and caffeine specifically protects the coffee plant. When insects drink it, they often bite the—" The hologram flickered again before continuing. "*RETURN TO FORMAL LANGUAGE*... Monsieur, caffeine is *regrettably fatal* for insects."

Jay had no idea what the little green man was talking about and, frankly, he didn't care.

"Whatever. I'd like to try one of these *Hot Caffeine Chocolates*. But where I come from, there's no money. Money is very odd to us. So in exchange for the drink, I'll give you these four *emerald-green* tail feathers from my sister – freshly plucked by myself!"

He waved the feathers in front of the hologram's green nose.

"Ha ha," the hologram laughed. "Monsieur is in the mood for jokes? We're neither a barter nor a welfare organisation. We are a capitalist hot chocolate chain and don't even pay our taxes. You won't get anything in our Chofé without money."

"Blimey," said Jay.

"However, I do like the feathers, Monsieur," said the hologram. "I'll give you a napkin for them."

"Hm, I'd rather have one little sip of cocoa," said Jay. "This could be our little secret. The beginning of a partnership even, because there are a lot more feathers growing where those came from. D'you get what I'm saying?"

"Yes, but it's a no."

"Oh, drat," said Jay, and flew off pensively. "Money is a confusing new invention. But so tempting, too! I'm starting to think it makes the world go round."

He returned to his furious sister.

"How dare you!" Popin scolded him. "You're so mean!"

"Here," replied Jay, handing Popin her feathers. "You can have them back."

"Very funny!"

"I'm serious. Maybe you can stick the feathers back on somehow, at least until you'll grow new ones in your next moulting period."

"I wish I was an only child," said Popin. "Then I wouldn't have been given such a silly name either."

She lifted off the ground and followed the dodos. When she realised that Jay wasn't joining her, she turned back.

"Are you coming now?" she asked. "The dodos are almost at the parking garage."

"No, sorry," Jay said seriously. "I'm starving and I need a change. I'll start looking for new feeders. A little girl and a little boy who will always stuff me with food like good feeders should! It's been nice knowing you, sis. Farewell! Stay safe! Wish you all the best!"

"Idiot!" said Popin visibly upset before she flew to the dodos on her own.

Jay knew the farewell could have been nicer, but it was easier for him this way.

He flew in the other direction and discovered a toy shop where a painting lesson was taking place. The preschoolers of Krejs and slime monsters were colouring pictures of their heroes, mainly comic and cartoon characters.

Jay took a rubber band, a red pen and a sheet of paper with the pre-printed face of King Reginald. He wrote on the white back and pierced two holes in the sheet with the tip of his beak. He then attached the rubber band to the sheet and left the toy shop as quickly as he had come.

"Parrot steals!" a kindergarten girl called after him. "Thieving magpie!"

Jay hung the sheet around his neck and stood in front of a fruit shop. With his sweetest puppy-dog eyes, he looked at the passers-by.

On his sign was written in Almendarin:

Si me dan cuatro buenas comidas al día,
no tengo que ir a la enfermería.

Translated it meant:

Four good meals a day
keep me out of sick bay.

A policeman whose uniform was as blue as his skin suddenly planted himself in front of Jay.

"Are you begging?" asked the policeman.

"Uh, *no?* No, no. Of course not," replied Jay with quick thinking.

"The penalty for begging is death."

"Whoa-ha! Then it's a good thing we cleared up that misunderstanding, Officer!"

"Looks suspiciously like begging to me, though," said the constable.

"Oh, baloney," said Jay. "I'm offering a service. I give comfort and affection in happy times, and if the food is amazing, even in bad times."

"I'm not aware of such a service."

"I'm a pet by profession. Surely there's something like that here, too?"

The policeman shook his head.

"Drat," said Jay. "Then I'll have to find another job quickly because I'm not a beggar and never will be! Have a nice day!"

He tore the paper from his neck, threw it into a waste bin and fled upwards.

"What to do, what to do, what to do..." he panicked.

He roamed through the airspace of the shopping street. Eventually, he remembered the cockatoo. A distant relative who might help him out.

When the dodos had found their parking space, Hookbeak looked around for the parrots. He could only spot Popin, who walked into him with her head down.

"Where's your brother?" he asked her.

"Argh! Don't know, ar–!"

"Stop it! You're not fooling me any more."

"Sorry," said Popin meekly. "Force of habit. And the whole truth is that Jay has left us both. He's looking for a new feeder."

"Oh," said Hookbeak, teary-eyed. "Then... well... I'm at a loss for words."

Anton waited at the lift for his colleagues.

"Captain," he said, "a language book was delivered. Nobody understood the first postbird, a pigeon, so she sent a parrot with a feather crest."

"Same thing happened to us in the restaurant!" said Dirk.

"You went to eat?" Anton asked hungrily.

"Just nibbles."

༄

The cockatoo Goliath stood at the table of a very difficult, regular customer, waiting to take his order. The guest was an Anvelar Crocopotamus, an egg-laying mammal that looked like a crossbreed between a hip hippopotamus and a ravenous crocodile and never knew whether its diet was meat or vegetarian.

"Do you," asked the crocopotamus, "have tender organic meat from happy Maledan zebra foals?"

"Yes, we do," said Goliath. "One serving, Mr Hipposnap?"

"Oh, wait, bring me a selection of your choicest grasses from the Tavojali pasture on Pastura IV instead."

"Yes, Mr Hipposnap."

"Wait a minute!" called the crocopotamus when the cockatoo was already in the air. "Bring me three large portions of the tender zebra foals too, just in case I get an appetite for organic meat."

Organic meat won't save your liver either, thought Goliath.

He tried to jump to the next table but was 'cleared away' by Jay before he could. Both parrots fell to the floor.

"I'm sorry. Can you help me?" asked Jay in Parrot.

The cockatoo did not respond.

"I'm sorry. Can you help me?" asked Jay in Almendarin.

"I heard you the first time," Goliath replied, standing up again. "What seems to be the problem, mate?"

༄

"Where is Jay?" asked Birdie as she took a seat on her folding chair. "We always need him on the bridge for the day shift now."

"The ungrateful wretch," said Hookbeak, "is looking for a new master or mistress at the spaceport." He was no longer sad but angry.

"I am sorry!" said Birdie. "So, um, we have to fly on without a translator? I think that's a mistake because of all the signs in this territory."

"Hmm," said Nala.

Dirk looked at the pilot. "You've got an idea?"

"I think so. We could ask the cockatoo. The little linguistic genius didn't seem happy as a waiter."

Anton objected, knowing that they were running out of time. "We need food *now*! The crew will soon start a mutiny – if they can find the strength. Let's go to Berdeil! We can still look for a translator afterwards."

༄

The temporary waiter, Jay, served juicy deer steaks to a tiger family of three.

The little tiger girl tugged at the parrot's waiter shirt with her paw.

"She's just playing," said her mother with a laugh.

"How reassuring," lied Jay.

"She's getting venison for the very first time today," explained the mother. "After that, she'll never want poultry again."

Jay nodded, acting friendly. Then he said, "You're mistaken anyway. I'm a wild bird. I'm not poultry!"

"We tigers eat all birds equally."

"You mean *treat*?"

"Yeah, that too."

"I see," said Jay. He took a cursory glance out the shop window and spotted three dodos who were chaining up their kick scooters in front of the restaurant. Birdie raised her little wing half-heartedly and waved at Jay. It seemed like a merely polite gesture to a former friend you no longer want anything to do with.

At another table, the pigged-out Hipposnap was just rising from his seat. The four-metre-long, thousand-kilogram crocopotamus made the floor shake. He quickly slipped into his anti-gravity slippers, which made him as light as a slime monster.

His waiter waited patiently.

"Another *Soul Heater* before you go, my Mr Hipposnap?" asked Goliath.

"Won't ever say *no* to that!" said the crocopotamus.

The cockatoo placed a glass of steaming brown liquid on the table and thanked his guest for visiting. Hipposnap whisked the liquor away and shuffled off.

Goliath looked after him with relief, but his expression darkened when he saw Nala, Dirk and Birdie walking up to him. "Well, at least your friends have had their fill?" he asked.

"We're in a hurry," said Birdie, "and only have three scooters."

"And what do you want? I have to work."

"That's why we're here," said Nala. "We're offering you a job on our ship."

Goliath suddenly began to fantasise.

He was on a space luxury liner, serving the dodos his latest invention: a cocktail of rum, pineapple juice and coconut cream. He doubted that the cocktail tasted good, but the dodos were his guinea pigs. Afterwards, he switched off the lights in the ship's restaurant as a supernova shone through the window. You had to cut electricity costs where you could.

Waiting tables on a cruise ship? At least I can see the world now, he thought. To his surprise, the dodos liked the drink.

"Yoo-hoo, don't dream," said Nala. "Do you fancy a change of career?"

"Yeeaahh..." replied Goliath, waking up. "I think of it more as a change of scenery."

"You don't even know yet what it's about."

"Sorry. The exact job title is what? Ship's head waiter?"

Nala shook her head. "Communications Officer for the ship Dodo Alpha Jet. Mostly translation stuff."

"Wow," said the cockatoo. "This actually sounds like work that suits my skills. What are the pros and cons of the profession?"

"We... er... we offer you a varied job in a respected industry," said Nala, advertising the position. "You will work with nice and qualified colleagues in a harmonious atmosphere. Moreover, we attach great importance to your health, for example in the form of regular preventive medical check-ups conducted by our ship's own company doc... uh, in-boat doctor. And most importantly: with us, you can fulfil your dreams thanks to a good work-life balance."

Birdie laughed out loud.

"Oh," she muttered when she saw that the others remained straight-faced. "I'm probably the only one who thought that was a joke."

Nala carried on unfazed. "Goliath, you just need communication skills for the work."

"And enjoy talking on the phone!" added Dirk.

"That's what I meant," whispered Nala to him.

Goliath felt underwhelmed in his work as a waiter, but he was missing the essential point in the job's description.

"Yes, understood, that's all well and good," he said, "but stop beating about the bush now."

"Excuse me?" asked Nala.

"You pussyfoot around the main point. What about the dough?"

"I don't quite understand."

"Bread, dosh, cash," explained Goliath.

"But," said Nala, "we already told you at lunch that there's no money in our society. That includes life on the ship."

"What now?!" the cockatoo asked, puzzled. "You were serious about that? I thought you were trying to bamboozle us out of food."

"We're not cheats!" said Nala.

Still, it seemed unrealistic to Goliath.

"No financial pressure at all, then?" he dug deeper.

"That's right," confirmed Dirk. "It's unnatural for an animal to amass wealth."

"But," countered Goliath, "for a clever animal that doesn't want to starve in the Almond Milky Way, wealth is a good start."

"Yes," said Birdie, "we've noticed that. For us, the idea of exchanging gold and silver coins is very strange. After all, you can't eat gold. At least not in the long run. You can trust me on this, I'm a doctor. A couple of hundred years ago our ancestors remembered that all the other birds on Earth don't use money. When they started to do each other favours, all jobs that only existed because of money disappeared overnight, like for instance saleshens and salesroosters. Admittedly, we have the advantage that we come from a small island. A land of plenty. Why buy fruits that we can get in the rainforests for free?"

"I must admit," admitted Goliath, "that I envy you. So you can live on your ship without money. What's the catch to your paradise?"

"*Paradise?*" asked Nala. "No, I wouldn't call it that. We hail from a real paradise and it was totally boring there. But on the ship, there's always a lot to do. Mainly cleaning work because parrots make a lot of mess. No offence."

"That's all right," said Goliath.

"If you don't take part in the tasks, you don't have any friends and become a loner," continued Nala. "That's why no one lasts doing nothing for long. A perpetual lazybones would get no recognition."

Birdie looked automatically at Dirk. *There's always an exception that proves the rule*, she thought.

The cockatoo cleared his throat. "You really wouldn't let the slacker starve?"

"No!" affirmed Nala.

"Well, in that case, I'm on board of course."

"However," said Birdie, "we will indeed starve in a few days if we don't find any food."

"Oh," said Goliath. "There's the catch."

🌿

Jay waited by the bright red scooters for the dodos.

"I want to come with you," he said, "and be a pet again. Serving meat to predators isn't my thing." His feathers were littered with food scraps and he belched. "I've eaten enough for a week now. It's amazing how rarely cats touch their salad garnish."

"You can come," said Birdie, getting on her kick scooter. "But Popin and Hookbeak don't take kindly to you."

"Oh, they'll get over it," he said.

"Great," said Birdie. "First we didn't have an Almendarin translator and now we have two."

"Why two?" wondered Jay.

At that moment, the cockatoo stepped out of the restaurant. He had fetched his backpack from the kitchen.

"Ah," said Jay, "you're coming with us?"

Goliath nodded. "I hope I won't regret it in a few days."

"You should regret it already. You've got green slime on you!"

"Yeah," Goliath said with a sigh. "The slime monster waiter hugged me goodbye."

The three dodos zoomed through the shopping arcade on their scooters while Goliath and Jay flew above them.

"Look at the two monsters at the feeding station!" the cockatoo called to the parakeet. "They were in our restaurant today! I don't think they'll get what they're looking for at that stand, though."

The two hot-headed monsters, one with yellow and one with blue fur, stood in front of the food stand.

"*Cake?!*" asked the yellow monster.

The Hondolanian vendor grabbed her head with her tentacles.

"For the last time," she said in frustration, "we don't have cake. We have cheap burgers and fries that sink into the fat and sometimes get lost in it too. Otherwise our fast food stall would hardly be called *Burgfries – The Good Fat Life at a Ridiculously Low Price*. And before your blue friend asks again, we don't have cookies either!"

The monsters could no longer contain their temper. They stormed the food stand and ransacked it for cakes and cookies. All they found were buns, mince, shrieking staff and fries.

Then they tried their luck at the kebab stand next door.

"I'll be a monkey's uncle!" exclaimed Goliath as he stood in front of the Dodo Alpha Jet. "Your ship's a sea cow!"

"Yo, totally, isn't it?" said Jay.

The cockatoo kept gawking. "A cyclops sea cow, to be exact. What punk designed that thing?"

"I think," said Birdie, "Hookbeak designed the ship that way to save space."

"Awesome! I always thought sea cows came from Deape-Bloo," explained the cockatoo.

On the water planet Deape-Bloo, sea cows had been swimming around with Eerian Fuddypuppies and Fliscan Leadgoats for five hundred years.

Jay used the comm tube and flew to his favourite rod next to the fusion reactor. The dodos went to the bridge with the cockatoo.

"All reunited," said Dirk as they stepped out of the lift. "We're ready to go. Where's Pops?"

"In your cabin," answered Dertie. "She's not doing so well. You know why."

"Then I'll bring her good news," said Dirk. "Jay's back. He's in the engine room."

"Oh really?" asked Hookbeak. "Good for him."

Birdie had heard the defiance in his voice. "Don't you want to go see him?"

Hookbeak shook his head. "No need for that. He'll come crawling back on his own."

The Sea Cow left the spaceport without immigration forms but with the new communications officer, Goliath.

Chapter 9: Witnesses of the Prosecution

More than a hundred thousand years ago, the Dumpians – green humanoids with pink hair – experienced an industrial revolution on their planet Dump.

After they had exploited nature over the next three centuries, an absolute climate catastrophe occurred. Within minutes, the planet's surface turned black as coal. The air heated up relentlessly and the water evaporated. Eventually, the atmosphere could no longer be held captive by the planet's gravity and fled into space.

While all the animals and plants died through no fault of their own, most Dumpians escaped in their spaceships.

The survivors found temporary refuge on Dump's blue neighbouring planet, which had a similar climate. Unconcerned, they continued their excessive lifestyle until their calculations showed that they would exhaust the natural resources of the new world after only two decades. Their financial and economic planners demonstrated credibly that it was not worth building a new civilisation for a paltry twenty years. So they generously left the planet to the indigenous flora and fauna and flew on with their tanks full.

The Dumpians had been given a second chance. And for a time, they behaved decently.

What was meant to be a short search for a new home turned into a six-month odyssey through the galaxy (similar to the odyssey the dodos were currently on). In the end, the Dumpians met an alliance of hundreds of worlds in the Almond Milky Way, which was about to establish a star republic.

When the Dumpians committed themselves to an environmentally friendly way of life, they were given permission to settle on Berdeil. Soon after, with the establishment of the new republic, they were made citizens. That *could* have been the end of their story. As Dumpians loved to do crooked business, though, they soon felt that democracy and the ban on bribery restricted them in their personal freedom. So it happened that thirteen days after the founding of the star republic, they were involved in the overthrow of the government on Berdeil. For their support in re-establishing the monarchy, they were awarded a third of the planet by the *Generous Despot*, King Louis XXI, and they named their country New Dump.

The next generations of Dumpians supported the Berdeil kings and queens in their ambitious project of conquering every planet of the short-lived star republic. Under Berdeil's rule, all the worlds of the Almond Milky Way were to be united forever and ever.

This goal was not achieved even after a hundred thousand years, but King Reginald the Present One lacked only eight... wait a second... seven planets at the far end of the Way, which stubbornly resisted his rule.

To this day, Dumpian businessmen regularly travel to their ancestors' solar system and abduct animals from Dump's neighbouring planet – Earth – to counter the kingdom's labour shortage. Often, the businessmen took their children with them to show them the old, uninhabitable Dump. For a few weeks now, the children had been disappointed. The planet was no longer to be seen. Granted, it was black, but due to its gravity, it wasn't undetectable either. The parents raised their eyebrows and gave their children cats and dogs as consolation.

The dodos knew Dump as the black planet *Vicinus*, which they had crumbled with their warp drive 45 days ago – long before the Italian astronomer Galileo would have been able to discover it for humankind.

🌿

The Sea Cow swam leisurely in its orbit around Berdeil and was overtaken by satellites, electronic waste and organic garbage.

Nala was reluctant to enter the atmosphere before she knew the way to their destination. In fact, she would have considered it extremely foolish. On an alien planet, you were looking for the proverbial needle in a haystack without a map. Just think of Earth and its alien visitors. Dumpians, for example, were ill-advised to begin their search for the South American llamas in China. Yet this happened three times a week.

A cockatoo did not spare a thought on maps or even a globe. He found his bearings with the aid of markers.

"We need to get to the border area between Kingstown and New Dump," Goliath told Anton and Nala. "We should find free food there."

"Do you know the way, *cockatoo*?" asked Anton, putting his feet up.

"Quasi, *dodo*," replied Goliath. "We have to enter the atmosphere first. I'll find my way based on the landscape."

"Okay," said Nala.

"Maybe," added the cockatoo, "it'll be hard for me to find my bearings at first because everything looks the same from above. But sooner or later, I should find my way around."

"Oh great," muttered Nala. "The needle in the haystack, after all."

Patiently but close to madness, Nala steered the Sea Cow two hours over forests, towns and an ocean – looking for a spot in the landscape which would help the cockatoo find the way to Kingstown.

Nala got an idea when they reached another town.

"How about we just stop and ask for directions?" she said.

"Yay!" whooped Goliath for a different reason. "It looks suspiciously like Kingstown to me this time. Let's see. Pretentious castle? Check. Public beheading? Check. Yep, we're here. The border area lies beyond the city walls."

"It's about time," said Dirk. "I'm so hungry I couldn't even take a nap."

Birdie could only bear the captain by mocking him. "Oh, Dirky, poor little chick, didn't have his afternoon nap. Now he'll become all fractious in the evening, won't he?"

"If you keep teasing me, I won't talk to you any more!"

Birdie smiled. "A dream come true," she said cheerfully.

"Don't you have anything to do?" asked Dirk. "No crash pilots at the animal hospital?"

"Strangely, no," said Birdie. "It must be like a morgue in the Tube. The parrots are all staring hungrily out of the windows. Of course I'd rather be working than talking to you."

"Very funny, Number Two. I'll find someone to talk to who actually likes me."

"Good luck with that..."

Dirk did not respond, for he knew he wouldn't stand a chance in a battle of wits against Birdie. He turned to the second folding chair instead. "Well, how's my first mate today?"

Hookbeak nodded and said, "Fine."

"Not a male of big words," said Dirk. "But I have a question, Hooky. Why can't you warm yourself up in a microwave when you're cold?"

"Because you'd die!" said Birdie. "Your head would explode!"

"I wasn't talking to you!"

Birdie moved her wing disdainfully as if to literally brush Dirk aside. "It's just as well that we have you as captain..." she began sarcastically.

"I agree," said Dirk.

"... and not someone who only asks silly questions," she concluded.

"He who isn't asking questions won't find answers to anything."

Birdie glanced at him. She had to admit that there was a certain logic in his rejoinder.

Dirk lay down. He was lying across his armchair with his back to Birdie so that he could ignore her better. Now it was up to Hookbeak to keep the captain entertained.

"Come on, Hooky," said Dirk. "Tell me an anecdote from your youth."

"You tell it. You were there," said Hookbeak.

The ship had reached the border area, a jungle of tall shrubs, bushes and turquoise flowers.

"*GUYS!*" shouted Nala abruptly, and everyone flinched. "We have a problem!"

"Do we?" asked Goliath. He hopped off the parrot perch onto her dashboard.

The scenery had puzzled Nala.

"Where am I supposed to land here?" she asked. "There's no space nearly big enough."

"But it's all clear," said Goliath.

"Joker. I see plants everywhere."

"On Berdeil it's only forbidden to park on trees. Nobody gives a darn about flowers and bushes."

Nala shrugged. "Alrighty then."

She switched off the propulsion jets and the ship plummeted more than thirty feet. It wiped out fifty bushes on its hard touchdown.

The captain criticised his pilot: "You've managed that more gently before."

"Had to be quick, I'm hungry," she said.

The Sea Cow wasn't the only spaceship that had just arrived in the border area. A Dumpian transport ship with involuntary immigrants landed three hundred fifty yards away.

Alien abductions happened much more often than people thought. The Dumpians always lured inhabitants of strange worlds onto their ships with free beer and clean drinking water. The king not only let the Dumpians have their way, he even encouraged them due to the shortage of skilled workers.

The abductees were automatically made *Citizens of His Majesty* with the same meagre rights and duties that all the king's subjects possessed. These new 'citizens' found paid jobs but were never allowed to fly home again, not even phone home (which made sense to them because their home worlds didn't have phones yet).

---

* "A secret study by the Royal Centre for Public Opinion Research concluded that Her Majesty's subjects were more comfortable with their fate when they were called 'citizens' instead of 'subjects'. As a result, Queen Louise CXIV ('The Smart Tyrant') changed the designation for the benefit of her absolute rule. She gleefully continued to have her population beheaded, but the victims were no longer as unhappy about it as before."
The Secret Service in its "In-House Eulogy for Queen Louise".

Despite the strict rules, the abductees didn't feel like prisoners since the Almond Milky Way had an advantage over the wild: those who obeyed the laws survived and enjoyed their retirement pensions.

As the transport ship was being unloaded, a Dumpian from the receiving department looked at the manifest.

"Whoa," he said. "New immigrants have arrived from Earth. The donkeys and camels aren't here yet, but all the birds have been flown in."

"What kind of birds?" asked his boss.

"Eagles and owls to fight the plague of mice on Berdeil."

"Yes, okay. But what else? *Songbirds?*"

"Blackbirds, finches, starlings and nightingales."

"Awesome! The opera houses of Sophistica are looking for new singers, and we'll get a big cash bonus!"

"Wow, boss, we got llamas. Our pilots actually found South America this time. But wait... they had to pay for them."

"Uh, what? *Payment?!*"

"Yep, the Incas wouldn't let the llamas be abducted for free."

"Hmm. Their ruler, Mayta Cápac, isn't an easy man to deal with."

"He's no Edward II, that's for sure. I once stole the horse of the English king while he was sitting on it."

"Really?"

"Didn't realise he was *still* on it until I opened the cargo hatch in New Dump. Had to fly him all the way back."

Although the Dumpians and dodos were in the same area, a direct encounter between them was prevented by the cosmic consciousness.

Hookbeak would have longed to know that Vicinus, or Dump, had been a dead rock even before his bracket error. The universe disagreed. The dodo was to live with the agonising uncertainty because he had destroyed a celestial body to which the universe had been very attached.

"Birdie wants to breed a parakeet-cockatoo hybrid," said Goliath in disgust.

"You mean Dertie," said Jay.

"And Dertie wants to give me an anti-radiation shot, when I only had my last one two years ago."

"Now you're talking about Birdie."

"And then the dodos all look alike!" exclaimed Goliath. "How are you supposed to tell them apart?"

"I always spot little differences," Jay said, pointing to a group of dodos walking sixteen feet in front of them. "No two eggs are alike."

The two parrots strolled through grass twice as tall as Goliath and in which Jay looked like an ant.

Flying lizards stuck out their tongues at the dodos and buzzed through the sultry air. The whole crew of dodos, parrots and geese marched through the jungle, scattering in almost every direction. Only to the southeast, where the Dumpians were, no one dared to walk any more. The dodos had turned back after a thousand Jandin Frogs had spontaneously gathered for a lively croaking concert. What had led the frogs to do so remained unclear. They remained in the dark themselves.

The flying lizards grew tired as dusk fell. They sank onto warm stones.

The birds were struggling to stay on their feet when a deep sound echoed through the landscape from the west. Someone was blowing a horn – it was the signal that they had discovered food or poisoned themselves with it.

The dodos ran with their last ounce of strength towards the west. Some parrots, too weak to fly, sat on the backs of their feeders.

Hookbeak's search party had come across a field of wild-growing stalks, their countless green legumes hanging in clusters.

"Looks like vegetables," Anton said warily.

"Ah!" said Goliath. "The good old Berdeil mulzbeans. Fatten up on them, they're not poisonous."

"What..." grumbled Dirk, "does Doctor Birdex Pert have to say about that?"

"Doctor Birdex Pert, called Birdie..." she said snarkily, "... thinks it doesn't matter at all whether we die of starvation or poisoning now."

"Besides," said Dertie, "that's my area of expertise. I trust the cockatoo. *Hey, parrots!* You get to eat first!"

All the dodos nodded in agreement. The pets had to be the food tasters as punishment for their centuries of deception.

After the parrots had pounced on the legumes and not dropped dead, the dodos did likewise.

Most of the birds agreed that the beans tasted terrible. Only the twelve geese asked themselves happily if they had ever eaten better.

"Yes, they're awful," said Goliath with his beak full, "but very nutritious."

While they were stuffing their bellies, the Western night sky suddenly exploded in bright colours. The birds looked startled at the fireworks.

"It's coming from Kingstown," said Goliath. "Today the monarchy must be celebrating something."

"I want to see that!" shouted Dertie. "Then we might as well take in the sights while we're here!"

"Well," reasoned Goliath, "surely there's nothing wrong with a little tour of the town while the crew gets the mulzbeans on board?"

"Great!" rejoiced Dertie. "What do you say, boss?"

"Sure, whatever," replied Dirk.

"I've spoken to Birdie," said Dertie.

"I, too, agree," Birdie said. "Anton will return to the ship with the crew and supervise the storing of the mulzbeans."

"Always me," moaned Anton.

Dirk had to show that he was in command, too. "Nala will help Anton. Two supervisors are better than one."

"Oh, come on," complained Nala.

Only Hookbeak returned to the ship of his own free will. "I need to start repairs on the warp drive. Take care of yourselves. Remember the king's motto: behead and let behead."

Goliath and Jay formed the vanguard, and the three dodos followed with a couple of metres' distance.

From time to time, Jay turned his head and looked back at Popin who was sitting at Dirk's back. He was ignored by his sister because he had left her at the spaceport.

After half an hour of walking through the hilly countryside, the birds stood before the silver gates of Kingstown. The fireworks over the city had not yet lost any of their power.

Jay thought of the parrots' New Year's ritual. "I'd totally be in the mood for *Get Away* right now."

"We haven't even really arrived yet," said Goliath.

"No, I was talking about riding the fireworks."

"Are you *insane?!*"

"Goliath," said Dertie, "please show us the sights of Kingstown now."

"You blind turkeys are standing right in front of the first attraction. Or have you ever seen swankier gates?"

Birdie disliked his tone. "What are turkeys?"

"Other birds," said Goliath.

"Then it's okay. Sounded like an insult to me first."

"That's how I meant it."

Two night watchmen in silver armour stood at the gate, leaning on their long swords. One of them waved the birds half-heartedly into the city.

The cockatoo led his five tourists along a cobblestone street towards the castle. On the pavement, residents had parked their horse-drawn carriages, cars and spaceships, depending on what a family could afford.

"Very well," said Goliath and cleared his throat. "Let's get started. Mesdames and Messieurs, my name is Goliath and it is my honour to show you around the city tonight."

"Huh?" said Dertie. "What's a *may-dam*? And what's a *mess-years*? Or was it *mess-yous*?"

Dirk shrugged. Birdie sighed.

"To your left," continued the cockatoo, "ye see four-storey brick buildings with solar panels on the tiled roofs. And on your right... ye see even more four-storey buildings with solar panels on the roofs. The king may be a tyrant, but he does care about climate protection. I bet ye did not expect that."

"Goliath," Birdie said calmly, "why are you saying 'ye' all of a sudden? For many centuries now, we've only used 'you' to address someone, no matter how many they are. Your Dodish is non-standard."

"I beg thy... I beg your pardon, Madame," said Goliath. "I was not aware of this regional custom. In other parts of the galaxy – notably in this one – parrots use archaic pronouns like 'ye', 'thou' and 'thee' on special occasions, for this is a very old-fashioned kingdom with a pretentious love for tradition."

"Aha. And this is supposed to be such a special occasion?" asked Birdie.

"A tour of the town for exotic earthlings? Certainly, Madame!"

"Stop addressing me in such a weird way!"

"Your wish is my command, milady," said Goliath. "Now let's get back to sightseeing. *Okay*, we've already had the buildings with solar panels! So now consider the... pavement. Traditional cobblestones!"

"Boring," commented Dertie.

"In that case, let's get straight to the streetlights," said Goliath. "The same ancient design as five hundred thousand years ago, but inside, they've changed quite a lot. At first, they were candlelit until one fine evening, half the city burned down. Then, for a very short time, they used a species of firefly from the planet Lumina Noctem. If they hadn't put the fireflies in airtight glass, it would even have worked. Well... their lights went out after a few minutes. So it goes. The plan was then to try other species of fireflies to see if they needed air, too, before some hippie suggested using electricity and light bulbs instead. As you can see, nowadays LED..."

Dirk interrupted the cockatoo. "I have to agree with Dertie. The sights in this street don't exactly knock our socks off. Are there any *exciting* things to see here?"

"Yes," said Goliath, "but they're not for readers under eighteen."

Dertie feared that the fireworks were fading. "We must hurry," she said and immediately picked up her pace.

They approached the castle, in front of which thousands of citizens had gathered. The Krejs stood close together, marvelling at the fireworks.

"Behold!" said Goliath. "Feast your eyes on the majestic splendour of *Louis' Palace*! Look at the green spaces on the sides. They lead to the castle park beyond!"

Birdie had had enough of this nonsense. "Goliath, could you please speak normally again?"

"Oh no, milady! I speak as beseems a guide! Or as befits a guide? Now I'm confused."

"By virtue of my office," said Birdie, "I relieve you of your duties as guide."

"Oh no," said Goliath. "Finally, I've had some fun at work."

Dirk pulled a face. "By virtue of *your* office?" he asked Birdie.

Louis' Palace was, contrary to Goliath's claims, not a feast for the eyes but rather a lacklustre castle from Berdeil's Middle Ages. Half a million years ago, King Louis I, the first global Krej ruler, had the high walls of the fortress torn down and the castle renamed Louis' Palace. Louis I had always maintained that a powerful king couldn't hole up in a fortified castle, but had to live in a palace, no matter how grey and ugly said 'palace' was. Today everyone referred to the building as a medieval castle again, and its official name was only kept to confuse tourists.

A sea of colour was reflected in Dertie's eyes because every second, three rockets exploded in the night sky. The dodos stuck to the heels of a group of children who were let through to the castle gate by adults.

A thirty-foot-high bronze statue of the current king had been erected in front of the gate.

Having quit his job as a tour guide, Goliath no longer needed to hide his distaste for the monarchy.

"New kings and queens always have the statues of their predecessors replaced by their own," he said. "Self-absorbed, conceited bunch."

The phrase *Natusestregula* was written on King Reginald's crown.

"What does that mean?" Jay asked the cockatoo.

"Uh, it's been a long time since I took Laddin lessons, but I think it means 'born to rule'. Humility is an alien concept to King Reggie."

Goliath noticed thousands more Krejs watching the fireworks behind the castle. He hopped over to a woman standing in front of the bronze statue with her five-year-old twin daughters. She made a friendly impression on the cockatoo.

"What's the celebration?" inquired Goliath.

"The planet Tafilka is joining our kingdom!" replied the woman with a bright smile.

She ran her fingers through her orange hair. On her blue forehead, Goliath saw a tattoo in the shape of a crown.

"Personally, I find politics totally boring," she said, "but the king really knows how to win kids over with fireworks."

"Joining our kingdom?" asked Goliath in wonder before a light dawned on him. "Oh, snap! Reginald has *conquered* Tafilka!"

The woman looked aggrieved at Goliath.

"Young bird," she said, "you should reconsider your attitude towards our ruler very quickly if you want to keep your head. You're lucky you're a stranger because I only rat on citizens who are close to me. But I know God will judge your sou... Hey, I'm talking to you!"

"And I'm not listening!" said Goliath as he walked away.

He rejoined the other birds.

"The Krejs are quite the jerks if you ask me," he said. "They're celebrating that Reggie conquered another world. Now there are just seven free planets left at the end of the Almond Milky Way. Let's hope your planet of choice is one of them."

"Well," said Birdie, "we might as well overthrow the king, now that we're here anyway."

Goliath laughed mockingly. "That'll be good! What are you going to do against thousands of guards? They're almost twice your size and armed to the teeth!"

"Oh, guys," groaned Dertie, "your talk's dampening the mood. Be quiet! I want to enjoy the fireworks!"

At that moment, the last rockets exploded in the sky. The spectacle was over and the Krejs went home.

"That figures," said Dertie, shaking her head.

Afterwards, Goliath persuaded the other birds to walk him in the castle park. Babymoon, the smallest of Berdeil's three moons, had risen and supported the light of the lanterns.

In the park, green peacocks came walking towards the dodos and parrots. The males had raised their majestic tail feathers to form beautiful wheels, but their females seemed unimpressed.

"Well, hello there," Jay said to the peacocks in Almendarin. "What kind of birds are you?"

The peacocks looked curiously at the little parakeet and opened their beaks in the hope that he wanted to feed them.

Goliath giggled. "Not all birds can talk, Jay. The peacocks live here by choice because they're fed by the king's servants. On top of that, they get pocket money to go shopping. All the lazy peacocks have to do in return is walk around the palace grounds and look beautiful. In other words, they work as models." The cockatoo pointed to the pond in the middle. "Reginald keeps other birds in the park that I'm sure you've never heard of. *Ducks!*"

"Why," asked Dirk, "is the king doing such a terrible thing to himself?"

"What do you mean?" asked Goliath.

"He keeps ducks!" said Dirk. "I haven't met a single duck yet that hasn't been mean to me."

"And I have never met a mean duck. I think we birds have to stick together against the mammals, lizards and monsters."

They walked down to the pond, and Dirk looked with great suspicion at the mallards.

Goliath sat down on the grass. "It's nice here."

"If it weren't for the ducks," Dirk said grumpily.

"Oh, Dirk," said Birdie. "You are too prejudiced. Almost all ducks are harmless. But if you look for nasty birds, you'll find them among dodos and parrots, too."

Dertie and Popin nodded.

"Well," said Dirk, "just because I'm paranoid... wait, what?... just because the ducks are nice to everyone else doesn't mean they're not out to get me!"

"*Right*... whatever you say, Dirk," replied Birdie.

"I think I deserve more respect as your dignified captain. And now I have to go to the loo."

He walked over to a large tree with a crown carved into its bark.

A *Berdeilian Foulmosquito*, whose tube-like mouth was twice as long as its body, spotted the dodo and took an instant liking to him. It flew to him to draw his blood.

The mosquito landed on Dirk's beak as he stood with his back against the tree trunk.

"Go away!" he grumbled. "Buzz off!"

He moved his head back and forth like a whirlwind to scare the little bloodsucker away.

The mosquito jumped onto Dirk's back and stung into his thick feathers. Despite its oversized mouthparts, it didn't manage to penetrate the skin. Quite disappointed with the world, it flew away, looking for an easier victim.

Dirk rejoined the group after finishing his business.

Dertie yawned, Jay rubbed his eyes, and their former guide lay in the grass, snoring.

"Let's call it a day," said Dirk. "We still have a long way back."

He nudged Goliath with his foot.

The cockatoo jerked awake, startled. "Where am I? Oh, I haven't been able to sleep in nature for a long time. The fresh air. Wonderful."

"Fresh air?" asked Jay, bemused. "We're in the city centre!"

"In a park!" retorted Goliath.

"In the middle of a big city!" said Jay.

Dirk nodded. "You're both right."

On the way back, Jay tried to reconcile with his sister, who hadn't said a word during the city tour.

"Are we friends again?" asked Jay.

"Nope," said Popin.

"Just family then?"

"That's right."

The earthlings had long since passed the city gate when they were suddenly called. Five armed guards came running from Kingstown. They formed a circle around the birds and stared at the three dodos.

Goliath and Jay asked the guards in Almendarin what the problem was. The captain of the city watch told them he had been tipped off by the ducks. A large male bird with blue-grey plumage had been doing his business on one of the King's Trees. There were four eyewitnesses.

Shocked, Jay buried his head in his wings.

Goliath kept his composure. "You don't need to make an ostrich out of a hummingbird, officer."

"My hands are tied because there are several witnesses," said the captain of the watch before he pointed at Dirk. "He's the only male, isn't he?"

Goliath replied with a little nod.

Dertie whispered, "What were you talking about?"

A guard grabbed Dirk by his head and butt and carried him away.

"*HEY!*" yelled Birdie. "*WHAT DO YOU THINK YOU'RE DOING?!*"

"Please calm down," said Goliath, "or they'll take us all with them."

With difficulty, Birdie managed to restrain herself. "Did the guards forbid us to go back into town?"

"No," replied Goliath.

"Then let's go. I want to know where they're taking Dirk. Now tell us already why he's being carried away."

The captain of the city watch glanced over his shoulder a few times, but he let the birds do as they pleased. He almost seemed to shrug once as if he was sorry.

When they arrived at the city centre, the guards disappeared with Dirk into a two-storey building.

Goliath translated a plaque next to the front door. "Police station, prosecution, court, executioner."

"How convenient," scoffed Dertie. "All under one roof."

Birdie spotted a ventilation shaft leading underground. "There seems to be a cellar!"

Goliath jumped to her. "Rumour has it that the Royal Dungeon is sixteen feet below the surface, but no prisoner has ever resurfaced, at least not with their heads on their shoulders. Sadly, they couldn't talk after that. So it could indeed just be a rumour."

"Let's try logic," said Dertie. "The building has no prison tower, and the windows are not barred. There is therefore every indication that we will find a dungeon in the cellar."

"I second that," said Birdie. "Now we need someone to get down the narrow shaft."

The officers' eyes wandered to Popin and Jay.

Popin sighed. "Always the little ones."

"It's settled then," said Birdie. "Does anyone happen to have a pen? I think I have a piece of paper with me. I just need to find it." She searched under her belly feathers. "Beak powder... external hard drive... Civil Code of the United Forests of Mauritius... and what's this? Oh! My claw file! That's very surprising. I misplaced it ages ago." She looked down at her feet, and her head turned red with embarrassment.

"You could have borrowed mine," said Dertie, waving her claw file. In her second wing, she held a pen. "Now, where's your paper?"

🪶

The two ~~parakeets~~ secret agents, Agent P and Agent J, argued about who should be first to go down the shaft.

"As they say, females first," Jay reminded his sister.

"But they also say: the pinhead pet goes ahead," said Popin.

"You just made that up, didn't you?" believed Jay.

Popin shook her head.

"Drat," said Jay, "I have to go, then."

As the siblings slid down the shaft, they felt like they were in an amusement park. Jay wanted to scream with joy. He barely managed to control himself, as he was on a secret mission and couldn't be caught.

The agents flew out of the end of the shaft at high speed and crashed into a shelf with cell keys. Still, they landed softly on the cold stone floor while the shelf swayed precariously.

Popin looked at Jay and put her wing on her beak.

"Shh!" she breathed.

"Okay, okay," her brother said.

They tiptoed down the dark corridor and found that only a few cells were occupied. A lizard was sleeping on its mattress. In the cell next to it, a Krej was talking to his reflection.

"What is he talking about?" asked Popin.

"They tell each other how their day was," said Jay.

"They?"

"Yep. A perfectly normal conversation between a Krej and his reflection."

The agents advanced only slowly on tiptoe but didn't want to get cocky.

"It's going pretty well so far," whispered Jay.

The very next moment, they heard a dull bang behind them, followed by clanking metal.

The agents froze in shock. They turned their heads in slow motion and had to swallow hard. The shelf had fallen over, scattering the cell keys on the floor.

"I guess we made…" began Jay.

"… it swing too hard," concluded Popin.

From the other end of the corridor, they heard footsteps approaching rapidly.

"Oh dear!" was Popin alarmed.

"What now?" asked Jay.

The two guards put the shelf up again and scratched their heads.

"Maybe a strong gust of wind from the ventilation shaft," reckoned the first guard.

"Let's play a game of poker," said his partner.

They got a table and chairs from an empty cell and sat down next to the shelf. Occasionally, the first guard looked out at the empty corridor.

"What is it?" asked the second.

"I'm probably hearing ghosts."

The agents hid on the ceiling.

"Shh?" whispered Popin.

"Whatup?" asked Jay.

"Back there in the last cell. Looks like a blue sack with feathers."

"Dirk!"

"*Shh!!!*"

Soon after, they heard the guards snoring. Even on night shifts, Krejs were diurnal animals.

The parrots crept up to the cell like a marten on a squirrel. As they slipped through the narrow bars, Dirk remained sitting on his mattress with his head down.

Jay took a piece of paper from his feathers. It contained some advice on how to build Dirk up before the trial. Then Jay looked back at the distressed dodo and sighed. "I clearly don't get enough treats for my work."

"Hello Pops, hello Jay," Dirk said gloomily.

"Captain Dirk. My name is Agent P, and this is Agent J. We're from a *top-secret* secret service, and it's important that you keep our real identities *secret* in case things get out of wing."

"You..." whispered Agent J, "seem to totally enjoy your new role."

"Hey," said Agent P, "if we have to risk our lives for a dodo, we might as well have fun doing it."

Dirk shrugged. "Okay, Popin. I'll take your secret to the grave. I'll be there in a few hours anyway."

"No names, moron!" said Agent J.

"All right, Jay," said Dirk.

Agent P shook her head in frustration. "He just doesn't get it."

"I'm not so sure," said Agent J. "Did he say J or Jay?"

"What?"

Goliath and Birdie made their way to the courtroom, which was on the ground floor of the multifunctional building.

"Oh, that reminds me of something!" said Goliath, taking off his backpack. "A time-travelling friend... her name's Gusu... gave me a letter from the future two years ago."

"A letter from the future?" marvelled Birdie.

"At least Gusu implied that this was the case. If I ever accompany a weird bird to court to get a second weird bird out of jail, I'm supposed to give the first weird bird this letter in advance. I guess she meant you."

Birdie opened the letter with her claw file. "Well, that's nice... it's in our language! *'Dear lawyer, in about a thousand years, Dr James Smith will discover a new kind of disease on Earth. It's called...'* Oh. Oh? Oh! Thank you, James Smith. That's an unusual name for a dodo, by the way."

"Perhaps he belongs to another terrestrial species," pondered Goliath, skimming the letter.

"Unlikely," said Birdie, "but who knows what the future holds. Hm, now I've discovered a problem."

"And that is?"

"The letter says only mammals can get the disease. This makes sense because mammals drink a lot."

"Surely the Krejs don't know that," said Goliath. "It's all about buying time now."

"I can manage that," said Birdie and went into the courtroom.

"The ducks squealed," Agent P told the captain.

"*I KNEW IT!*" growled Dirk. Suddenly, a fire flared inside him again, smothering his self-pity. "When I was a little chick, the ducks stole my ice lolly. A few months ago, they turned my dreams into nightmares. And now they want to see me on the scaffold. We have to get back at them!"

"That could hardly have been the same ducks," said Agent P, "and if I remember correctly, you pushed three ducks off the ship before we left. That was *mean*. Besides, it might be because of your prejudices that ducks have appeared in your nightmares."

"You're already talking like Number Two," said Dirk. "Don't you worry about my feathers?"

"Of course I do," she replied as her tears rolled. "I'm sorry. I've blocked out the thought that soon you'll…" She broke off her sentence and took a deep breath. "The fear would paralyse me. In that case, I would be no help to you."

"I see," said Dirk. "Unfortunately, I have no idea how you can help me."

"Don't worry," said Agent J. "Your lawyer is in court right now, seeing what she can do."

"Number Two?"

The agents nodded.

"Pops," said Dirk, "fly to the Dodo Alpha Jet and tell the crew to come here. Wait, I've got a better idea. Have Nala fly the ship to Kingstown and land in the castle park next to the pond. That will intimidate the ducks."

"No names!" said Agent P.

🪶

"Your Honour, a trial?" asked the blue prosecutor in disbelief. "The request of the defence must be a bad joke?! Trials are only held in cases of petty crimes that subje… slav… I beg your pardon… that citizens commit against each other. Never for a serious crime. After all, we're talking about 'lese majeste' – an insult to our majesty! Dirk Dodo has no right to a trial. Besides, his execution has already been scheduled. Just think of all the paperwork if it has to be cancelled now."

When Goliath had translated the prosecutor's remarks, Birdie was seething with anger. However, she knew better than to show it in front of a judge who could barely keep her eyes open.

"I..." Birdie said softly, "I have here in my left foot a report from... ahem... Dirk's psychologist, Doctor Pert. Dirk has a *Water Illness*. Thus, he has an urgent need to go to the bathroom whenever he sees a large amount of water – like a pond, for example. That's a bad thing. Those who suffer from it live in constant fear that they won't make it to the nearest tree in time. Your Honour, due to his illness, Dirk was of unsound mind at the time of the crime. He simply let nature take its course. And, to my knowledge, there were no prohibition signs in the park. Therefore, I demand the immediate release of my captain!"

"Your Honour, please," said the prosecutor. "The executioner has postponed his holiday just for the accused."

The judge yawned and looked out of the window. Dawn was looming on the horizon. The night was over, and she had been deprived of her sleep by two birds. Enough was enough.

"Mr Prosecutor," she said, "please step forward to my desk for a moment. *No*, just the prosecutor. You stay in your seat, Counsellor."

"Wow, great legal system," scoffed Birdie. She squeezed Goliath's beak before he could translate it for the judge.

"Sorry," said Goliath. "I forgot these fools aren't supposed to hear everything."

"Find out what they're whispering about," said Birdie.

Goliath pricked up his invisible ears and heard snippets of conversation.

"...declining approval ratings of the king... deceive the population... pretend to have a fair legal system... show trial... The king's dignity is inviolable," said the judge.

"And?" Birdie whispered. "Did you hear anything?"

"Er... no, no, I couldn't understand anything at all," fibbed Goliath, believing that Birdie would otherwise have ruined her only chance of a trial.

The prosecutor returned to his seat, smiling.

The judge cleared her throat. "Pleading insanity because of a new disease is very clever, Counsellor. Water Illness... Well, I'm curious to hear about it. Of course, it's almost impossible to prove such a thing, but you shall have your chance to convince this court otherwise. The trial will take place the day after tomorrow, after lunch. The prosecution may have its own expert opinion prepared by that time. And now everybody out! Good night!"

🌿

Dertie had been waiting outside the building for Birdie and the parrots.

"So," Popin began to say, "what are we going to do now?"

"We need a crazy plan," suggested Dertie. "If we don't take high risks, Dirk has already lost."

Popin nodded. "I'll fly to the Sea Cow. We don't have much time."

Birdie preferred to send the cockatoo. "Goliath is faster than you and knows the planet better. He can tell Nala to park outside the city gate."

"But Dirk said..." replied Popin.

"Dirk's not a lawyer," said Birdie. "Trust me."

Goliath saluted. "Park outside the city gate, aye-aye, sir!" He rose into the air.

The parakeets watched the cockatoo until they lost sight of him over the rooftops.

"So, we carry on being secret agents," believed Jay.

"Agent," Popin said dreamily. "This is so exciting!"

Birdie told the siblings they had to say goodbye to their secret identities, for a better life awaited them.

"I need two paralegals," she said. "Ta-da! You've got the jobs. Paralegal is a most honourable and responsible position."

"Boring as hell," said Popin.

"This is animal cruelty," added Jay.

As paralegals, the parrots entered the dungeon the next afternoon – with some delay – via the main entrance.

The baffled guards had heard the job title for the first time and looked up dictionary after dictionary. It was their captain who eventually allowed the parrots inside. He had once read about a paralegal in the banned novel *Fair Trial* but had assumed the profession didn't exist in the real world.

Popin informed Dirk that the prosecutor offered him a plea bargain. "Fifty years of labour service. You'll work in street and sewer cleaning."

Dirk was shaken by the news. "*Working?!*" he asked. "I go along with a lot of nonsense, but that's too much! They should rather behead me, then!"

"That could happen," said Popin, "if you don't accept the plea deal."

Dirk hesitated nevertheless. "What does my lawyer say?"

"She wants you to agree," replied Jay. "The crew will free you while you're sweeping streets. And then we vamoose."

"Doesn't sound like Birdie at all," noticed Dirk.

"Dertie helped with the planning," said Jay.

"*Ah*... that explains it."

꧁꧂

Dirk was given stale bread by the guards the day before the trial, but his stomach wouldn't have coped with it because he was a dodo, not a duck. He didn't sleep a wink that night because he was so hungry.

When he was led into the courtroom with ankle chains the next day at noon, he was surprised at the number of spectators. He estimated that about one hundred Krejs had come, and he wasn't the only bird among them.

He recognised Hookbeak from a distance by his featherdo. Nala, Dertie and Anton had taken their seats in the front row next to the chief engineer.

On the other side of the aisle sat four mallards. The ducks were the witnesses for the prosecution and made Dirk's blood boil.

Birdie was waiting for Dirk at the defence table with Goliath and her paralegals. His eyes wandered to the empty prosecution table.

"The prosecutor should be here any minute," said Birdie. "Then we'll explain to the judge that you're only pleading guilty to one thing: 'desecration of royal property by reason of being cuckoo'. The prosecutor will agree, and you will be sentenced to forced labour. We'll set you free in a few weeks when you pick up trash from the street."

"In a few *weeks?*" Dirk asked in dismay. "What am I supposed to do until then?"

"Work," Birdie said dryly. "You have little experience with that, but it shouldn't hurt you."

Shortly afterwards, nine soldiers entered the hall and spread out along the aisle. Under their golden armour, they concealed knives that had been tried and tested over the last five hundred thousand years. In their hands, they held the latest generation of laser guns because you had to keep up with the times, too.

"Yikes!" said Goliath. "It's the King's Guard. Reginald appears in person."

"Why is that?" asked Birdie. "And where's the prosecutor?"

"Goodness knows," said Goliath.

A tall, muscular Krej appeared in the doorway, strode down the aisle and sat behind Anton Pavlovich in the second row. It should not go unmentioned that he wore a black mask and held a sharp axe in his hands.

"And who's that now?" asked Dirk.

"Just someone who postponed his holiday for you," said Goliath, "but obviously, nobody told him he could've taken the day off."

"Really?" asked Dirk. "So what's his profession?"

Last but not least, Reginald the Living came through the hall door. The middle-aged Krej sported a grey beard to distract from the fact that he was a thin, almost scrawny man. It was too much to ask of a beard. The birds got the impression that he was nearly crushed by his heavy crown. But appearances could be deceptive.

The Krejs and ducks rose from their seats more out of fear than respect. The dodos remained unmoved. Goliath wanted to get up as well, but Birdie pushed him down on his chair with her foot.

"Only honour to whom honour is due," she said. "I must admit, though, I had imagined the tyrant differently."

"How so?" asked Goliath.

"Taller, better fed... but above all, more menacing."

"Don't let his appearance fool you," said Goliath. "He's a very bad boy."

The king sat down at the prosecution table and looked over to the birds with a grin. Then he saw the empty desk of the judge and burned up with anger.

"*The judge shall come in!*" he yelled. "*You don't keep me waiting!*"

After five seconds, the judge hastily appeared from her room.

"Excuse me, Your Highness," she said, "I didn't hear you enter. Only shouting." She sat down and banged her hammer on her desk. "This Honourable Court is now in session. Four distinguished citizens accuse Dirk Dodo of desecrating the king's property. How does the defendant plead?"

"Your Honour," said Goliath, "please allow me to translate everything aloud into Parrot for the dodos present, as they do not speak Almendarin."

"Yes, I remember. Motion granted."

"And now to your question, Your Honour," continued Goliath. "Dirk Dodo pleads guilty to desecration of royal property by reason of being cuckoo."

"Aha," the judge said indifferently. "What's the *new* charge, anyway? Your Majesty?"

The king leaned back in his chair. "The charge is violation of my royal honour. The head of the ugly bird must roll!" he said, pointing at Dirk.

Birdie cleared her throat when she heard the translation. "Your Highness, we had agreed on a plea bargain."

"That was with the Kingdom Attorney," said the king. "The agreement is off the table. For the insult of yours truly, my humble self, I demand just punishment."

The executioner rose from his chair. He proudly showed his axe to the audience like a trophy. The audience roared and threw confetti at him. He bowed to them in gratitude.

In the midst of the spectators was a blonde peasant woman holding her pitchfork in the air. Blondes were extremely rare among the Krejs and were held in high esteem because of their intelligence.

"First," shouted the blue blonde, "you have to wring a goose's neck and hang it on a tree to dry! Then it is beheaded, plucked, and in the evening, you have roast goose!"

"Haha," laughed Jay. "She thinks the dodos are geese."

"I didn't want to translate that part," said Goliath, "so as not to hurt the dodos' feelings."

The king called his first witness. "Mr Donnie Drake, step forward!"

"Objection!" said Birdie. "That's—"

"Objection overruled!" said the judge.

Birdie raised an eyebrow. "Don't you want to know first why I object?"

"No!" shouted the judge. "Sit down, Counsellor, or I'll have you taken away for contempt of court!"

Birdie smiled because she had expected a dirty trick. It didn't worry her in the least that the king was now leading the prosecution.

Donnie Drake, a well-known liar in town, waddled over to a cosy armchair next to the judge's desk.

The duck told his listeners the truth for a change. He had seen with his own eyes how Dirk had done his business at the King's Tree. At the time of the crime, Donnie had been swimming a few laps in the pond with his friends Daisy, Achmed and Gladstone.

The king had no further questions and Birdie waived her right to cross-examine the witness.

Meanwhile, Goliath was breaking a sweat from translating and recruited Jay as a second interpreter.

"Next," said the king, "I call the accused, Dirk Dodo, to the stand."

"Objection!" called Birdie. "Captain Dirk exercises his right to remain silent!"

"Counsellor," said the judge, "you can't just make something up. Remain silent? You're funny. There is no such right here. Captain Dirk, sit down in the armchair."

"Well," said Birdie, "maybe you call it 'refusal to testify' or the 'privilege to clam up'?"

"No," said the judge, "we don't have anything like that."

Dirk was only too happy to swap his regular wooden chair for a cosier seat. He felt comfortable in the armchair. Only one little thing was missing. A hole for the tail feathers. But it was perfect for lying down.

"Dirk!" called the stunned Birdie.

"*WILL YOU SIT UP!?*" yelled the judge.

"Sorry," said Dirk. "Force of habit."

Birdie was ashamed of his behaviour but she wasn't surprised. She turned to Hookbeak.

"Contingency Plan Alpha Omega Thirty-Six Dash Cuckoo And Three-Quarters Madcap?" she asked, trying to remember which loony bird had come up with the code name.

"Good idea," said Hookbeak.

He stood up, took his phone in his wing and filmed his feet while he calmly strolled out of the courtroom so that neither the king nor the guards would suspect anything.

A tiny bird shadow circled in the square in front of the building.

Hookbeak looked up at the sky, raised his little wing and waved to Herbert.

The parrot gained altitude.

When Herbert was above the city, he waved to Papagayo, who was sitting on a tiled roof a hundred metres away. Papagayo passed the signal on to the night watchbird Tomny. The parrot chain continued along two dozen more parakeets until the signal finally reached Nochnaya. The second watchbird flew directly above the Sea Cow at the city gate.

Hookbeak returned to the courtroom. He saw that King Reginald had built himself up menacingly in front of Dirk.

"Captain Dirk, have you ever abused a tree as a toilet?" asked the king.

"I'm a bird," said Dirk, shrugging. "When I'm in nature, I do my business there."

"So you admit that you have defiled my tree?" echoed the king.

All of a sudden, there was silence as everyone was expecting the translation for the dodos. However, it didn't come. The whole room looked at Goliath and Jay, who then stared at each other.

"Whose turn is it to translate now?" asked Jay.

"All right, I'll do it," said Goliath, exhausted.

King Reginald was losing his patience and shouted, "Captain Dirk, have you desecrated my tree? Yes or yes?! Don't wait for the translation! Yes or yes?!"

There was scattered laughter in the audience. With a few seconds' delay, Goliath translated it into Dodish.

Birdie didn't feel like laughing. "Your Honour, I object. Is that really the king, or did he send his court jester? Who cares about a white spot on a tree trunk? Everyone knows that a little fertilizer never hurt a plant. That's why it has become a tree. As a tree, you have to live with things like that. I didn't even hear it complain about it!"

"Objection overruled," said the judge. "Your captain has smudged the king's property and doesn't even deny the crime. I therefore pronounce the sentence at once. Guilty! Dirk Dodo's execution will take place tomorrow after lunch."

"*HAVE YOU GONE STORK RAVING MAD NOW?!?!*" screamed Birdie. "We don't accept this sentence!"

"Counsellor," said the judge, "I sentence you to twenty years of labour service for contempt of court."

"No, thanks. Sorry to decline."

"Fifty years' labour service!" yelled the judge.

"Oh, girl," retorted Birdie as disrespectfully as she could. "In your mind, bats are being eaten by insects. You've got a few things mixed up, you see? You really need to lie down on my couch."

King Reginald believed Birdie was angering the judge on purpose. "She's trying to stall. Guards! Arrest all birds!"

"Quack quack?" asked the four ducks anxiously.

"Only the dodos and parrots," the king corrected himself.

Before his men could grab the earthlings, a huge flock of birds poured in through the hall door.

Seven hundred and fifty parrots swooped down on the king, the guards and the judge.

"Guards! Guards!" screeched the king.

The guards made a wise decision and withdrew their limbs and heads into their armour like a tortoise into its shell.

"The birds…" cried the judge, "…they attack us for no reason at all! I think I'm in a bad horror movie!"

"Could become a classic," disagreed Goliath.

The blonde peasant woman, who had been keen to wring Dirk's neck just a moment ago, raised her pitchfork again. "Let's abolish the king and the monarchy!" she shouted. "We won't get another opportunity like this in a thousand years!"

The audience began to roar loudly, forming an angry mob, joined by the quick-thinking executioner. In his profession, one received higher recognition for a royal head than for the pate of an ugly goose.

"Killomajesto! Killomajesto!" the mob shouted in a peasant dialect.

"They shout: Kill the king!" translated Jay.

"Yeah, I might have guessed that," said Birdie. She climbed on her chair and started singing the Mauritian peace hymn.

The flock of parrots immodestly put on the king's golden crown and streamed out of the courtroom.

King Reginald was lying flat on the floor. His blue skin had turned fiery red because the parrots had bitten him all over his body.

"He doesn't have blue blood at all!" shouted the blonde, and the crowd went wild. "He's no better than us in any way!"

The King's Guard rolled out of the hall in their armour while the king was surrounded by his subjects.

Reginald opened his eyes when he felt a pitchfork and axe at his throat.

"What a show!" he said with a smile. "The trial is over! Dirk Dodo and his lawyer are free, for I'm a kind-hearted king and pardon them!"

The blonde leader of the pack told him he could drop the act. His head would roll tonight.

"Free beer?" replied the king tentatively. He had broken out into a cold sweat.

The Krejs whispered. Three nuns lowered their nail-studded clubs but didn't put them back in their handbags yet. The executioner shrugged his shoulders and took the axe from the royal throat. Only the blonde was suspicious.

"Free beer for how long?" she asked.

"A whole day!" the king whooped.

"You despicable miser!" yelled the blonde and pushed the prongs of her pitchfork against his neck.

"Free beer for a month!" cried the king in desperation.

"Oh, cool!" said the blonde, dropping her pitchfork. "Free beer for a whole month, for all your subjects. Very generous. You already would've won me over with two days."

In jubilation, but completely without thinking, the nuns threw their clubs up.

In the meantime, the dodos gathered at the defence table. They wondered what had happened after Goliath and Jay hadn't translated a word in all the commotion.

"Well," said Goliath, "to cut a long story short: Dirk is free. And more importantly, there's free beer for a month. Beer is a vegan drink that lifts your spirits, similar to fermented grape juice. It will blow your minds!"

"No," said Dirk, "we won't stay here for another hour, let alone for a whole moon. We've wasted too much time already."

Goliath explained to him that a month on Berdeil was only three weeks on Earth and that a longer stay for free beer was well worth it.

The captain thanked the cockatoo for the very interesting information and told him that he didn't give a darn anyway because they would be leaving immediately.

Goliath then asked for a half-hour delay. "I must get something to eat, and you surely don't want to travel through the Almond Milky Way without a cultural expert."

"Why?" asked Dirk. "Do you know one?"

"I was talking about me, of course."

"All right. You're a very good negotiator," Dirk praised the cockatoo.

"Great," said Goliath. "Then I'm going to hit the sauce for the next thirty minutes."

"Goliath, wait," said Birdie.

"But it takes away from my booze time," he feared.

"No, it doesn't," replied Birdie. "I'm going to take two weeks of shore leave in return for leading Dirk's defence."

"You can't do that," said Dirk, "because then we'll all have to stay here! Without a doctor, lawyer and so on, we cannot fly!"

"Yay!" cheered Dertie. "Two weeks' shore leave for everyone!"

"Yippee!" Nala joined in.

"Terrific," said Goliath. "If we're not pressed for time, let's go see King Reggie again. I remembered something."

"Why?" asked Dirk. "Shouldn't we keep away from him now?"

"Just come with me," said Goliath.

The king was still lying on the floor while his subjects told him one by one what sorts of beer they preferred.

Goliath jumped the queue and spoke to the king in Almendarin. "I think there should be a compensation payment – and a fat one at that – for Dirk's stay in the dungeon."

"Twenty grand," said the king. "Take it or leave it."

"Sixty grand! Accept it or be overthrown. Our parrot troops are still in the vicinity."

"Forty, final offer," Reginald said in a weak voice, as if begging the cockatoo for mercy.

"Very well," said Goliath. "Congratulations, you'll remain the Living One, Reggie."

King Reginald straightened up. He handed the banknotes to the cockatoo, but the latter pointed at Birdie.

"She's got *a lot* of room in her feathers," said Goliath.

The king put the money in the wing of the surprised Birdie and wrote down the cockatoo's beer order.

Birdie didn't know what to do with the paper notes and tucked them under her belly feathers.

"What did the king give you?" whispered Nala.

"Green pieces of paper with his mug," Birdie said, shrugging.

"Does he want you to pass the paper out and promote him?"

"Probably. But he can wait for it till hell freezes over."

Chapter 10: About Time

As a free dodo, Dirk walked out of the courtroom and multifunctional building with his six officers. For the first time in three days, he felt the warm sunlight on his feathers.

Hookbeak looked around.

"Has Jay run off again?" he asked Birdie.

"He just left for the Sea Cow with Popin because he was hungry."

"Captain," said Anton, "would you like to say something about your lawyer's performance?"

"Well," replied Dirk not charmingly, "Birdie's lawyer skills didn't do much good against the king and the biased judge."

"You ungrateful good-for-nothing!" Birdie said, disappointed.

"The parrot rescue was Birdie's plan," said Dertie. "Mostly, at least. I came up with the code name."

Dirk looked genuinely surprised. "Oh, really? I thought the parrots just went nuts. All right, Number Two. Thank you very much for saving my feathers. And thanks to everyone who helped her along the way."

Goliath shook the heroine's little wing. "You're sort of our MVP."

"MVP?" asked Birdie.

"It's an acronym from team sports," explained the cockatoo. "It means you're the most valuable parrot in the competition."

"Ah! You mean I'm the most powerful piece on the chessboard. The queen who must protect her king because he can't cut it alone."

All eyes fell on Captain Dirk, then landed embarrassed on the floor.

"Our captain," said Hookbeak, "is sometimes smarter than you think. He just likes to fool his fellow citizens."

"It's all tactics," Dirk said. "I want the crew to think that I'm exactly as stupid and helpless as they are. So no one can take a second term away from me. Keep dreaming, Number Two. The rank and file want an imbecile as their repressident, and I'm good at acting."

"Representative," retorted Birdie.

"All right, Dodish has never been my strong suit," admitted Dirk. "In school, I only got an A minus in it."

"*You* had A's in school?" asked Anton.

Hookbeak confirmed it. "He sometimes let me copy his work."

"I'm quite amazed," muttered Birdie, "that he even went to school."

"There's something else I need to ask," said Goliath. "You do mean Earth weeks when you say two weeks of shore leave?"

"Of course!" all dodos said in unison.

"Great. As I mentioned before, the weeks are a bit shorter here."

Nala was especially happy about the holiday. "I'll turn eighteen in four days! And since we don't have to work, we can start my birthday party that midnight and celebrate for twenty-four hours! I know someone who could provide music. Simba from my running group used to be a disc jockey. I'll ask him whether he has time. You're all coming, right? There'll be formal invitations tomorrow."

"You're turning eighteen?" asked Dirk. "I thought you were already twenty! That's what your application said."

"Oh, no!" Nala acted innocent. "Tell me I didn't put the *Year of the Flying Dragon* as the year of birth? I meant the *Year of the Dragonfly*, of course. I get it mixed up sometimes. I think I made the same mistake when I registered for the Mauritius Grand Prix, which is why I could race and came third at my first attempt last year."

"Our chick is pretty cunning," Dertie said with appreciation.

The street they were walking through looked familiar to Dirk.

"Where are you taking me?" he asked.

"To the ship, where else?" said Anton. "Nala parked the Sea Cow on a grassy area outside the city gate. That's why the parrots were in the courtroom so quickly."

"Nala," said Dirk, slightly miffed, "didn't the parrots tweet you to land at the duck pond?"

"Yes, they did," said Nala, "but our MVP... our boss thought it was a stupid idea to provoke the witnesses and overruled you."

Dirk startled and looked at Birdie. "I'm still in charge, am I not?"

"Of course you are," said Birdie. "As long as you make decisions that I like."

Dirk was grateful to Birdie for the rescue, but he loved his captaincy even more than his head. He took Hookbeak aside and walked with him to a fountain in the middle of the street.

There, Dirk stood on an iron grid with a shaft leading underneath into the darkness. He didn't care about the shaft because he thought it was a water drain belonging to the fountain. Still, he overlooked the warning sign the city watch had put up two metres in front of the grid.

The sign depicted a dragon sitting in the shaft, breathing fire upwards and heating a cooking pot on the grid. The dragon was only a symbol, of course, because the fire had been generated by solar energy since the dragons had migrated to another dimension four years ago. The unusual hotplate (officially: cooking grid) was still used by a few traditional Krejs who were completely unwilling to buy a cooker with induction or glass-ceramic hob.

The best thing about the cooking grid was that you didn't have to switch it on. It was enough to put something on it. After a minute, flames came shooting up explosively, heating the water in the pot *immediately* to one hundred degrees Celsius.

"Hooky," said Dirk, "you're my Number One. You have to protect me from a mutiny."

"I should do what's good for the crew," reasoned Hookbeak. "Dirk, just ask yourself before making any decision: What would Birdie do now? It's probably the exact opposite of what you would do."

Hookbeak walked on and returned to his colleagues.

Dirk stayed at the fountain and stubbornly shook his head in disagreement. "What would Birdie do now? The exact opposite of what I would do," he repeated. "As if I've ever made a bad decision. My tenure has been absolutely flawless so far!"

A family of nine ducks waddled past him. The mother duck stopped abruptly when she noticed what Dirk was standing on.

"Hey, watch out!" she shouted in Almendarin, but Dirk couldn't understand her.

The father duck leapt towards Dirk and pushed the much heavier dodo off the iron grid with his momentum. Metre-high fire shot out of the shaft before duck and dodo landed unroasted in the street dust.

The mother came running to them with her seven chicks. Dirk was shocked.

"Oh my goddess!" he cried. "Thank you so much!"

"Ah, you speak Parrot," said the mother duck. "If I'd known that, I would have called you in the parrots' language right away. It was my first foreign language at school."

Dirk was more than surprised. "Thank you. You're very nice for ducks."

The mother's eyes widened. "Have you ever met a duck that wasn't nice to you?"

"Yes," said Dirk with a broad smile. "That must have happened once or twice."

"Hard to believe! But I guess there's an odd bird in every family."

"That's true. I haven't always been fair to ducks either."

His officers rushed over.

"Dirk, what happened?" called Birdie.

"It all turned out fine," he said cheerfully. "I got pushed into the dirt by a duck just in time!"

᭜

Meanwhile, the parrots were plundering the cargo hold.

"Mulzbeans, I've got mulzbeans!" Herbert cried while distributing them among his hungry fellow parrots. "Mulzbeans over mulzbeans, torture for the tongue, so disgusting your stomach won't keep them in!"

The two former paralegals sat on a cooler.

"Do you remember," Jay reminisced dreamily, "how well we used to do as pets? Hookbeak used to steal a late-night meal from the kitchen for me after his parents had already fattened me up at supper. Be honest, sis, don't you miss those days? That's when I felt loved. A schoolboy's pet. Today, all we get is cold average food."

"You're still as loved as you were then," said Popin. "Although I think you were completely spoilt as a chick. I always had enough to eat with Dirk's family. He just wouldn't let me overeat. You had stomach aches all the time!"

"Still, everything was better in the old days," claimed Jay. "How I'd love to be a pet again that's pampered from morning till night. Kids are so easy to manipulate."

"Oh, brother dear, did you really think this would last forever? Then you're pretty gullible."

"You should know that my longing for the old days was the reason I ran away on the space station. It had nothing to do with you. If one day I do start looking for a younger feeder again, you're welcome to come along."

"I could never leave my family," said Popin.

"Great!"

"Dirk and Hookbeak are also part of our family. That's why I would stay with them, Jay. I'm sorry."

"I partly understand," said Jay. "But come on, you're my sis!"

"And you're a sissy. You can't have your cake and eat it too."

"This saying never made sense to me. Why should I get a cake I can't eat?"

"No. You either have to keep the cake or eat it," explained Popin. "You can't eat it and keep it for later."

"Wait, are you trying to say I can't have the best of two worlds?"

"Exactly."

"Why didn't you say so?"

The next morning, the officers met in the cafeteria because errands had to be run during shore leave.

Goliath turned up late for the meeting.

"Awesome news, everyone!" he said, settling on the breakfast table of the six dodos. "The computer and I finished the first translation chip for dodos tonight. I call it *Instant Almendarin Crash Course for Dodos*, or *Iaccfd* for short. A real tongue twister. Who wants it?"

Birdie was concerned about the safety of the microchip. "I should check it first... Strange. The chip looks like one of mine."

Goliath smiled. "That could be because I found it in your data centre."

"But... but all the microchips contained important data!" shrieked Birdie. "What did you erase for your language stuff?"

"Don't worry, on this chip was only some weird pop rock music, or weird punk rock music for that matter."

"Oh, no!" cried Birdie. "You deleted all my Queen Day albums! I can't live without Pop Rock Punk!" She sank from her chair to the floor.

Her colleagues bent over the table. They thought Birdie had gone into shock.

"Don't panic!" said Hookbeak. "I have all the Queen Day songs. Even the B-sides."

"Oh, really?" Birdie asked with relief. She stood up again. "With my workload, music is the only thing that gets me through the day. Let me say I'm sorry *if* I've lost it for a moment."

"That's all right," said Dirk. "No dodo's perfect! Even I made a mistake once, many years ago!"

"Er, yes," said Birdie. "Thank you very much, Dirk."

Dertie sneered. "Queen Day only had two good songs. 'We will rock you when September ends' and 'Bohemian Idiot.'"

"I strongly disagree," said Birdie.

Hookbeak nodded. "I second that disagreement."

"What," asked Dirk, "is a Bohemian, by the way?"

"Gosh," said Birdie, "someone from a fantasy land. It's just a made-up word."

"All right!" said Goliath. "Whatever. Now, who wants my chip?"

Nala shook her head, and the other dodos stared at the ceiling.

"Volunteers, come forward," said Goliath.

He looked at Anton, who reflexively closed his eyes and began to snore.

"Bad actor," grumbled the cockatoo.

"Hm," mused Dertie. "I think he really fell asleep." She lifted her foot and kicked Anton in the side. "Hey, sleepyhead, what are you doing at night?"

"Sorry," said Anton, yawning. "Nochnaya and Tomny were listening to loud country music all night. It was unbearable. They haven't got used to the normal day-and-night rhythm yet and only went to bed an hour ago."

"Country music, of all things!" said Dertie. "How horrible. Why didn't you send them to the bridge?"

"I wanted to," replied Anton, "but they refused, claiming the acoustics in our bathroom were better."

Goliath sighed deeply. "This is all insanely interesting. Unfortunately, it doesn't get us anywhere. Who's going to take the translation chip? Consider this: we're travelling the Almond Milky Way in search of a planet where we can settle ... settle down even. Sooner or later, each of you will need a chip. You're far too lazy to take a language class."

"Is the microchip safe?" asked Nala.

"Probably," replied Goliath.

Birdie wasn't convinced. "I should run some diagnostics first."

"Nonsense," said Goliath. "The computer has already done it. This translation chip is as harmless as Jay's."

"In that case," said Hookbeak, "I'll take the chip. Jay's been swearing in Almendarin lately when something doesn't please him. Next time, he'll be in for a nasty surprise."

"Great!" said Goliath and pressed the chip to Hookbeak's skull.

Visible data streams flowed like lightning into Hookbeak's brain.

Birdie was worried. "Doesn't look like a harmless form of data transmission to me."

When the transmission was complete, Hookbeak stared into space for a moment.

"Úbisum?" he inquired.

"The Almendarin," noticed Nala, "sounds stranger this time."

"Whoops," said Goliath. "Why is he suddenly speaking Laddin?"

"You tell us."

Goliath held the microchip to the chief engineer's head once more.

"Dondeestoy?" asked Hookbeak after a final flash had streamed into his brain.

"Ah, Almendarin," said Goliath. "You're still in the cafeteria."

"Quéhasdicho?"

"Uh-oh! Now he doesn't understand Parrot!"

"It's called Dodish," claimed Hookbeak. "I understand everything. I just pulled your leg."

"Very funny," retorted Goliath. "Great, now we can start mass production. What was the name of the ship's computer? Fortifor? Fortisicks?"

"His name is Fortitoo," said Birdie, and she reprimanded the cockatoo. "From now on, you'll save all data onto my computer in the animal hospital before you delete it from microchips. Is that clear?"

"Crystal," replied Goliath.

"And don't you dare share my password with the parakeets!"

Nala gave a small cough. "Guys, what did we want to talk about? I'm a little busy with preparations for my party."

"It will have to wait," said Birdie. "We need to get food and we need a plan. That's why we're here."

"Great!" said Nala, standing up. "Let me know when you've worked out a plan. I'll go print out the invitations for my party and give them to express mail. You should have them in your wings by noon. See you then!"

She ran out of the cafeteria.

"Quite defiant," commented Dirk, and his officers nodded dutifully.

"You should have a word with her," Birdie said. "As your second deputy, I can do it too. After her party, of course."

"Yep, after the party," confirmed Dirk. "I don't want her to disinvite me."

"Same here. Let's move on to food. If we take only mulzbeans with us, the crew will start a mutiny. I guarantee it, *my captain*. Then your office will be history."

Birdie had already called Dirk 'captain' on occasion, often as disrespectfully as possible. By putting a 'my' before it, she had just admitted for the first time that he was her boss. He knew what she was trying to tell him. He had to make wise decisions from now on, or she would personally lead the mutiny.

"We cannot allow that to happen!" he said. "Does anyone have an idea where we can find tasty food?" He looked hopefully at the cockatoo.

"Every Tuesday there is the Galactic Market in Kingstown," Goliath said. "Fortunately, tomorrow is Tuesday. We can get some food from Earth, but be careful: Dumpians like to rip you off."

"How many days is a week on Berdeil?" Birdie asked.

"Berdeil has four days a week," answered Goliath. "Startweek, Tuesday, Endweek and Sunday. On Sunday there is no work because Krejs are busy—"

"Worshipping their gods?" asked Birdie.

"No, they're busy lying in the sun, of course. Hence the name. Fun fact: One day is thirty-one Earth hours long. That is why four—"

"That's why four weeks on Berdeil is almost as long as three weeks on Earth," calculated Birdie in her head. "That's right. If only the days on Berdeil were half an Earth hour longer. Well, well."

"What then?" asked Dirk and Anton.

"Mathematics, guys, mathematics," Birdie said dreamily.

"I got it!" said Hookbeak.

"And I don't care!" said Dertie.

🪶

By noon, the rest of the crew and pets were up and about.

The birds quickly realised that there was nothing special to see when you spent your shore leave on a green space outside the city walls. They shot video footage of the grass and of themselves posing with the stiff guards at the gate. Shortly after, they lost interest.

Dodernicus and Dodileo Dodilei fetched their deckchairs from the engine room and placed them in the hot midday sun. The next crew members followed on their heels, and after half an hour, the entire ship's company had spread out on the green space. There was neither sand nor sea, but the birds spent their first vacation day as they had spent their lives in Mauritius. Lazing around and getting dull in the mind in the process.

It showed Birdie that an idyllic life was exhausting everywhere in the galaxy. She wanted to experience something on her holiday and not be mentally stunted.

"There's a neighbourhood meeting," Goliath told her, "although the term is used very broadly because all the planets in the Almond Milky Way are considered Berdeil's neighbourhood."

The neighbourhood meeting was a cultural exchange for space pilots in the north of the city, far from the castle and its royal tyrant.

Hookbeak joined Birdie for a walk up North. Goliath was allowed to act as their guide again – on the condition that he kept his beak shut throughout the tour.

After they had passed the city gate, Hookbeak pulled out a letter from his feathers.

"Have you seen the invitation yet?" he asked. "Nala's parrot delivered it to me."

"No, not yet," Birdie said. "My mail always goes to the animal hospital. The parrots seem to think I live there."

"The party starts the day after tomorrow in Nala's cabin. Half an hour before midnight, our time."

"*Our time?*" Birdie wondered. "Well, it's afternoon here then."

"I know, but it says Dodish Mean Time. Look." Hookbeak showed Birdie the end of the letter.

IT'S GOING TO BE A HUGE 24-HOUR PARTY.
START: ***SATURDAY NIGHT, 11.30 DMT***
PLACE TO BE: ***CABIN 17, DECK 5***

BE THERE OR BE SQUARE.

RSVP!

"Oh, my," said Birdie. "She's serious about the whole twenty-four-hour thing, isn't she?"

"That's no problem for me," said Hookbeak, "but we have to respond soon if we get sick at parties."

"*What?*"

"It's just what RSVP means literally. *Respond Soon* if you *Vomit* at *Parties*. It's an abbreviation from old times, when party guests used to drink too much and hosts wanted to get enough buckets in advance."

"Ahem," Birdie cleared her throat. "Actually, RSVP means 'Respond soon via parrotmail.'"

"I always thought it means 'Respond soon if you—"

"I heard you," said Birdie. "Who told you that?"

"Dirk," replied Hookbeak.

"He fooled you, or more likely, he was fooled by someone else."

"Ah."

The cockatoo turned left, with the dodos following close behind.

Hookbeak looked ahead on the narrow street. "It seems Goliath is leading us on rat runs past the castle."

"Definitely," said Birdie, "and I'm grateful that most rats are running away from us."

One rat stopped and looked back at the birds. It squeaked and shrugged as if to say, "Sorry!"

They reached the North, where a harsher wind blew. Snakes spat venom from the rooftops and drunken lizards vomited into buckets after parties. It was, in short, not the poshest neighbourhood.

The birds entered an old industrial area with warehouses and disused chimneys.

"This is the old Foam-Wool Spinning Mill," Goliath said. "I know I should keep my beak shut, but foam-wool sheep used to be farmed on Berdeil. Now many artists use the site. Painters, writers and sculptors, for example."

"The scum of society, then," said Birdie.

"Yes," said Goliath, "but you meet educated people here too because there are pubs and martial arts halls for the space pilots."

"Hooray, culture at last!" cheered Birdie.

Dirk read the invitation on his deckchair. "RSVP. Respond soon via Popin," he said.

"Parrotmail," said Nala.

Dirk nodded. "It's the same thing for me."

Dertie had no pets. "Nala, I'm coming to your party. Now you know."

"No," said Nala. "Write me a letter and borrow someone's parrot to deliver it. Or bring it to my cabin yourself. I can't remember every oral answer."

"Can I borrow one of your three parrots?"

"No way! I love my parrots too much. Besides, you would only try to use them for your experiments!"

"Hehe," giggled Dertie. "I was going to do your feathers for the party. Now I'd better ruin them sometime when you're asleep."

"Don't you dare!" cried Nala. She moved her deckchair closer to Anton.

Dertie was jealous of any female who talked to Anton. She narrowed her eyes and listened to the pilot's and navigator's chat.

"Do you think," asked Nala, "that we'll still find our dream planet? We've been travelling for months!"

"That's just the way it is," Anton said. "If you want to reach the oasis, you have to walk into the desert first."

"Very poetic," said Nala.

"The fastest way doesn't always lead to the cake."

"I understood you the first time. And now I'm hungry, too."

They watched the geese flying overhead.

The parrots were sleeping in the shade – under the dodos' deckchairs.

Three birds walked into a bar. Said one bird to the others that he knew someone.

"Gusu! My time-travelling friend!" Goliath called a humanoid woman from the planet Dalmatia. Her snow-white skin was covered with black spots.

"Shh! Are you trying to kill me?" Gusu asked, startled. "This place is crawling with scoundrels just waiting to rewrite history."

This was unfair to the scoundrels. They were smugglers who had been wallowing in money for a long time but didn't retire because there was a lack of trainees. Young people nowadays preferred to study instead of learning an indecent profession. Furthermore, the weekend and night shifts in the smuggling business were an additional deterrent.

Time traveller Gusu needn't have feared for her spotted skin. Smugglers were rich (some even richer than the king) and didn't fancy the idea of an alternative timeline. On second thought, Gusu should have been terrified for her life.

"Don't worry, Gusu," said Goliath. "I deliberately spoke to you in Parrot. No one here understands it but us."

Birdie looked at the time traveller up close. "Where did a wingless life form learn Dodish?"

Gusu was confused. "Dodish?"

Goliath coughed. "That's what those giant weirdo chickens call my language."

"Oh, I see," said Gusu. "I speak fourteen languages fluently. The right language can save your life. Parrots, in particular, are very helpful."

Birdie and Hookbeak doubled over with laughter until their eyes watered.

"*Parrots, helpful?!*" they called out in turns. "You're killing me!"

To their surprise, Goliath and the time traveller showed no reaction.

"Oh, you were serious?" Birdie said after the ten-minute fit of laughter. She looked at Hookbeak. "What crazy world have we entered?!"

Gusu stroked Goliath's crest. "I owe him my life," she said. "Let's talk outside. The scoundrels have been staring at you for ten minutes."

They stood in the ship park in front of a dirty black spaceship. The ship was actually pink but appeared to be black because there were several layers of dirt on it. On top of these layers of dirt was an additional layer of dirt that made the 'black' ship look dirty.

"Wow, Gusu," said Goliath. "Your spacetime ship hasn't looked this inconspicuous in years. Where did you find so much dark sand?"

"A mile and a half to the north, there used to be mining under Queen Margaret. I found more than enough dirt there. I can't wait to fly back into space so it all comes off again."

"I don't understand," said Hookbeak.

"No problem, bird mister," said Gusu. "I'll explain. Queen Margaret, Reginald's mommy, had revived mining. She was a climate change denier. When Reginald ascended the throne, he went back to renewable energy like his granny, Queen Hildegard. One could almost like Reginald if he wasn't so addicted to executions and conquests."

Goliath nodded. "I could have told you all about it on the tour, but I had to keep my beak—"

"No!" said Hookbeak. "I don't understand why Gusu willingly dirties her own ship."

"Camouflage, I suppose?" guessed Birdie.

"That's right, bird lady," said Gusu. "I learnt that from Goliath. A professional spaceship thief can crack even the best access key, but who would think that a valuable ride was hidden under that rust bucket?"

"Ingenious," said Birdie. "And the idea came from you, Goliath?"

"In a manner of speaking," replied the cockatoo. "I'm actually black."

"You're blue," said Hookbeak.

"You see!" Goliath felt validated. "I fooled you all. I cover my upper plumage with the blue powder of my lower plumage."

Birdie couldn't make heads or tails of it. "You camouflage your black feathers with dark blue?" she asked. "*Seriously?*"

"Yeah, sure," said Goliath. "What's wrong with that?"

"Well, er... I can't figure out a reason why you would do that."

"I don't want to be stolen."

"That doesn't make any sense at all!"

"All right, it's a mating ritual," said Goliath. "Supposedly, females find powdered males more attractive."

"And? Is it true?" Birdie was curious.

The cockatoo hung his head. "If there's an effect, it fizzles out immediately because all the males do it," he whined.

"I'm so sorry to hear that," said Birdie with much sympathy.

Hookbeak was interested in how the spacetime ship worked, but Gusu was reluctant to let the dodos in on the secret.

"You can trust them," said Goliath.

"All right," Gusu said, looking into Hookbeak's innocent face. "I take it you know about warp drives?"

"Yes, we also have a warp drive," said Hookbeak. "Our spacetime distortion machine."

Gusu nodded. "I built a warp drive that warps spacetime backwards when I put the ship in reverse. So, naturally, I travel back in time."

"That's completely impossible!"

"No, it's not," replied Gusu. "I'm just amazing."

"I've been hearing that sort of self-praise a lot lately," realised Hookbeak. "Are you possibly related to mushrooms?"

The time traveller shrugged. "Not that I know of."

Hookbeak's thirst for knowledge wasn't quenched yet. "And how do you get to the future?"

"I put in a seventh gear," explained Gusu, "that lets me travel into the future faster than we're doing right now. We mistakenly call it the present, but actually, we're always travelling into the future."

"That's an interesting way of looking at it," said Hookbeak. "My understanding is that the present is always the time you are in right now."

"Well, I'm neither a physicist nor a philosopher," Gusu humbled herself. "I'm merely a highly gifted inventor and engineer. When I shift into seventh gear, time becomes distorted so that I overtake it with my ship. Thus, I end up in the future."

"Totally imposs—" Hookbeak interrupted himself because he remembered the Badians' crazy technology. "Hm. I think it's *unlikely*."

"I can live with that," said Gusu. "I'm afraid I have to get going. I have a dentist appointment in three days ago and I don't want to miss it."

"Is your appointment in three days?" asked Goliath. "Or was it three days ago?"

"Neither. My appointment will be in three days ago. There is no good grammar for time travellers."

Birdie was disgusted, but not just by the grammar. "There are doctors for teeth? Yuck, yuck!"

Hookbeak screwed up his face in revulsion. "We're lucky then that we don't have teeth. Are we staying for the slime fight of the Giant Snails?" he asked his colleagues.

"Definitely," said Birdie.

"You guys go ahead," Goliath said. "The slime fight only started five years ago. I'll catch up."

"Remember," said Gusu, "there's going to be a thunderstorm tonight. So don't stay too long. You don't have to stare at the blue sky, I really know better."

The dodos said goodbye to the time traveller and strolled towards the martial arts hall.

"Gusu," said Goliath, "I have a request. Can you build me a space-time ship? A small one will do for me."

"It would take me many years."

"Oh, come on. Don't forget how I saved you on Backwoods from the Backwoodsfolk. If I hadn't translated *for free*, you wouldn't have had to worry about your future for a long time."

"True, but..."

"You said you were in my debt," added Goliath. "Now you can pay it back."

"I thought I already had," said Gusu. "The dodo is alive."

"I didn't ask you to do that. Not yet, anyway."

Gusu relented because she knew how stubborn a cockatoo could be. "Okay, but after that we're even. When do you want me to bring the ship over?"

"Right after you finish building it."

"I realise that," said Gusu with a sigh. "With my spacetime ship, I can bring yours over whenever you like. Even in your past. Though they say deliveries to the past cause confusion for the recipients because they haven't placed the order yet."

"I see," said the cockatoo. "Then bring me the ship as soon as I'm settled on a planet with the dodos."

"Do you mean before or after the War of the Starworlds?"

"Excuse me?!" Goliath was shocked. "A star war?"

"Never mind," Gusu said quickly. "I got the time all wrong. Occupational hazard."

"Thank God! You just gave me a good scare." He offered her his wing. "So we'll meet again before long?"

Gusu smiled. "Time is relative," she said. "You'll meet me again sooner."

The next morning, Birdie and Goliath went to the Galactic Market with fifty crew members pushing a wheelbarrow each. Popin and Jay joined them at first, but then flew ahead because for some reason Jay was in a hurry.

The wheelbarrows had crossbars at beak height. This allowed the crew members to rest their wings and steer the wheelbarrows with their beaks.

"We need pandanus fruit," said Birdie.

"I don't know if they have any of it," said Goliath, "but pineapples didn't kill you either. It's important to look at all the fruit first. Never buy a pig in a poke in this market."

"Why would anyone want to buy a pig in a… is that one of your exotic phrases?" she asked, frowning. "I'd appreciate it if you could hold back on those a little. Dodos only know pigs or monkeys from seafaring accounts. Besides, you've forgotten that we can't buy anything. We'll have to trade furniture from our ship."

"Birdie," Goliath said, shaking his head, "the green paper the king gave you is money."

"*Really?* Printed paper?? You don't use gold coins??? Gosh!!!!"

"Yes, we use coins, too. You can take the bank notes out of your feathers now."

"I gave them to Jay," said Birdie. "He said he had a use for them. Seemed a bit odd to me, but since the notes are green, I thought he wanted to stick them on his sister as replacement feathers. The poor thing has lost a couple of tail feathers on the space station."

"You didn't give him the whole forty thousand crowns, though?" hoped Goliath.

"Oh. That's a lot, is it? Well, you could have told me sooner what the bundle was all about. Money! I would never have thought of that! To me, it was just paper that was taking up valuable space in my feathers."

"*When?!*" cried Goliath in horror. "*When did you give it to Jay?*"

"Ten minutes ago," said Birdie.

"Oh?" Goliath said, a little relieved. "Then he can't have spent it all yet. I hope he hasn't. I'll find him!"

He rose a hundred feet into the air and got a rough overall view of the hundred and fifty market stalls. Still, his eyes were too weak to make out a forty-centimetre parrot.

How I'd like to be an eagle now, Goliath thought.

He descended swiftly and flew to the food and drink stalls. *I should have thought of that right away!*

"I'm not actually hungry," said Popin, who was walking with her brother past a waffle stall. "But it all looks so delicious."

"Jay!" called Goliath, who was circling over the parakeets. "How much money do you have left?"

"Shh!" said Popin. "Don't shout! We don't want everyone to hear."

"Sorry," whispered Goliath. He landed between the siblings. "So, what's left of the forty thousand crowns?"

Jay calculated in his head. "Thirty-nine thousand nine hundred and ninety-six! I only got myself a Hot Caffeine Chocolate at the Chofé stall. Boy, I'm bursting with energy and drive! Let's race each other. Whoever gets to the castle first. On your marks, get set..."

"Stop!" said Goliath. "Give me the money first. Birdie and I need to buy food and coffee."

"No problem," said Jay. "How much do you need?"

"Thirty-nine thousand nine hundred and ninety-six."

"Nah, no can do. I'd be broke if I did."

Popin sighed. "Just do it, and I promise to fly around with you until the poison wears off."

"That wasn't poison," said Jay. "It was full of yummy... ooh, there's something wrong with my stomach."

Goliath had a sneaking suspicion. "You didn't drink a plant-based milk substitute, you drank cow's milk, did you?"

"Yeah, sure," said Jay. "The stall owner told me she was a cow and that her milk was an in-house production. It would've been rude to say no to that."

"Birds can't tolerate milk," explained Goliath, "but who can resist a good cocoa? With the right medicine, it ain't no problem at all. Keep fifty crowns and fly to the pharmacy in Charlatan Street. If you hurry, Jay will survive."

"SURVIVE?!" cried the siblings.

"If you hurry," repeated Goliath. "They sure got an antidote."

The pharmacist's orange mane reached to the ground, which is why she had to hop along to avoid tripping over her hair.

"Good afternoon, how can I help you?" she asked.

"My stomach... I feel sick... I drank hot chocolate," stammered Jay, who had to be supported by Popin.

"Well, well," said the pharmacist. "Birds shouldn't drink milk at all. It can end badly."

"*Oh, really?*" retorted Jay.

"I recommend drops from the Salvation Pharmy. They'll break down the cocoa milk in no time and damage your stomach walls only a paltry thirty to fifty per cent."

"Give me that!"

The pharmacist hopped to the back and took a long box from the shelf. "That's nineteen crowns and ninety-five pennies."

"*Extortionate price!*" claimed Jay. He had picked up the term at the market and had quickly realised that it was actually always true.

"What did you expect?" asked the pharmacist indignantly. "We are the Cut-Your-Throat Pharmacy on Charlatan Street. We stand by our name! Oh, you know what? Let's say fifty crowns instead."

"You counted the notes in my wing, didn't you?" asked Jay.

"Yep," said the pharmacist. "Fifty crowns is still a snip when it comes to life and death."

Popin didn't understand Almendarin and didn't need to because she knew her brother all too well.

"*NOW GIVE HER THE MONEY ALREADY!*" she yelled.

🌿

"Look," said Goliath, pointing to a sweets stand. "There's great food there."

Birdie counted eleven children queuing for chocolates. "If kids love it, it's too sweet and unhealthy. That's the golden rule. We should all watch our diet a little bit."

"Well, you dodos definitely should," said Goliath.

"No fat shaming," warned Birdie. "At least we're not skinny midgets like some other birds."

"Hey!"

They passed a bakery stall.

"Mmm," said Goliath. "Stollen tastes great."

"This pastry looks like a sugar and fat bomb," argued Birdie.

"No, no. You're looking at it all wrong. Stollen is extremely healthy. It consists *largely* of dried grapes, called raisins, and is therefore considered a fruit."

"We'll keep walking for now. Where do we find the real fruit, Goliath? I hope they have pineapple there. And what's the name of the dessert you served us at the restaurant?"

"Apple sauce."

"Right," said Birdie. "We definitely need the fruit that's used to make apple sauce."

"Apple."

The cockatoo turned his head, casting a glance at the never-ending queue of dodos and wheelbarrows.

"Oh, it's going to be fun with that troop," he said.

"What do you mean?" asked Birdie.

"We'll have to go through the whole marketplace once. They always hide the healthy food in the back section of the market."

"But... why?"

"Because no one wants it."

The siblings sat on a step in front of the pharmacy.

Jay raised the vial from Salvation Pharmy to the light.

"I only needed half the antidote!" he said. "I can still drink one Hot Caffeine Chocolate! Where can I get some?! Back to the market! Let's go! Come on!"

"Wait," said Popin. "What's wrong with you? You're totally hyper. It's a good thing you don't have any money left."

"Oh, right," remembered Jay. "Cockatoos and pharmacies took all my money. The pharmacist mentioned that the caffeine has a stronger effect once the milk has been broken down in the stomach. That's probably why I feel so awake. The only thing that helps is exercise! Let's get to the ship! Last one to sit next to the fusion reactor is a lame duck!"

He took to the air, raced up the building's wall and vanished over the roof.

"Good grief!" said Popin and chased after her brother.

The sun reflected on the solar panels of the ten thousand roofs of Kingstown. That late morning, the siblings had the airspace to themselves as the commuters had already flown to work in their spaceships.

After three minutes, they reached the Sea Cow. They shot through the cargo hold before turning into the Parrot Communication Tube System.

Popin had caught up with her brother but couldn't overtake him in the Tube because he was flying in the middle on purpose.

"You blocked my way," she said, sitting down next to her brother's regular seat. "I'm faster than you, and you know it."

"That's logical," said Jay. "You're more slender and weigh less."

"Have you had enough romping for now? Are you feeling better?"

"No. I feel ready to take on anything. On to the next round!" he shouted.

He jumped off the bar and flew back into the Tube.

"Aw, come on!" exclaimed Popin.

Birdie and Goliath were already doing a second round around the market. They had three dodos left in tow. The other crew members had marched to the ship with full wheelbarrows.

Birdie had a pen in her beak and a piece of paper in her wing. She had noted down the amounts of food and calories. Now all she had to do was calculate in her head how long the food would last. She put the pen back in her feathers.

"It's a pity the Dumpians didn't have fruit from Mauritius," she said. "I'm relying on your knowledge that bananas, melons and pears are non-toxic."

"You should be glad," said Goliath, "that the Dumpians have never been to Mauritius, or they'd also have abducted dodos regularly. Always in small groups so it wouldn't be noticed."

"You're probably right. I don't like the kingdom," Birdie said. "Crooks and cheats on one side, and citizens who don't fight back on the other. Everyone's only looking out for their own gain. I can understand why you want to come with us. Over the last few months, we've become a family that sticks together. Even the parakeets helped with Dirk's rescue – after I did a lot of convincing."

"You threatened that they would have to treat themselves in future if they didn't help."

"Oh, yes! Because some of them acted like the king himself. Of course it was an empty threat. *You* are well-behaved for a parrot, but imagine the chaos the parakeets would cause in the animal hospital. All right, back to food. I've finished my calculations. We have enough food for three months. Surely, it won't take us that long to travel the Almond Milky Way."

"Wait a minute," said Goliath. "We still have three wheelbarrows and more than twenty thousand crowns left. We're not done shopping yet."

"Why not? What have we forgotten?" asked Birdie.

"We still need sugarcane, coconuts, pineapples and cows."

"Excuse me?"

"Oh, forget the sugarcane. We'd better buy ready-made rum instead. But a cow – not a bull! – is absolutely essential. Cream doesn't stay fresh for long."

"Are these all groceries that you need for a healthy diet?" asked Birdie.

"No, but I have this idea for a new drink," said Goliath. "Why do you ask?"

"Because *I'm* your new vet, and I'm putting together your menu. And we're not taking a cow with us!"

"Then I'd rather stay on Berdeil."

"Just make your drink without cream," said Birdie. "We're not kidnapping a bouncer and mother."

"Well," pondered Goliath, "I guess a little more coconut cream will do, too. Then we'll incidentally save the money on the antidote."

"There you go," said Birdie. "A cow wouldn't have fit in the wheelbarrow anyway."

"Right! My mistake."

Chapter 11: Lost in Space Vortex

The warp engine was fixed, for now. Hookbeak had spent the whole morning checking it for further signs of wear. A warp engine was like a bicycle. You could patch the bike's inner tube if it had a flat. It was even better to replace the old, holey tube with a new one. However, you rarely took a spare tube with you on a cycling tour. Hookbeak hadn't brought a second warp engine with him either. It would take him at least ten days to build a new one, provided they found the necessary materials.

The chief engineer knew he couldn't repair the engine indefinitely. Before patching a bicycle's inner tube for the fifth time, it was better to throw it in the rubbish.

Birdie and Goliath had just returned from shopping when Hookbeak sprang the bad news on them in the cargo hold.

"We can't afford to go to every solar system like we did at the beginning of our journey," he said. "The warp drive can't take it. And the ship's computer can't calculate a course until we have star charts of the Almond Milky Way."

"Hm, hmmm," mused Birdie. "We should be able to get maps somewhere. Right, Goliath?"

"There are star navs for sale," said the cockatoo. "They're small navigation computers for spaceships. But they don't help us because they won't tell us anything about the nature of the planets."

"Oh dear," said Birdie. "So we really have to fly to every planet, one at a time? Then we should get spare parts for the warp drive first."

"It's not that simple," said Goliath. "There are over a thousand habitable worlds in the Almond Milky Way. It would take us years to visit them all! And for the most part, they're already *occupied* by intelligent life forms. Although the intelligence of some higher life forms is debatable. The Donkkies of Moron IV, for example, found indoor swimming pools boring, which is why they built outdoor pools instead – completely covered with roofs, of course, because it's raining cats and dogs on their planet. A little Antzibal girl later asked the

Donkkies why there were only indoor pools on Moron IV and no outdoor pools."

"Goliath," Birdie said, "we need..."

"Fun fact: It's only raining one day out of five hundred on Moron IV. The cats usually land on their feet, but sadly, the dogs don't. So it goes."

"Goliath," Birdie said firmly, "we need information on the gravity of every single planet. Then, perhaps, we can rule out some worlds and star systems before we continue our journey."

"Top idea. There's an institute for astronomical nonsense where we can ask about the gravity of celestial bodies. If I'm not mistaken, the institute is just a few streets past the city gate. A two-minute flight, tops."

"We're more interested in the walking distance," said Birdie.

"Oh, right! I always forget that," said Goliath. "I just have to imagine you're ostriches or emus because they can't fly either."

"That's really rather interesting," replied Birdie snappily. "Keep twisting the knife in the wound!"

Popin returned from her seventeenth round trip. Her exhausted brother followed a moment later and settled on Hookbeak's back. The effects of the caffeine were beginning to wear off.

Dirk lay on his deckchair and enjoyed the sun. Then, from one second to the next, the sun was gone. He opened his eyes and saw three bird silhouettes fluttering above him. They belonged to Popin, Goliath and Jay.

"Hey," said Dirk, "you're in my sun!"

Birdie appeared on his right side, just as he was used to.

"You've been lying in the sun all day, Dirk."

"There's no TV here," he said. "What else am I supposed to do? I'm on holiday."

"And this holiday has culture in its programme," explained Birdie. "Let's go to the Institute for Astronomical Nonsense."

"That's a strange name for an institute."

"Yeah, I thought so too," Birdie said, puzzled. "Come on, get your bum up. We're all waiting for you."

"Nah, I'm not a culture vulture," said Dirk. "You guys have a good time."

Hookbeak appeared on his left side. "Dirk, don't you want to see our new home? Your dream planet?"

"But right now, it's the perfect afternoon sun for napping. Can't we go in the morning?"

"No," said Birdie, determined. "Tomorrow morning, you'll want to sleep in again because you're on holiday."

Dirk pondered. "Now I'm faced with a real dilemma, Number Two. Sleeping in or taking a nap."

"Let's go, get a move on."

After a quarter of an hour, the six birds reached a temple made of sandstone, the Royal Institute of Astronomy and Aerospace. The temple was forty feet high and fifty feet wide, and its roof was supported on the front by eight pillars. Behind the two central pillars lay a modern steel entrance door.

Goliath flew to the information booth that had been squeezed between the temple and the bowling centre.

The other birds admired the temple. It had once been built for the supposed goddess of luck, Miss Fortune, and had never attracted many visitors. Doubts about her suitability as goddess of luck first arose on a Friday, the 13th, when a black cat lured her under a ladder. Afterwards, a bucket of salt fell from the ladder onto Miss Fortune, causing her to walk blindly on clear ice and skid against a mirror, which shattered into a thousand pieces. As a result, her followers died in tragically-curiously ways over the next seven years. Miss Fortune was retitled the 'goddess of bad luck' at the next Gods Con but was allowed to keep her name as a consolation. After that, the temple was no longer much use as a tourist attraction. It was now occupied by astronomers who didn't believe in gods, which is why Miss Fortune didn't care a smidge about them. Visitors, however, should beware of her streak of bad luck.

"Boy, oh boy," said Dirk. "If we had built a structure like that for Loony Polly, I'm sure she would have let us fly straight to paradise."

"I don't believe in gods any more," said Hookbeak. "My only religion is science."

Dirk pitied his old school friend. "I'm really sorry about your soul. I'll miss you in paradise."

"Ahem!" Jay said to Hookbeak. "If I were you, I'd give your faithful pet five huge meals a day. Because if you're wrong and the gods do exist, I could put in a good word for you with Mama Polly."

Popin chided her brother. "You're only thinking of yourself, glutton."

Goliath returned before Jay could think of a justification.

"We may go in, but we are to excuse the mess," said the cockatoo. "They had their summer party yesterday evening and had to celebrate inside because of the thunderstorm."

What the birds saw in the research facility couldn't be described as anything but wild chaos. The paper plates and leftover food from the summer party were dismissible, but the nine Krejs running around frantically couldn't be ignored. The Krejs received their instructions from a creature standing on a lab table. It was a New Zealand kakapo.

"Now this is terrific!" Goliath said because he didn't need to translate the words of a kakapo. "I can put my feet up for once."

Birdie marvelled, "Another exotic giant parrot!"

The dodos looked at the green parrot in a white children's jacket as if it were a zoo attraction. Goliath jumped up on the table next to it, and they met at eye level.

"What's going on, mate?" the cockatoo asked the kakapo.

"There's quite a lot going on around here," said the bird astronomer. He was talking in his mother tongue for the first time in months. "We are trying to create a space vortex to shorten the travel time from A to B. The Royal Transport Company has already announced another increase in ticket price, which angers my boss. He flies halfway around the planet three times a week on shuttle ships. But you probably didn't want to know that. Tell me, who are your friends? Are they from Earth? The infamous dudus who almost started a revolution?"

"Dodos. Yes, that's right," said Goliath. "And two green parrots."

"Ah, now I see the two parakeets. Aww, they're so small and cute!"

Jay felt insulted. "Hey, you gangly whopper!" he retorted. "How's the air up there?!"

"I don't know," replied the kakapo. "Thank goodness I can't fly because you're proof that high-altitude air is damaging the brain."

Popin shook her head. "Trademark male behaviour."

Birdie sighed. "When the gentle-birds are done exchanging pleasantries, perhaps we can make our request."

"All right," said the kakapo. "How can I be of service?"

"We want to phone home," said Goliath. "Little joke. We need information about the gravity of the planets. My chubby friends here want to fly. Do you think that's possible or laugh-out-loud funny?"

"Both," replied the kakapo. "I don't quite get it. In space, they can fly around weightlessly in zero gravity."

"Well," said Dirk, "it's just not the same. And we can't stay in space forever. We're looking for a new place to live… er, what's the word?"

"Residence?" came Hookbeak to the rescue.

"A new home?" added Birdie.

"Yes!" confirmed Dirk. "My, if I didn't have you guys. You are like books that explain words!"

"Dictionaries?" asked Birdie, annoyed.

"Yes, but dictionaries that are moving!"

"Walking dictionaries," said Birdie, most annoyed.

"Exactly!"

"Hmm," the kakapo brooded over the dodos' wish. "Could you glide on Earth when you took a running jump off a cliff?"

"Not even a bit," replied Birdie. "And the broken bones didn't look very appetising."

"Okay," said the kakapo. "According to what you just told me, we can disregard all habitable planets that have a gravity acceleration of more than five metres per square second."

Hookbeak nodded. "I had arrived at the same conclusion. That's about half of Earth's gravity. How many planets does that leave us?"

The kakapo called his two assistants and instructed them to continue the experiments in his absence. Then he turned to the other birds, saying, "Follow me into our 3D Star Room."

He led them through an archway to the back of the research area and down a dark corridor. They came to a red door. A note stuck to it.

"Guided tours..." translated Goliath, "for visitor groups by appointment only. Thirty crowns per every creature with a nose, trunk or slime sniffer... Oh, I don't know if we have a hundred and eighty crowns with us."

"No problem," said the kakapo. "I'm happy to help distant relatives."

"What's your name, by the way?" asked Goliath.

"Kiwi."

"But..." began Goliath, thinking of the kiwi, a completely different bird species from New Zealand.

Kiwi, the kakapo, shrugged his wings. "That *is* my name," he said. "My parents purposely gave me a name associated with my home islands."

They entered a circular room, fifty-five yards in diameter. The roof was in the shape of a dome, and Hookbeak knew in an instant that he was in a gigantic observatory.

Kiwi closed the door, and his wing brushed over a few sensors on the wall.

"Computer," he spoke into the room, "show us the holographic projection of the celestial bodies, Almond Milky Way Delta Fourteen."

Billions of planets and moons appeared as small dots in space.

"Show only the habitable planets and moons," said Kiwi.

What remained were about a thousand illuminated dots.

"Blimey!" Dirk said. "So many worlds and so little time to visit them."

"Now," continued Kiwi, "display the objects on whose surface there is an acceleration due to gravity of less than five metres per square second."

"What's going on?" asked Dirk. "Why do I only see six dots all of a sudden?"

"It's not that surprising," said Kiwi. "You have to understand that habitable planets need a certain gravity to be able to hold their atmosphere. However, you do have six planets to choose from. Try your luck."

"Hooky," said Dirk, "you're an astronomer too. Couldn't you have given us a heads-up?"

"We've already combed three Milky Ways without success," replied Hookbeak. "It should have been obvious for weeks that there aren't many planets on which we could possibly fly."

"Guys," said Birdie, looking on the bright side. "Six targets is still better than, well, five. At least we'll have an answer soon." She turned to the kakapo. "Thanks, Kiwi. Can you print out the coordinates for us?"

"Of course. Will do."

They left the observatory and stopped dead as they entered the laboratory area.

The Krejs had created a space vortex they couldn't control. It hovered three feet above the ground, swallowed light objects (for example paper plates with leftover food) and transported them to an unknown location.

Suddenly, the space vortex turned towards the birds.

"Duck!" said Kiwi, which offended Dirk because he wasn't one.

They ducked until the vortex had spun away from them.

"Stand very still," said Kiwi to his flock of birds, "and nothing will happen to you."

In truth, he thought it was possible the whirlwind would swallow them all.

Kiwi saw his co-workers cowering behind a computer and ran under the lab tables to join them. A Krej lifted him onto the computer keyboard.

The space vortex turned again towards the dodos and parrots. Jay panicked. He spread his wings and flew towards the ceiling.

"*No!*" shouted Kiwi. "The pull of the vortex is too strong on the ceiling!"

But it was too late. The space vortex caught Jay and swallowed him. It had only taken a second.

"Where did he go?" cried Popin. "*Where did he go?!*"

Kiwi hastily pressed buttons on the keyboard with his claws until he managed to contain the space vortex with a force field. The monster vortex shrank and dissolved.

"Where did he go?" asked Popin again. This time, she sounded desperate. Her brother had disappeared without a trace.

Birdie looked with sadness at Hookbeak, who stared into space with his beak wide open.

"Well," said Kiwi, picking up a phone from the table. "If the experiment is successful, he'll show up on the other side of the planet. I'm going to call our branch office there."

He let the phone ring five times, then the answering machine picked up.

"Maybe they're taking a nap," pondered Kiwi. "They were at our summer party and only returned to their hemisphere this morning. But I'll try again."

Eventually, the kakapo reached someone on the other end of the line.

"Yes, hello there, it's Kiwi. No, I'm not a talking fruit. Yes, sure, I always laugh at your silly joke again and again. Tell me, have you by any chance received a parrot? What does it look like? Small, green... *Yes, green like the inside of a kiwi. But with a bill and wings... No*, not a bill for chicken wings, a parrot with a beak... Nothing arrived at all? Not even food scraps and paper plates? All right. Let us know if the parrot still turns up, or parts of him... What kind of parts? Well, feathers for instance. Or feet. Or a head. Okeydokey, we'll see you in half a year for the summer party on your hemisphere."

"*Parts of him?!*" Popin shouted angrily. "Where's my brother?"

"Oh, I'm sorry," said Kiwi. "That was mean of me. The Krejs in our branch office make stupid jokes all the time and I got infected by it. Your brother is probably not missing any body parts. Still, the outlook isn't rosy, I'm afraid. He could have landed anywhere in the universe, and that's why it's quite possible he was pulled into the vacuum of space. We'll continue our search, but please don't get your hopes up too high."

"Didn't we call it shore leave?" asked Dirk. "Why's Jay on a space holiday?"

"Dirk!" exclaimed Birdie, shocked.

"Sorry, I wasn't listening."

Popin couldn't hold back the tears any longer.

Birdie and Dirk stroked and reassured her that they were not giving up yet.

"Maybe," said Birdie, "the space vortex spat Jay out again if he didn't taste good. We'll use the ship to scan a thirty-mile radius. And if we don't find him here, we'll fly to the northern hemisphere and continue our search at the branch office."

Popin nodded gloomily while Hookbeak gathered all his strength.

"Let's go then," he said. "What are you waiting for? Let's start searching."

There was tremendous consternation among the parrots. Jay had enjoyed a great reputation after winning the prize for the most broken bones in the hammock hopping race.

The officers were shaken as well, and Nala postponed her birthday party indefinitely.

The birds searched for Jay all over the province of Kingstown (as well as in the greater Nwotsgnik area on the opposite side of the planet) but in the end, they didn't find even a feather. They called the institute every day in the hope there was a new lead.

The kakapo Kiwi took full responsibility for the mistakes of his doltish Krejs, although it hadn't been his fault.

After two weeks, he told the dodos to give up. "We have Hookbeak's number and will get back to you if we find a green parrot. But, to put it bluntly, there's no hope left. I'm sorry. Take your time to process your loss."

The officers and Popin sat on the bridge, downhearted. As captain, Dirk had to make the hard decision.

"We must fly on, my friends," he said to Popin and Hookbeak.

Birdie agreed with him. "If we stay on Berdeil, the king will – sooner or later – frame us for something. I'm sure he's just waiting for a chance to take revenge on us. We should finish our mission."

"Do what you want," Popin said bitterly before she flew into the comm tube.

"Oh, the poor thing," said Nala.

"Goliath?" asked Dirk. "Do you still have the planet list? Fortitoo needs it. I asked Birdie if we could use the random number generator again, but she said no dice."

"Already done," said Goliath. "Fortitoo knows the list *by heart*."

"Ahoy!" the computer called with delight. "That's correct! The cockatoo gave me the coordinates so I could calculate the fastest sea routes. You can sail to the six ports within three days – if two shore missions a day are convenient for you. I've planned your first mission tomorrow after breakfast. Then lunch, nap, second shore mission and supper. What do you say, mate?"

Dirk almost warbled a song out of joy. "You thought of my nap? Excellent, Fortitoo! I hereby appoint you my Third Officer: Number Three!"

"*Excuse me?!*" said Nala, thinking she was in the wrong movie.

"What about me?" asked Anton.

Dertie shook her head in disbelief. "So this is what it feels like to be passed over for promotion."

"All right," said Dirk. "No Third Officer then if you're jealous of Fortitoo."

He turned to his chief engineer, who sat in his chair, distressed.

"Hey," whispered Dirk. "Do you want me to come over after work? We can just hang out like we used to. Have a little snack and watch a film? The parrots had secretly made a disaster movie out of a classic – called *Gone with the Winds: The Shark Attack Edition* – and they're willing to share it with us as part of their redemption for playing dumb."

"No," replied Hookbeak. "I don't want any guests in my cabin at the moment. I need some time on my own."

"Okay, no problem," Dirk said sympathetically. "Just let me know when you feel like company."

That night, four parrots met in sick bay for a round of games. Herbert and Papagayo wanted to distract Popin from Jay's disappearance. Popin brought along the cockatoo as the fourth player.

They played Parrot Ludo. It was a mixture of checkers and chess, but with cards, so basically nothing else but Blackjack.

"I'm sorry," said Goliath. "I'm afraid I have to place my seven on the queen of hearts."

Papagayo had no seven and had to put on a straw hat as punishment.

Popin coughed. "Herbert is looking at your cards again, Papagayo."

Papagayo laid his cards facedown on the floor and scowled at Herbert. "What is your problem? Can't you lose fairly? Because you're going to lose no matter what!"

"I'd rather win unfairly," replied Herbert with a grin. "The hat suits you."

"At Parrot Ludo," said Popin, "everyone could show you their cards. That still wouldn't mean you're getting the upper wing."

"Why's that?" asked Herbert, placing an ace. Goliath had to tie a bandage over his eyes and play the rest of the game blind.

"Well," answered Papagayo, "it's because you can't predict which card a player will lay down next, as long as they have several options. Let's say I have a seven of hearts and a seven of clubs on the wing. Then it wouldn't matter to me with which of the two cards I respond to a seven of diamonds. But my choice has unknown effects on how the game develops."

"Chaos theory!" realised Popin.

"No," said Papagayo, "I don't think chaos theory can be applied to our card game, dear Popin. We can ask our medicine bird, though."

"Yes, Birdie is very clever," said Popin. "For a dodo."

"*My* feeder," Herbert said with pride.

Goliath felt left out of the conversation. "Can someone tell me what the chaos theory is?"

"I can explain it to you metaphorically," said Papagayo. "When a turtle in Hawaii hits the water too hard with its foot, a tidal wave occurs off Mauritius. That's the so-called turtle effect."

"You only know Hawaii from reports," objected Herbert. "We're in space! There are no turtles here…"

"It's just an example," groaned Papagayo.

"…and there's no sea here either…" Herbert continued.

"It's only an illustration of the theory!"

"…so there can't be a tidal wave either…"

"Your train of thought is as brilliant as it's unnecessary."

"…because I've heard tidal waves consist of a lot of water," continued Herbert, "which means your theory is complete nonsense. *Hey, where are you all going?*"

Herbert suddenly sat alone on the floor.

"Apparently," he groused, "no one can bear it any more when you point out a flaw in their thinking."

The Parrot Communication Tube System was lit even at bedtime. Papagayo was taking Popin home.

"I'm sorry," Papagayo said as they stood over her cabin. "Herbert spoilt our evening."

"That's okay," said Popin sadly. "I couldn't really distract myself anyway."

Papagayo wanted to cheer her up. "I don't think Jay's dead. He'll be fine on Berdeil."

"But he probably is dead!" retorted Popin and began to cry. She turned away from Papagayo without another word and slid down the exit tube to her cabin.

Papagayo put his head in his wings. "Silly me!"

Dirk woke up. "What? Why? Huh?"

"It's just me," said Popin, sobbing. She flew to her hammock.

"Are you all right?" asked Dirk.

"No!"

"Do you want to talk about it?"

"No!"

"Jay will be fine," said Dirk.

"Why don't you all shut up!" shouted Popin.

"Sorry." He turned onto his other side and fell asleep again.

"Dirk?" asked Popin.

"What? Why? Huh?"

"I'm sorry I yelled at you. But it's better if you leave me alone for a while. I need time to myself."

"Of course," said Dirk.

"Starting now," explained Popin.

"You got it. Sure thing."

"As of this second!" gave Popin a broad hint.

"Er."

"I'm sure one of your officers will take you in."

"Oh, I see," said Dirk.

He got up without enthusiasm, snatched his pillow and headed for the door.

"Good night," said Popin.

"'oo' 'igh'," mumbled Dirk with the pillow in his beak.

Dirk begged Anton, Nala and Dertie for a place to sleep, but they all turned him down. He didn't need to ask Birdie. He knew she didn't like him very much.

In the end, all he had left was his armchair on the bridge.

"I got thrown out of the cabin by my own pet," he grumbled and closed his eyes.

He had just fallen asleep when the night watchbirds Nochnaya and Tomny woke him up again.

"We're hungry. D'you have food?" asked Nochnaya.

"Nope," said Dirk. "Could you please let me sleep?"

"You do have access to the food chamber!" said Nochnaya. "Open the chamber for us, and we'll leave you alone."

"No, you can't get extra rations. Food doesn't grow on trees."

"Yes, it does!" said Nochnaya.

"True," said Dirk, "but we don't have any trees on board."

"Give us Jay's ration!"

"The cockatoo ate it."

"Then give us yours!"

"Leave me alone!" cried Dirk.

"Food first!"

It was a wonderful Sunday morning in space. Calm and peaceful. The soft light of an enchanting red nebula was shining through the windows. Unfortunately, no one was awake to admire the nebula. The dodos were sleeping. The parrots were sleeping. The geese were sleeping. The whole ship was asleep. Even the night watchbirds, whose only job was to be awake, were snoring on the bridge.

But just a few minutes later, at 5 o'clock on the dot, Birdie's alarm clock rang, as it did every morning.

When the alarm sounded, the doctor literally hit the ceiling. She fell back into the nest, grabbed the culprit with her foot and hurled it full force against the wall. The alarm clock didn't even get a scratch and gleefully continued to make a noise. It was unbreakable. Hookbeak had built it for Birdie after she had destroyed seven alarm clocks in the first week of travel.

Herbert had also been roused from sleep and was lying in his hammock, shaking his head. Of course he would fall asleep again in twenty minutes when his mistress left for work. And yet, the daily morning madness was getting on his nerves.

"Birdie, the alarm clock is still ringing," he said and looked down at her.

Her head was buried under a pillow, but at least she was stretching her legs out of the nest now. Her feet searched the floor, looking for the source of the noise. After a few seconds, they found it.

To turn off the alarm, Birdie had to press the clock gently ten times. A whole ten times. One day she would get even with Hookbeak.

She stretched and opened her eyes since Sunday was just another workday for her. Nevertheless, her fatigue still kept the upper hand.

"You won't last without a dip in the bathtub," she said to herself. An ice-cold bath was her only remedy so far to perk up after five hours of sleep.

If Birdie had known the effects of the roasted brown beans that Goliath secretly stashed in his room, she would've become a thieving magpie. She would have confiscated the coffee as *medicine* because it would've made her life better and worse from the very first cup.

After her bath, she shook herself dry, like a wet dog, and once again cleaned herself thoroughly with her beak.

Half past five, Birdie turned on her computer at the animal hospital. While it installed a time-consuming update, she went to the storage closet to get bandages for the parrots. She looked in the closet and sighed because it was empty. No clean bandages. She'd had the laundry baskets with the dirty bandages picked up the night before, but it had completely slipped her mind that the laundry staff didn't work on Sundays. There were no days off for the officers. Still, apart from Birdie, no one else seemed even minutely overworked.

There would be no rush hour traffic in the comm tube today, but the parrots made regular Sunday trips to the gyms and tennis courts on Deck Seven. Birdie would certainly need fifty bandages.

She closed the cupboard and left the animal hospital with quick steps. Fortunately, her sick bay for dodos was one deck below.

As Birdie walked into the large dormitory, she accidentally stepped on a straw hat. There were playing cards on the floor, all scattered around the hat. They looked familiar to her.

Huh, can you believe it? she thought. *I have exactly the same pack of cards! And the little straw hat... Well, that's really crazy, my parrot has a hat like that, too...*

"Herbert!" she said angrily. "Have you been secretly playing poker with my cards?"

She didn't get an answer. Not in the proper sense. She hadn't expected an answer at all because she was standing alone in the room. Still, she thought she had heard a muffled sound. A faint wail.

She looked around the room but saw only the seventy empty beds. *No, it's all in my imagination. I'm alone.*

After locking the pack of cards and the straw hat in her desk, she opened the closet and breathed a sigh of relief. Five hundred bandages would last a week.

Suddenly, she had an eerie feeling.

She turned her head and looked at the second bed at the entrance. And she shuddered. Something was moving gently up and down under the sheet.

Maybe just a palm thief? Maybe just a spider? she told herself as she mustered up the courage to sneak up to the bed.

As she stepped closer, she could better assess the proportions of the body. The *thing* was much bigger than a crab or a spider! Birdie got scared and didn't know what to do about it. She wondered how a dodo normally reacted in such a situation. *Oh yeah, right*, she remembered and stuck to the tried and true.

Her panicked screams woke the whole deck.

Dirk was trembling with fear under his sheet. As the screams wouldn't end, he panicked and began to scream at the top of his lungs, too.

Then there was silence.

Dirk took a deep breath. For once, attack had been the best form of defence. He pulled the sheet off his head and caught sight of the terrified Birdie. When they recognised each other, they burst into screams of horror again.

"For crying out loud!" Birdie scolded. "What the heck are you doing here?"

"Popin threw me out, sort of," explained Dirk.

"Oh. I guess she needs…"

"Time to herself," he said.

"Everyone copes with loss in their own way," said Birdie. "Shutting everyone out rarely helps, though."

"Tell her and not me."

"Anyway. You'll have to find another cabin. You can't stay here."

"But we don't have any cabins left," said Dirk. "The ship is completely booked up. The cockatoo has taken a whole room for himself because we don't pay him – despite the fact that he eats three times as much as our parrots. And he's only twice as big, mind you."

"Dirk, the cockatoo weighs five times more than Herbert. He doesn't really eat much for that."

"Wait, *five times more?* What does it mean?" asked Dirk. "Is 'five times more' the same as 'five times as much'?"

"To me, it isn't," said Birdie. "Let's say I eat one delicious pineapple today, and you eat three times as much. How many pineapples do you eat?"

"Three!"

"True," said Birdie. "And tomorrow, I eat one delicious pineapple, and you eat three times *more* than I do. Then how many pineapples do you eat?"

"Still not enough."

"Yeah, well…"

"Anyway, I have no other place to sleep," Dirk pointed out.

Birdie groaned. Her good heart made a suggestion that displeased her mind. But surely there was still another option. "In sick bay, everything has to be kept sterile. Why don't you ask Hookbeak? He has more room now, after all."

"Excuse me?" said Dirk.

Birdie bit her tongue. "That was a stupid thing to say. But I'm sure he'll let you sleep in his cabin."

"He wants to be alone at the moment as well. Jay's disappearance has taken a lot out of him."

"What about your captain's office on the bridge?" asked Birdie.

"Redecorated into the cockatoo's cabin."

"Oh, I see. Hm. Hmm. Hmmm. Well, you sometimes fall asleep in your chair during the day. Wouldn't that be something for you at night, too?"

"Do you have any idea," asked Dirk, "how uncomfortable it is to spend the night in an armchair?"

"Oh my, you little hatchling! Then you'll sleep in my cabin for a few days," Birdie said, already regretting it. "I hope Popin lets you move back in soon, or I'll probably go crazy."

"And where are you going to sleep?" asked Dirk.

"In my nest, of course," she said. "You'll get a hammock next to Herbert's."

"But my hammock has to be bigger than the parrot's."

"I realise that," Birdie said, eyes rolling.

"That's really nice of you," he said as he forced his feathered body out of bed. "I always thought you didn't like me."

"Oh, that's an understatement," she said with a smile. "I can't stand you, but unfortunately, my benevolence is sometimes infinite."

"Well, I'm lucky then. The other officers are mad at me for trying to promote Fortitoo."

"That really was a crackpot idea."

"My first stupid idea on the whole voyage," claimed Dirk.

"Aha," said Birdie. "Would you rather sleep in the cargo hold?"

Chapter 12: Hatched to Survive

After breakfast, the crew flew to the planet Crownus, which had only forty-seven per cent of Earth's gravity. The dodos had high hopes that their space journey would end that day. Birdie and Dertie looked at Crownus' readings and gave the green light for a 'shore mission'.

Nala landed the Sea Cow in a world of snow and ice.

If the birds had thought the temperatures on Imleria were freezing cold, they were now proved wrong. When the cargo hatch opened, they all started shivering. The parakeets and geese went straight back into their warm nests.

The dodos denied themselves this comfort in pursuit of their dream. They saw snow as far as the eye could see. It covered the entire landscape and eight hundred birds' feet which were sunk in the wet whiteness. And promptly it began to flutter down from the sky as well.

"Snowdrops?" asked Nala.

"Snowflakes," said Goliath.

Dertie jumped around to warm herself up for her first flight test while the other dodos huddled close together ('group cuddling') to protect themselves from the icy wind like emperor penguins.

Dirk started to doubt.

"We've never been this light on a planet before," he observed. "Still, I feel a lot heavier than at Dertie's successful test in the cargo hold."

"Whether we can fly," said Birdie, "depends not only on gravitational acceleration but also on air properties. Lift plays an important role. How well does the air carry our bodies? A feather and a stone fall at the same rate in a vacuum on Earth. In normal air, a feather sinks to the ground much more slowly."

"And we have lots of feathers," noticed Dirk.

"Exactly."

"Half the gravity but far too cold to live... Is this planet really in the habitable zone?"

"Of course," said Birdie. "Otherwise we would already be dead ice pops. Under the sea ice, there are liquid water and oxygen-giving plants. For a period of three months a year, temperatures should be above ten degrees, so fruiting plants can grow on land. During that time, we would need to gather enough supplies for the long winter."

"Nine months of winter?!" asked Dirk in terror. "There's no way we can stay here. We'd better try the equator."

"We're at the equator," said Birdie.

"Quit joking."

"It's too cold to live in any other region."

"You don't say," grumbled Dirk. "We'll have to do a global warming on this ice planet if we're going to live here. That means pumping lots and lots of greenhouse gases into the atmosphere by setting fire to everything that burns."

He moved a few steps away from the warming group and ordered Dertie to carry out the first flight test.

Dertie spread her wings and took a two-metre run-up before she jumped. She came out of the snow, she saw the snow, she lay in the snow. Gravity conquered.

Thereafter, the rest of the flock attempted to fly – failing as miserably as their science officer. Dodernicus and Dodileo criticised each other for their technique and parted arguing.

When Birdie saw the astronomers, a thought flashed through her mind. She skidded and sailed on flat, trampled snow to Dodernicus, tried to slow down with her two little paddles, and fell hard on her stern.

"Hello, Dodernicus," said Birdie after she had struggled to her feet. "When I was at school, my history teacher told me that you hadn't just been a great astronomer and mathematician... I'm sorry, you *are* still alive. Is it true that you're also an experienced physician? Or was my teacher wrong about that?"

"No."

"*No?*" wondered Birdie. "Which of my questions did you answer *no* to now?"

"To your second, of course," said Dodernicus, "because it answers the first one too."

"Very clever. Would you like to assist me?"

Dodernicus nodded. "I haven't worked as a doctor for decades, but I'll be happy to help you whenever Hookbeak can do without my experience and ingenuity. Do they still use hammers and pliers for heart surgery?"

"By Jove!" cried Birdie and fell with horror into deep virgin snow. "Forget it! I'll be fine on my own. Somehow." She sighed, discouraged, and just kept lying there.

※

After lunch in the cafeteria, the officers returned to the bridge.

"On we go," said Dirk. "Wake me when we arrive at the planet Majestus."

The pilot tried to launch the ship, but it put up a fight.

"Holy hawk!" called Nala. "The propulsion thrusters are frozen! They have full power, but we're not moving."

Dirk opened his eyes again. "What? We can't fly?"

Nala shook her head. "The jet engines have to warm up first. This could take a while! According to ground control, we're stuck on Crownus *until further notice. Please inform the passengers.*"

"I don't get it," said Dirk, looking at the chief engineer. "It's much colder in outer space, isn't it? Why haven't the engines ever frozen up there?"

"Because there's no atmosphere in space," said Hookbeak. "Heat can only be lost in the form of radiation. Here on Crownus, the problem is the icy air and the high humidity. The engines aren't immune to that. I couldn't foresee that we would land in such a cold region. We've only ever heard of snow from horror stories."

"All right," Dirk said with a sigh. "How long will it take the jet engines to warm up? Your guess, Hooky?"

"I expect they'll be back to operating temperatures in five to ten hours. We can probably do the second shore mission tomorrow morning."

"Oh dear Polly," said Dirk. "We're losing half a day."

Hookbeak shrugged. "After nine weeks, half a day's delay doesn't really matter any more."

🌿

On the next four rocky planets, the dodos had no success with their flight attempts either, but since they could jump high and far, they didn't give up hope. There was only one problem: they were slowly running out of planets.

The fourth day since their departure from Berdeil had dawned, so to speak, and the Sea Cow was on its way to the sixth world.

"Good morning," said Dirk as he came onto the bridge just before 11 am. "What's our next destination?"

"Rockus," replied Nala. "Fortitoo sent me the coordinates two hours ago – when our duty began, Captain."

Dirk looked around. Of his officers, only Nala and Dertie were present.

"I had a hard time getting out of bed," he said. "Birdie's alarm clock yanked me awake in the middle of the night."

"In the middle of the night?" asked Dertie.

"Yes, five o'clock! Can you believe it? Tell me, ladies, where is Anton?"

Nala turned to him. "Nochnaya and Tomny had breakfast in the cafeteria after their shift. In other words, they raided the kitchen."

"I see," said Dirk. "That means Anton...?"

"...was ordered to clean up by angry cooks," Nala said.

Birdie came out of the lift, looking anything but happy.

"*Dirk!*" she called. "Ever since the cockatoo started using the Tube, the animal hospital has been more crowded than usual!"

Goliath was so big that there was too little room for oncoming traffic when he flew through the comm tube. The parakeets were always squeezed against the walls by the cockatoo.

"A third of our pets complain of pain," continued Birdie. "If you ask me, Goliath should only be allowed to use the lift. I'll break the news gently to him."

"Make it so, Number Two," said Dirk. He hadn't been listening.

"You're welcome to sleep on the bridge tonight if you keep ignoring me."

"Sorry, but I basically just told you that you can do what you want. In the end, you'll do it anyway!"

"Hm, you're right about that, of course," admitted Birdie. "Still, I want you to listen to me."

"All right!" said Dirk. "I'll do better. I promise!"

"Oh, a promise! We'll see if you remember it tomorrow. I'll go and find Goliath then, because I can't keep up with the extra work for long."

She hurried back to the elevator.

"Where are you going?" asked Dirk.

"Where am I going?" retorted Birdie. "Did you listen to me at all? I just told you..."

"...that you were looking for the cockatoo," said Dirk. "But his cabin is over there!" He pointed to his former office on the right side of the bridge.

"Oh," said Birdie, turning back. "Yes, you mentioned it. Sorry. I have to remember too many things as it is."

She stood outside Goliath's room and raised her foot to knock. At that moment, the cockatoo opened the door, and her foot landed in his face.

Goliath yawned. "Your loud blathering woke me up," he said sullenly.

"It's eleven," rejoined Birdie.

"I'm a parrot."

"What's that got to do with it?"

"With sleeping in?" asked Goliath. "Nothing at all."

"I don't follow," said Birdie.

"It's called *Parrot* Communication Tube System," explained Goliath. "A cockatoo is a parrot, and that's why I fly through the Tube! Lifts are stupid. *Got it?*"

"And I'm your superior," countered Birdie. "You use the lift from now on! *Got it?*"

Goliath lowered his head. "Yes, of course, sorry," he replied meekly.

"Great!" Birdie said cheerfully. "Then I can take care of my patients now."

She ran to the lift.

Dertie called the cockatoo from the other side of the bridge. "Please come over here for a minute!"

"Hold on!" he said. "First I have to do my early morning exercise."

Goliath flew a few hundred laps in circles, using the entire bridge radius. Afterwards, he landed on Dertie's panels and began to stagger.

"Whoo, I'm still spinning around," he said, feeling giddy. "It wouldn't have happened to me in the comm tube."

"Have you given any more thought to my offer?" asked the science officer.

"Dertie, for the last time, I'm not available for a parakeet-cockatoo hybrid."

"Oh, too bad," said Dertie. "I guess I'll need another hobby for our new home then."

"I hope we find that home quickly," said Goliath, "because I'm expecting a delivery there."

"Don't worry. We'll reach it today!" Dertie was convinced. "Rockus has the lowest gravity of any habitable planet, with a gravitational acceleration of 1.1 metres per square second. I'll be almost eighty-nine per cent lighter there than on Earth. I've already flown under similar conditions, shortly after we left. That was only in the cargo hold, but with updraft or tailwind, it will be even easier! Oh my Polly, tomorrow I'll be famous. Isn't that crazy? The first dodo to fly. Woohooo!"

"You really think you can do the mammoth task?" asked Goliath.

"What's a mammoth now?" inquired Dertie, rolling her eyes.

"Something similar to an elephant. You know, the huge grey animal from the restaurant that trampled the universal translator? Mammoths are relatives of him and have brown fur."

Suddenly, Dertie looked at the cockatoo through narrow eyes and smiled menacingly. "To be honest: As a biologist, I'm more interested in dissecting animals and less in the animals themselves. I've always been keen on exotic creatures in particular."

"Why are you looking at me so funny then?" asked Goliath.

"I am a scientist," replied Dertie. "So please don't take it personally. It's just my duty to find out if a cockatoo's guts look the same as our parrots'."

"*HELP!!!*" screamed Goliath and flew towards the ceiling.

"*Dertie!*" Dirk and Nala shouted before hearing their colleague giggle with delight.

Goliath sighed and dropped back onto the panels. "Very funny indeed, ha-ha."

"I thought so too," said Dertie with a grin. "But now back to the mammoths. Did they come from Earth? They'd have to be if they're related to the infants."

"Elephants," said Goliath. "Yes, mammoths originally lived on Earth until they died out there a few millennia ago because it got too hot for them. But luckily, they were also among the first animals taken by the ancient Dumpians.* It's considered extremely difficult to defeat a mammoth because it's so big."

"And that's why you call my mission a mammoth task, I get it," said Dertie. "But you will see me defy gravity! I know I will!"

The planets Rockus and Krong appeared before them. Krong presented a rare sight, having a red-blue surface due to its red rock and blue oceans. The dodos, however, didn't care about beautiful Krong as it possessed one hundred and fifty per cent of Earth's gravity.

Nala switched off the autopilot and steered the Sea Cow into Rockus' orbit.

🌿

When the birds stepped out onto Rockus, the air made them feel warm all over. Birdie pulled a thermometer from her feathers, which climbed to 45 degrees Celsius within a few seconds, even though the two suns

---

* The descendants of abducted mammoths live on Aeona, a cold world at the end of the Almond Milky Way, where they're hunted by the descendants of abducted sabre-toothed tigers.

were hidden behind thick clouds. Nala hadn't landed in a subtropical desert, but at the South Pole, in the coldest region of the planet.

The crew looked at the half-withered grassland. Goliath spotted a small fruit bush that must have felt very lonely.

Anton was breathing heavily. "Oxygen is pretty scarce here."

"Oh, well," said Goliath, "I find it sufficient."

The parrots began bouncing around gleefully as if the planet was a giant trampoline. However, as with any hobby they practised, an accident was bound to happen. Thus, Goliath collided with three parakeets in mid-air and fell awkwardly on his wing.

The dodos didn't notice the parrot crash. They watched with excitement as Science Officer Dertie prepared for take-off.

"Beat them!" shouted Anton, who had his phone camera ready to capture the historic moment for posterity.

"Who do you want me to beat up?" asked Dertie, confused.

"Gravity and drag!"

Dertie shrugged and began to concentrate fully on the mammoth task, as Goliath had called it. She would be the first dodo to fly in the sky.

This is the moment, she thought, *when I secure myself a place in the history books! My chance to make myself immortal and go down in history! Okay, there might have been some repetition in that train of thought, but never mind.*

With a mixture of running and hopping, which was only possible in low gravity, Dertie started moving. She *runhopped* along the runway, wings flapping, while the crew cheered her on.

My time to shine has come, knew Dertie. *This is the moment!*

She leapt out of the grass, flew five metres – so close to the ground, so far from the sky – and made a belly landing on the only grass-free patch for miles around.

The crowd fell silent, and cameras disappeared into feathers.

Dertie lay on the ground. "The air is much too thin for sport!" she gasped, making no effort to get up again.

The other dodos were ashamed of Dertie's disgraceful performance. But they, too, got into trouble as soon as they put one foot in front of the other.

"It..." Hookbeak said, "...makes... you... lose... your... breath."

"Apparently..." said Birdie, "we... need... more... oxygen... than parrots... because... we... are... *bigger.*"

"Back... to the ship!" shouted Dirk. "And will... someone take... Dertie with them... She fell asleep... on the ground."

The crew crept up the ramp.

Birdie and Hookbeak went to sick bay with the injured Goliath while their colleagues returned to the bridge.

🌿

"Well, that went down like a lead balloon," said Dertie when she sat back in her seat.

"You did indeed," Anton agreed.

"Fortitoo?" asked Dirk. "Give Nala the coordinates for the next planet."

"Hello there!" answered the ship's computer. "That was the last planet with low gravity."

"What? That can't be it," said Dirk.

"Yes, it can," said Fortitoo. "You didn't count? Crownus, Majestus, Stoneus, Pebblus, Boulderus and Rockus. Six planets."

"Oh no," Nala was dismayed. "Now what?"

"Oh, guys, don't take it too hard," beeped Fortitoo. "Sailors like yourselves are at home on the sea. You can turn off gravity and float through the ship if you like! Only flying is better! Oops, sorry."

Dirk sighed. "We don't want to spend our whole lives on the cosmos boat. I don't want to float through corridors. I want to fly to the clouds."

"You could still offer the galaxy an Oat Milky Way," joked Fortitoo, "and conjure up a few billion stars."

"Give it a rest," said Dirk, annoyed.

"Just sail on, seafarers! On and on towards the sunset! Now if you'll excuse me again. Beep."

Dejection spread like a plague across the bridge.

"Let's fly off," said Dertie, "somewhere into the vast, desolate void. I cannot go back to Mauritius."

"The disgrace would be far too big," concurred Anton.

Dertie repeated Fortitoo's last words and snorted contemptuously. "'Just sail on. On and on towards the sunset!'... *Pah!* Do you know where the suns really set? Forever?"

Dirk nodded. "I know what you mean. Nala, set a course for the black thingy at the centre of the Milky Way."

"You mean the black hole?" asked the pilot. "Hookbeak called it the *Beast*, didn't he?"

"Yes, exactly," said Dirk. "A black hole it was. I want to know if it's as beautiful as Hooky thinks."

"Aye, Captain."

"Let's hope for a view that lifts our spirits."

Dertie shrugged indifferently. *If the black hole doesn't lift our spirits, we'll just fly straight into it*, she thought. She put her feet up on her panels, closed her eyes and said, "*Crack!* the egg shoots 'gainst the wall. The Grim Reaper's having a ball."

🪶

Birdie gently smacked Goliath's wing with a hammer.

"A little further back," Goliath said.

Hookbeak was once again pacing thoughtfully, albeit for the first time in sick bay. "We could still try planets in other galaxies," he said.

Goliath shook his head. "First we'd have to get out of our own galax... *Ouch!* Watch it!"

"Don't be such a cry-chick," said Birdie. "Your wing is only slightly twisted, not broken."

"Space vortex!" recalled Hookbeak. "On Berdeil. The giant green parrot..."

"Kakapo," breathed Goliath, his face contorted in pain.

"...wanted to create space vortexes!" said Hookbeak. "That's how we can get to other galaxies!"

"I take it you've already forgotten what happened to your pet Jay?!" Goliath asked insensitively.

Birdie coughed. "More likely repressed. My diagnosis. I'm sorry."

"That's okay," said Hookbeak. "You are of course right. But we can still ask the highly evolved mushrooms if they see any possibility with their teleports."

Goliath could no longer follow. "Teleports? Highly evolved mushrooms? I don't understand."

"Badians. They gave us the universal translator. Anyway, one thing is certain: no dodo will want to go back to Mauritius. The mockery from our fellow citizens was unbearable even before we left."

"That's true," said Birdie. She stood on her right leg and wrapped a wound dressing around Goliath's wing with her left foot. It was a routine treatment for her, which is why her eyes wandered to the window.

"We're flying with warp," she noticed.

Hookbeak looked out the window. The stars raced past the Sea Cow.

"At top warp speed even," he said.

"But where to?" Birdie wondered. "Fortitoo, what's our new destination?"

"Ahoy!" said the computer. "It looks like we're *sailing full steam* into the black hole in the Galactic Centre! Stupid idea if you ask me. You better drop anchor real quick!"

The three birds ran to the lifts.

🌿

"One minute and five seconds to go," said Nala, "until we get caught in the Beast's pull. I'll have to brake soon."

They could see the outline of the black hole. A dark circle surrounded *and* divided in half by thick waves of light. And yet it was an optical illusion – a dodo's distorted view of the Beast because its gigantic mass warped space and time.

The black hole snatched up matter and starlight like a relentless, gluttonous monster.

The feast for the eyes stole the officers' minds.

"Wonderful," said Dertie.

"We should brake now," Dirk said enchanted.

"Yes," said Nala, her eyes reflecting the black hole. "We really should."

Braking is totally overrated, whispered a dark, attractive voice into the officers' ears. *Come to me, and all your wishes will be granted. I'll make you fly as you have always dreamt.*

No one was able to move. Thrilled, they stared at the looming doom that had cast a spell over them. A spell from which they could no longer free themselves.

⚜

At the other end of the ship, Hookbeak hurried out of the lift. He jumped over the bannister and landed one level down, next to the warp machine. But he was standing on the wrong side. Without hesitation, he threw himself onto the machine and slid across its smooth surface. When he fell down on the other side, he saw the pedal he had attached to the foot of the machine. A note stuck to the pedal:

"WarpEmergencyBrake. DON'T EVEN THINK OF IT!"

Hookbeak shrugged. He ignored his own warning and stepped on the emergency brake in the nick of time.

The ship tugged violently at spacetime, and the warp bubble burst.

The Sea Cow was hurled through space and whirled on its axis as if chasing its own tail flukes. The black hole slowed its spin but still pulled the ship closer. The crew had a paltry three hundred kilometres to escape the Beast with the old-fashioned jet engines.

On the bridge, the officers had been vigorously shaken.

"I didn't do anything!" asserted Nala. "What happened to us? I can't remember why we're here. Oh no! The warp drive isn't working any more! Someone must have applied the emergency brake. And the engine room has shut down the normal jet drive, too!"

"But why?" asked Dirk, who, like his officers, had awoken from the spell. "If I see Hooky, I will... well, I will demand an explanation."

"Guys!" said Dertie. "Aren't we a bit too close to the black hole?"

Birdie stormed out of the lift and was already giving her colleagues a dressing down from afar.

"*Are you completely out of your minds?!*" she shouted. "How can anyone be so stupid?"

Goliath had a hard time keeping up with her but argued along the same lines. "Honestly! You're not suicidal lemmings, *are you?!*"

"Er... right," said Birdie. "*We are dodos! Hatched to survive!*"

Nala now remembered. "But... but..." she stammered. "It was like in... a wonderful, beautiful dream. With the evil Beast, though."

"There's always a new dream," said Birdie. "Just because flying didn't work out doesn't mean you have to take the whole crew down with you!"

"We didn't mean to," said Dertie, trying to sort out her thoughts. "Granted, I didn't care about anything half an hour ago. I was down in the dumps. I would have called in sick tomorrow, spent a few days in the nest with my books and then everything would have been fine again. Just like everyone does to recharge their batteries. But the black hole smells very fishy to me. It sensed my sorrow and promised to make me happy. I've never believed in magic before, but that was *strange*."

"*Oh?*" asked Birdie with a sneer. "So now it's all the Bea... all the black hole's fault?"

"YES!" replied Anton and Nala.

Dirk nodded. "I felt it too."

"See?" said Dertie to the doctor.

Birdie hadn't expected this. "It's curious that you all agree with each other for once."

Come to me, said the dark, attractive voice. *Me poor black thing am all alone.*

"*Oh,*" Birdie said sadly. "The black hole is very lonely. Perhaps we should fly to it for a moment and comfort it... *What the Krubbermarf!*" she repeated Smock's expression. "The Beast wants to devour us. It's using black magic!"

"That's unscientific," said Goliath. "There's no such thing as black magic."

"Yes, yes, of course, I know," Birdie said, uncertain. "It's all imagination."

"That enchanting view," said Nala, pointing to the bridge window that showed only empty space. "Well, I mean the black hole that's about to reappear after the Sea Cow has done its round. Ha, there it is. We shouldn't look directly into it any more, only watch it from the corner of our eyes. I don't want to die!"

"Great," said Fortitoo. "I don't want to either. That's why I'd like to inform you kindly that the ship's still heading for the huge black whirlpool."

"Fortitoo," Birdie said quickly but without panic, "tell Hookbeak to turn on the propulsion thrusters."

The computer told the birds that there were no speakers in the engine room. Besides, his job description hadn't said anything "about delivering messages."

Goliath didn't think twice. With his powerful beak, he bit through his bandage and shook it off the wing. "Request permission to use the comm tube for this emergency."

"No," said Birdie. "You need to rest your wing. I'm going to the engine room."

"Without permission, then. Today I'll be the hero saving the crew from a beast," retorted Goliath and flew into the Tube.

⸎

The Sea Cow swam through the vastness of space.

Two days had passed since the birds narrowly escaped the black hole.

"How much longer to the Almond Milky Way?" asked the captain.

"About seventy thousand years," said Nala. "Whose idea was it again to fly to a black hole?"

The warp drive was out of order after the emergency brake.

"You played along!" Dirk reminded his pilot.

"Yes, I did. But a captain has a duty to act wisely and responsibly."

"Seriously?" Dirk asked in surprise, for this was news to him. "Why didn't someone tell me this before? I always thought you had to be able to make quick decisions based on your gut. *Act wisely?* Then I was totally unsuited for the job."

"Yes," said Anton. "From the very first day."

Nala and Dertie nodded silently. The pilot then took her phone out of her feathers.

"Do you want to see Dertie's big moment again?" she asked.

They gathered around Nala's seat and watched a video of Dertie's failed flight attempt on Rockus.

"It's not history-making footage," said Nala, "but at least something to laugh about."

Dertie made eyes at Anton. "Didn't you make a video too, my dickybird?"

"Yes," Anton replied shyly. "But I wasn't sure if you wanted to see it... my *little birdie.*" He put his wing on her back.

"Oh, sure," said Dertie, as she started to beam with joy. "I can laugh at myself for a change."

While the ship flew on autopilot, the entire crew met in the cargo hold. The dodos had voted by postal ballot on where they wanted to settle permanently.

"Well, Hooky, old chap," Dirk tried to kiss up to his chief engineer. "How's it going, how do you do? When will the warp drive be whole again?"

"In ten hours," said Hookbeak.

"Great, I'll give you twenty hours."

"All right, I can do it in five."

"Good boy!" rejoiced Dirk.

Anton Pavlovich announced the result of the election. "All 400 dodos were eligible to vote. 401 votes were cast. However, the result is so clear that I don't give a bat's poo about the one fraud. First, the good news: no one wants to return to Mauritius."

All the dodos cheered while over a hundred parrots booed.

"Only a small minority of parrots," said Anton. "Would the masters and mistresses please get their pets under control?"

The security officers told Anton that Nochnaya and Tomny were the ringleaders.

"It's their lack of sleep," explained Anton with a shrug. "Let's get back to the election results. 56 dodos want to settle on Berdeil and be oppressed by the king. The overwhelming majority – with 344 votes – prefers to emigrate to the hospitable mushrooms on Imleria."

Dertie ran out of the hold, screaming. "*I'm not going to jail! I'm not going to jail!*"

Anton paused for a moment until his girlfriend could no longer be heard.

"And one individual," he continued, "wrote *New Guinea in Oceania* on their ballot paper and put a cross next to it. Well, there we have our election cheat. Goliath, pets aren't eligible to vote."

"What the...?" wondered the cockatoo. "I'm not a pet! I don't belong to anyone!"

"A cockatoo is a parrot and therefore a pet," said Anton. "Even without a master."

"Hmm," pondered Goliath, "this makes no sense. Unless... I belong to myself? I'm my own pet? I can live with that. Much better than being a subject for another day. It's frightening that fifty-six dodos prefer Reggie's tyranny. You already lose your head on Berdeil if you get caught three times with a parking violation."

No one had listened to Goliath. He would now experience this all over the ship whenever he talked about Berdeil's reign of terror. "I need to find more pleasant topics of conversation."

Birdie joined Dirk and Hookbeak at the lifts.

"Imleria is a good choice," she said. "However, it's going to be hard to convince President Baycap because we hadn't turned Dertie over."

Hookbeak nodded. "She won't be welcome on Imleria."

"But," said Dirk, "to pacify Baycap, Dertie really should sacrifice herself for her crew. I'm sure she'll only go to prison for a few years." He looked at Birdie. "Besides, she's got a good lawyer and psychologist."

"Crawler," Birdie said with a smile. "Well, at least Dertie didn't kill anyone in her madness. It will still be a challenge to prove her insanity in court. Don't worry, I'll succeed somehow. Because I'm good."

Chapter 13: Soar in Peace

The Sea Cow flew to Imleria the next day after Hookbeak had repaired the warp engine in record time.

Dertie had holed up in her cabin and not shown up for duty on the bridge.

Her captain was anything but pleased about this.

"She didn't call in sick either," he said. "I guess I'll have to reprimand her then."

"Boy," marvelled Goliath, "things sure are harmonious around here. In the kingdom, an officer immediately faces a firing squad."

"Goliath, please," Nala said irritably. "We happen to hail from a progressive society. You don't always have to draw comparisons to a tyrant's empire. Captain, we'll be arriving in seven minutes."

"*Oh, great,*" said Dirk. "Now I'm supposed to conduct negotiations with Baycap on my own, or what? Where are my first mate and Number Two when I need them? Those lazybones."

Goliath cleared his throat. "They're fully behind you."

"Well, I should hope so!" said Dirk. "Otherwise it would be mutiny."

"Turn around!" said Nala.

Dirk did as he was told, and his eyes fell on his two highest officers. It did not embarrass him by any means. "Well, well! Where did you come from all of a sudden? I didn't hear you enter."

"Obviously," Birdie said, narrow-eyed and scowling.

"We just arrived," explained Hookbeak, "and didn't want to intrude on your conversation."

"In future," said Dirk, "you'll take your seats as soon as you come onto my bridge."

"Yeah, sure, Dirk," Birdie said with a grin.

"That's 'Aye, Captain.'"

"Yeah, sure, Dirk. You're only captain for six more minutes. And then I'll throw you out of my cabin."

They reached Imleria's solar system.

Hookbeak pulled his phone from his feathers. "I think it's best if we call them and briefly mention why we're here."

"Too late!" exclaimed Anton. "A welcoming party is already on its way to us!"

"That's nice," said Dirk. "I was rather expecting bombs."

"Congratulations," said Nala. "The welcoming party is four fighter jets. I'm glad you're not surprised, Captain. What do we do now? Turn around?"

In that moment, Hookbeak's phone began to ring. He looked at Birdie.

She nodded. "Put it on speaker. I'll deal with them."

This time, Baycap dispensed with any pleasantries. "What are you doing here?" he asked.

The four fighter jets circled the Sea Cow in Imleria's orbit.

"A very wonderful day to you," said Birdie. "Thank you, Mr President, for being so kind to send four fighter jets to escort us. I'm well aware that, after our sudden departure, our visit today must be a most unexpected surprise for you..."

Dirk rolled his eyes because Birdie was speaking in such a high-flown manner.

"... but we would like to give you something as a token of our appreciation. Firstly, I am pleased to inform you that I have cured Dertie of her illness and she'll never hurt a fly ag... well, okay, she is a biologist, so flies should continue to be wary of her... but she will never ever threaten a Badian again. She's so ashamed of what she tried to do to Amanita and Aguaricus that she doesn't even leave her cabin any more. She's ready to answer for her crime in your courts. That's why we're bringing her to you as a gift."

"Okay, see you in a minute," replied Baycap and hung up.

"That's all?" Birdie wondered at the curt reply.

"Maybe," said Hookbeak, "the call was billed to him as long distance again."

"He probably knows," muttered Dirk, "that prattling is much like personal hygiene: Sometimes less is more. Now we just have to drag Dertie out of her cabin."

Ten minutes later, the captain and Birdie stood outside Dertie's cabin door with three security guards.

Birdie knocked. "Yoo-hoo, we just landed. Would be nice if you got to know our new home."

"I've already seen it!" shouted Dertie. "Didn't like it much. I'm not going to jail!"

"How," asked Dirk, "do you even know you're going to prison? Maybe they've got the death penalty here."

"You're no help!" Birdie scolded him. She turned back to the door and shouted, "Oh, Dertie, don't worry about that! You were totally batty, and now you're just as crazy as an average dodo. I even got Dirk off for desecrating a tree. Just let me do my thing."

"Then do it!" shouted Dertie. "Don't forget to tell me how it went. I'll stay in my cabin until I'm acquitted."

"But I must call you to the stand, dearest. To prove that you're sane again."

"Nope. Buzz off!"

"How cured do you think the Badians will regard you if our security has to drag you into the courtroom?" asked Birdie.

"You wouldn't dare!" cried Dertie, but she didn't sound convinced.

"*Open the door!*" shouted the head of security. "*Or we'll kick it in!*"

On their second arrival at Imleria, almost no one was interested in the birds – apart from Baycap, three judges and a handful of policemen.

Anton shivered. "If only we'd remembered the weather before the postal vote."

It was pouring with rain at nine degrees Celsius.

"Nope," said Goliath. "There's no way I'm moving here. I don't mind rain, but it should be warm."

Baycap stood with the law-shrooms outside his presidential hut. They had waterproof universal translators with them.

Dertie hid behind Anton until Birdie and Hookbeak pushed the science officer forward.

"I... I..." stammered Dertie. "I don't even know where to begin. I can't believe what a bad dodo I've been. After three hours..."

"Ahem!" Birdie cleared her throat.

"...After three weeks of therapy, I didn't recognise myself any more. I hate the dodo I was before. I hope the toadstools..."

"Ahem!"

"...I mean Aguaricus and Ama... Anit... the Chief of Staff are doing well," said Dertie, bowing deeply to Baycap. "I turn myself in of my own *free* will."

Baycap looked to the judges, three female mushrooms in black robes, who turned, bumped their shroom heads together and conferred.

"In a few seconds," said Baycap, "the verdict and Dertie's sentence will be announced."

"What the..." began Dertie in horror. She looked at her lawyer with despair.

"What do you mean?!" asked Birdie. "How can the verdict and sentence be announced already? Dertie pleads insanity by reason of serious mental illness!"

"Now don't get carried away!" whispered Dertie.

"We were expecting a trial!" continued Birdie. "Come to think of it, a hearing is all I'll need!"

"She confessed," said Baycap. "The fact that she shows remorse and has undergone therapy will be taken into account by the judges. Perhaps."

"Oh, great," muttered Dertie.

The judges turned back to Baycap and the birds.

"Have the honourable judges reached a verdict?" asked Baycap.

"Not yet," replied the presiding judge. "We lack a psychological report of the accused and proof of successful treatment. We need to interview her therapist, otherwise there are no mitigating circumstances."

Birdie took a step forward. "I'm Dertie's psychologist."

"And also her lawyer?" wondered the judge. "That's... convenient. Come with us, then."

"Take my living room for the interview," said Baycap.

Birdie followed the judges into the hut.

The parrots stood in the clearing. They kept a close eye on their feeders, except Herbert, whose mistress had disappeared when he had glanced up at the grey sky for just a second.

"And what happens now?" asked Popin.

"Nothing," answered Herbert. "We have to wait. In the cold rain."

"Well, that's nothing new," Popin said. "What's it like with two dodos in *your* cabin?"

"Exhausting. Do you want Dirk back?" Herbert asked hopefully.

"No. Not yet. But soon."

Birdie and the judges returned after half an hour. To the dodos' surprise, Amanita and Aguaricus followed them.

"In light of the confession," said the presiding judge, "as well as the credible remorse of the defendant, Dertie Dodo, and taking into account the statements of her treating therapist, boss and family doctor, Dr Birdex Pert, who is also an excellent lawyer, there will... will... damn it, fungus goofus, now you've forgotten the only important part of the sentence."

"Every time," said the other judges groaning.

The presiding judge coughed and began again. "No prison sentence will be imposed. However, there can be no acquittal by reason of insanity. Dertie Dodo wasn't treated by a local therapist. Therefore, her illness and full recovery aren't proven beyond reasonable doubt."

Dertie rolled her eyes. *Get to the point*, she thought.

"Dertie Dodo," continued the judge, "will go to the Badian City University Hospital every tenth day, from sunrise to sunset, for her treatment. Either until the end of her life or until it is confirmed by the head of the clinic that she poses no danger to the Badian population. Furthermore, Dertie Dodo has a criminal record as of today and must therefore remain resident on Imleria for the rest of her life. She is only allowed to leave the planet for a maximum of fifty days per year."

"Dear dodos," said Baycap, "for your information, a year on Imleria is four hundred and eleven days long."

Dertie felt hoodwinked. "Being trapped on the same planet clearly is a prison sentence," she muttered.

Hookbeak raised an eyebrow. "You spent the first twenty-three years of your life on only one planet. Won't be much of a change then."

Anton stroked Dertie and comforted her with his words, "Compared to Mauritius, this planet is a huge home."

"The verdict," concluded the presiding judge, "is already final because we don't allow appeals or reviews. We wish everyone a great afternoon."

The judges climbed into their sports cars and raced into the woods.

Nala looked after the speedsters. "Not bad."

Dertie took a step towards Amanita and Aguaricus. Everyone else held their breath, startled.

"I also want to apologise to you personally," said Dertie. "I had only seen mushrooms in you and not the sentient and intelligent individuals you really are. I beg your forgiveness. I was indeed insane – even to a degree that is unusual for a dodo." She bowed her head.

"Thank you for your words," said Amanita. "In the past, we also had madshrooms and criminals who were convinced that the end justifies any means. I'm glad you know better now."

"I'm glad too," said Aguaricus.

"Great!" exclaimed Dirk happily. "Then it's all settled!"

Birdie sighed. "Dirk, you've ruined the moment," she said. "*Oh, Baycap?*"

The mushroom president turned to her. "Yes, Birdie?"

"Now that Dertie has to live on Imleria, we'd like to keep her company. We've grown into a family after our long journey."

"I have no problem with that, but you must abide by our laws if you wish to live in our forests or Badian City."

"To be honest," said Birdie, "I was thinking more of an unpopulated area near the equator. Also, that way we won't be in your feathers."

Baycap looked surprised. "You want to live somewhere in the vast wasteland?" he asked, scratching his cap-shaped head.

"Hmm, I have a feeling we mean different things by the term *wasteland*." Birdie looked at Baycap's universal translator with suspicion.

"That's what we call the tropics and subtropics," said Baycap. "In those regions, it's too hot for us. All you find there are bleak rainforests, palm trees and sandy beaches."

"Whoopee!" shouted Birdie. "Let's go to the tropics!"

"Many dangerous insects live right in the tropics. You might not survive their stings. How'd you like a subtropical climate instead?"

"Yes, that's even better," said Birdie, "because there should be less rain than in rainforests."

"But chilly nights!" objected Dirk.

Hookbeak could live with that. "We can sleep on the warm ship. Then we don't need to build huts."

"But you like building so much," said Dirk.

"I won't get bored," said Hookbeak. "I'll take care of the fusion reactor, and I'll also attach solar cells to the ship's hull. It should provide electricity for us and the next generations for ten thousand years."

"All right, agreed," said Dirk. He turned to the mushroom president. "Thank you for letting us hang out on Imleria."

"And thank you for coming back with Dertie," said Baycap. "However, we still have one condition. You have to take your crabs with you!"

"What crabs?" asked Birdie.

"The brown gang of troublemakers. We took them to the Underworld so they wouldn't freeze to death. They live by the Underworld lake and steal scientific instruments all the time."

The dodos hadn't even noticed that the palm thieves had disappeared from the ship.

Birdie, who loved all creatures, great and small, was also the dodo who had missed the crabs the least. Naturally, she didn't like the idea of getting them back, but since she had no choice, she nodded weakly.

Baycap clapped his hands. "Great. Then go see if you like the place at the following coordinates: 20 degrees south and 57 degrees east. And only eat the *red* fruits. They're made for dreamers. The green fruits are poisonous!"

"Got it," said Dirk.

"We'll catch the crabs and bring them up to your ship," said Baycap.

"Hmm, all right," Dirk replied without enthusiasm.

All officers were on the bridge. They stared at a calm ocean.

"A year has four hundred and eleven days on this planet?" Nala asked, groaning. "Then I'll have to wait even longer for my next birthday."

"We should keep our Earth calendar," suggested Anton. "As a tradition. And we could create another calendar for the Imlerian year."

"Good idea!" said Dertie. "That way, we can celebrate New Year twice!"

"Well," said Hookbeak, "a day on Imleria is seven minutes longer than on Earth. I'll just build a clock that shows the date and time of both worlds. But I'll likely need two hours for that."

"I'll even give you four hours!" said Dirk.

"All right, I can do it in one."

"Guys, look!" shouted Nala. "We're reaching the coordinates. There's indeed land in sight!"

Dirk's eyes widened. "It's only an island," he whined. "Barely bigger than Mauritius."

"Still," said Dertie, "this island I have to share with far fewer dodos! Just with you 398 odd birds! And Anton."

The entire coast of the island was covered with fine yellow grains of sand, and the captain wanted to feel them under his feet as soon as possible. He told Nala to bury the Sea Cow in the sand, but she found his choice of words more than unfortunate. Besides, she had already realised that the coastal strip was too narrow for the ship. In the end, she landed directly behind the sandy beach and uprooted twelve palm trees.

Dirk was the first to step on his new home. He watched the high waves breaking and foaming off the coast before they rolled in and out on the beach.

"Looks like Mauritius!" exclaimed Hookbeak, who came walking down the ramp with Birdie.

Birdie breathed in deeply. "Ah, the sea smells like home. What do we call the island? New Mauritius? Mauritius 2.0? Foreign Planet Mauritius? Or rather *Mauritius, Imleria,* as opposed to *Mauritius, Earth*?"

"I'd prefer a name," said Dirk, "that doesn't remind us of the losers we left behind on Mauritius."

"Well, we're *dodos*," observed Hookbeak. "And the island is our *new land*. Why don't we call it *New Dodoland?*"

What a stupid name for my island, thought Dirk, screwing up his beak in distaste.

"I'm all for it!" said Birdie, and Dirk had to admit defeat.

The dodos dug their phones out of their feathers and took selfies with the local green palm trees. They were pleased to note that on New Dodoland, as on the whole of Imleria, there were no other birds, who could have mocked their inability to fly.

The parakeets and geese explored the island from the air, while the palm thieves stole Birdie's music collection and buried it in the sand.

After an hour on New Dodoland, hundreds of dodos lay on the beach in the sun. As they all looked the same from a distance, it was difficult to find the one you were looking for. Hookbeak only recognised Dertie and Anton because they were nestled together in the sand.

"Hey, lovebirds," said Hookbeak. "Have you seen my scientific advisers? I'd like them to take a look at my draft calendar."

"They're on beach holiday too," said Anton, pointing to two small dots more than a hundred yards away.

Once again, Dodernicus and Dodileo Dodilei had been the first to settle into their deckchairs in the sun.

"This is the way to live," said Dodernicus, sipping Goliath's new cocktail invention. The cockatoo had named the drink somewhat unimaginatively 'Pineapple-Rum-Coconut-Cream Mix'.

"You bet," confirmed Dodileo, also holding a cocktail glass in his wing. "That's a nice twilight for you, old guy."

Beneath the palms grew hundreds of fruit bushes, their red fruit resembling peaches.

Dirk sat between the Sea Cow and a palm tree that Nala had spared during the landing. He looked back on the journey and became happy and sad at the same time. It was a bittersweet feeling. The adventure had freed him from his dreary daily routine, but the mission had failed. Birdie had said there was always a new dream. Dirk wasn't sure if that was true for him. But he would keep his eyes open.

He hoped that the fruit on this island would be delicious. Yes, this was his next little dream, and in a moment, he would know if it came true. He reached with his foot to a bush and picked a fruit that gleamed in the sunlight. He sniffed it, found its scent pleasantly sweet and devoured it in three bites.

Soon after, he felt surprisingly light. Ten times lighter than on Rockus. He spread his wings and flew to a white cloud that crept lonely along the blue sky.

What a feeling! This was how he'd dreamt it would be! Free as a bird, he whizzed through the cloud. His wings were as small as ever, but this time, he didn't lose height. And he didn't wake up either.

"Whoa, dude, I can fly?!" he asked in amazement because his greatest wish had come true after all. He let the wind carry him to the beach, calling out to the other dodos, "The red fruit! Boy, this stuff is awesome, dudes! I can fly!"

"Uh, Captain?" said Dertie with bemusement and concern.

Anton held Dirk by his wing so he wouldn't run into the sea.

Dirk began to stumble. "*Let go of me, or we'll crash!*" he shouted. "*Uh-oh, too late!*"

He fell forward at the very moment when the tail end of a wave approached. His head landed in the seawater and the illusion was over.

"What the heck?" asked Dirk. "The red fruit made me fly!"

"You didn't fly," said Dertie.

Wrinkles formed on Dirk's forehead. "You're kidding?"

Anton shook his head.

"But I felt it with all my senses," Dirk said. "The airstream, the colder air at altitude, everything seemed so real. Come along to the fruit bushes and try it yourself."

Dertie and Anton ate a red fruit and instantly felt the wind beneath their wings.

Not five minutes had passed before all dodos were nibbling on the fruit. They *flew* over the beach and the palm jungle that stretched out beyond.

When the parrots returned from their excursion, they didn't have the slightest idea what was going on.

Herbert sat down in front of Birdie.

"Get out of the way!" Birdie ordered her pet. "You're in my flight path."

"Birdie? What's wrong with you?" he asked as his mistress ran past him, wings flapping wildly.

Goliath flew in from his beach bar and explained to Herbert what had happened.

"The red fruit causes hallucinations in the dodos."

"Hallu-what?" asked Herbert.

"Sensory illusions," said Goliath. "The dodos are imagining things. They think they can fly. Their eyes only see what they want to see. And not just that. They can hear the airstream and feel it on their feathers. The fruit deceives all their senses. In other words, the dodos are hallucinating."

"Oh my goodness," said Herbert. "And what do we do about it? How do we stop them from eating the fruit?"

"We don't. Not at all," replied Goliath. "Think about it. This is what your feeders have been dreaming of. When they believe the illusions are real, they're happy."

Herbert grew thoughtful but agreed.

"Birdie always says happiness is a state of mind," he recalled. "Now I understand what she means. By the way, the fruit bushes are all over the island. I've eaten a red fruit myself, as have all the parrots. It contains a lot of sugar, but no poison, I think. Why don't we get illusions?"

"I wonder the same thing," said Goliath. "I guess the fruit sugar doesn't go to our heads because we don't have dreams that are beyond our reach."

Nala celebrated her eighteenth birthday that same evening, almost three weeks late. Thanks to the fruit, it turned out to be a mixture of beach and cloud party.

The pilot greeted Dirk exuberantly. "The great visionary has finally arrived!" she exclaimed to her guests. "Hurray for Dirk!"

When the cheers had died down, Hookbeak joined his old school friend.

"I'm curious, Dirk. Do the hallucinations feel better than your dreams of flying?"

"Absolutely, Hooky," said Dirk. "It seems more real than reality, don't you think? Of course the best thing is that the dream doesn't turn into a nightmare. And it's healthier, too. Without the crash, my blood pressure doesn't rise as much."

Gusu, the time traveller from Dalmatia, arrived during the party in her spacetime ship. Goliath noticed that her black hair had turned grey at the temples. She delivered a small flying saucer to the cockatoo and drank cocktail after cocktail.

"I didn't know," said Gusu, "they had piña coladas in this time. I thought the drink wouldn't be invented for another six hundred years."

"Excuse me? Peena-kolada?" asked Goliath.

"Piña colada. What do you call this cocktail?"

"Pineapple-Rum-Coconut-Cream Mix."

"Yeah... nah," Gusu said. "Piña colada sounds better. Where did you get the recipe?"

"It came to me in a little daydream," said Goliath, "when I still thought the dodos were going to hire me as a waiter."

"Hmm," said Gusu with a shrug, draining her fifth cocktail glass. "Thousands of worlds have created warp drives independently from each other. So it's not that unlikely that the same drink would be invented on two worlds. *Hmmm*. Actually, piña coladas and cockatoos originated on the same world. Anyway. This could all work out for the best for you. Offer the cocktail to anyone who wishes you harm. You'll gain allies that way. Now then..." She lifted the cockatoo into her arms and hugged him. "...time to say goodbye."

"Why are you saying goodbye to me?" asked Goliath. "Will we never meet again?"

"Probably not," she said, "but we both have spacetime ships, so never say never."

After Gusu flew away, Goliath pushed his ship up the Sea Cow's ramp.

Suddenly, a large dodo shadow loomed over his small parrot shadow. The cockatoo quickly turned around.

Birdie scowled and pointed at his saucer.

"What's that?" she asked in her lawyerly interrogative tone. "Your one-bird time ship?"

"My one-cockatoo *space*ship," asserted Goliath. "You know. Just for short trips."

"Aha," she said suspiciously. "Don't change history, will you?"

"You'd never know, would you?"

"Oh, believe me, a vet learns everything from her patients."

Goliath grinned. "Like how your patients have played dumb their whole lives? You wouldn't have guessed that in a hundred years."

🌿

On the fifth day, Dirk once again 'flew' through the palm forest of New Dodoland. The last 96 hours had been the happiest of his life.

On his flight back to the beach, he got hungry due to bad management of food supplies for the journey. However, he could only find green fruit at the landing site.

It's probably not quite ripe yet, he thought and bit into a green fruit because he hadn't listened to Baycap.

Dirk yawned and became sleepy. "That's crazy, it's all getting so quiet," he said. His body began to relax, and he bit into the fruit once again. Time seemed to stand still; his heartbeat slowed. He kept walking through the palm jungle until his muscles went limp. The rest of the green fruit fell out of his wing and he crawled under a palm tree for his afternoon nap.

"Tomorrow starts our new calendar," said Hookbeak. "Fortitoo told me not to be so modest, so I've named it *Hookbeak's Imlerian Calendar*. But we can leave my name out if it seems too boastful."

"Oh, nonsense," said Birdie. "It's a good name. Credit where credit is due. I'm going on a trip. See you later." She gobbled a red fruit and spread her wings.

"Bye-bye, Birdie. I'll show Dirk our calendar."

Hookbeak walked up and down the beach for two hours in search of Dirk. He asked the sunbathing dodos if anyone had seen the captain.

Afterwards, he went on the Sea Cow and knocked on Birdie's cabin, where Dirk still lived.

Eventually, he knocked on Popin's door.

"I can't find him anywhere," Hookbeak said.

"Maybe," said Popin, "he went for a walk on the island."

"Possibly. But it's not like him to be gone so long. The island is big. I'll ask Goliath to search for Dirk from the air."

Popin had a sinking feeling. "I'll help Goliath look," she said.

They found the cockatoo behind a pile of fruit crates – his beach bar.

Popin's concern for Dirk grew with every second. Since arriving on New Dodoland, she had stayed in her cabin. Even now, it escaped her notice that the dodos were running around like odd ducks because they had fledged.

"It will be dark soon," said Popin. "We must hurry while we can still see everything."

"Let's go then," said Goliath. "Dirk can't have wandered more than six miles."

"I'll wait on the beach," said Hookbeak, "in case he shows up here."

Goliath and Popin flew low through the palm trees.

They spotted Dirk less than a mile from the beach and landed on his belly.

"Do you think he's...?" began Popin, horrified. "Is he still breathing?"

"I don't know," replied Goliath.

They tried to shake him awake. Without success.

"I think he looks happy and peaceful," said Goliath. "He's probably just sleeping. Stay with him, I'll go get help."

After forty minutes, the cockatoo returned with Birdie.

Birdie laughed when she saw Dirk under the palm tree.

"That sleepyhead," she said. "He is asleep, isn't he?"

"You're the doctor," said Goliath.

"Wait, what? Oh, that's right. But, well, I'm flying right now, so we'd better make an appointment at my ship's medical practice."

"Please land," Goliath said with all the patience he could muster.

"Okay," said Birdie. "Just a minute... just a sec... I'm landing... HEY, ARE YOU FREAKING BLIND?! USE YOUR EYES AND STAY THE HECK OUT OF MY FLIGHT PATH! YOU MUST HAVE WON YOUR PILOT'S LICENSE IN THE LOTTERY, YOU MORON!"

Popin looked up from Dirk and turned to Goliath. "Who is Birdie talking to?"

"To a dodo crossing her flight path," explained Goliath.

"But dodos can't fly," said Popin. "She's standing right next to us!"

"At the moment, all dodos are off their rocker. It's a long story. You missed some stuff in your cabin. *Oh, Birdie?* Are you on the ground yet?"

"Don't distract me, cockatoo!" she retorted. "You can see I'm on approach to land. Oh, darn... HELP!!!"

"I think she's got a screw loose," said Popin as she watched the gentle flaps of her doctor's wings.

Goliath nodded. "The illusion doesn't seem to make the dodos any smarter," he said, vastly understating the matter.

"Phew!" Birdie breathed in relief. "So, here I am. A bit of a bumpy landing, but oh well. Only practice makes perfect."

"Then examine Dirk, please," said Goliath.

"Do I have to touch him for that?" asked Birdie.

"I'm no expert, but YES! YOU HAVE TO!"

"Stay calm, Goliath," she said, hurt. "No need to get loud right away."

The cockatoo sighed and looked at the sunset. *If only I had stayed in the kingdom*, he thought. *Life as a waiter had been easier.*

Birdie rested her head on Dirk's chest. The more seconds passed, the more her expression darkened.

"Oh sh... sh... sh... sugar!" she said, shocked. "He's not breathing, and I can't hear his heart beating."

She saw traces of the green fruit in his beak. The poisonous fruit Baycap had warned the dodos about.

Popin pleaded with the doctor. "Do something!"

"He'll be all right, won't he?" asked Goliath.

Birdie shook her head as tears rolled from her beak.

Dodos wasted no time planning funerals. The reason was likely the hot climate. Or perhaps it was because of their belief that after death, a dodo's soul would present itself to the Loony Polly. The supreme goddess either raises her wing and the dodo is allowed to fly to paradise or lowers it and the soul has to walk another round of life in a fresh body.

By now it was deep in the night but it seemed as if dusk had just begun. The birds on New Dodoland witnessed a natural spectacle that only happens once every thirteen years: the full moons Satluna and Lunellite were in the sky at the same time. Every cloud, no matter how small, was visible to the naked eye because of the moonlight. Sadly, no one could enjoy the view at the moment.

The funeral service for Dirk began four hours after Popin and Goliath had found him.

He was lying in a black nest on the beach and looked happy – almost as if he was only sleeping.

In his honour, all dodos were physically present, even though most of them were mentally whooshing through the clouds. Several dozen parrots also appeared – including Herbert and Papagayo, who tried in vain to comfort Popin.

All officers were deeply shocked.

Hookbeak was unable to deliver the eulogy, so Birdie took on the hard task.

"Dirk was an extraordinary dodo," said Birdie. "On Mauritius, they called him a freak because he wanted to realise his dream of flying on a distant planet. But thanks to his determination, we can actually feel the wind on our wings today. Who needs reality when the illusion feels much more real. Dirk has... Excuse me, the effect is wearing off and I don't want to crash." She bit into a red fruit and resumed her speech while munching noisily. "Dirk believed there was a way. After the failure on Rockus, his disappointment was merely short-lived... Well, okay, he almost led us to our black doom at the Galactic Centre, but it's to his credit that we embarked on this journey at all. For that, we shall be eternally grateful to him. We will build a monument to Dirk and honour him as the founding father of our society on New Dodoland. And I'm sure he would be very pleased that we're holding his funeral service in the middle of the clouds."

Birdie paused briefly and bit into the fruit again before continuing.

"Today we are sad," she said. "Sad because Dirk was only able to live his dream for a few days. But starting tomorrow, let us at least rejoice that he spent the happiest days of his life at the end."

Before Birdie closed her speech, she issued a warning to her fellow dodos.

"Please remember: *don't take poison! Wings off the green fruit!* Thank you. And now I wish you all a pleasant flight home. Please don't all shove out of the clouds at the same time. Happy landing and good night."

In the early morning, Popin was still sitting on the beach with her friends Herbert and Papagayo. They were watching the sun rise.

"I'm sorry about Jay and Dirk," Papagayo said.

"Yes, I know," said Popin and sighed. "I think Jay's happy wherever he is. And I sincerely hope Dirk doesn't embarrass himself in paradise in front of Loony Polly."

"Shall we take a look at the island?" asked Herbert. "The three of us? Popin, you haven't even seen New Parrotland yet."

"It's a beautiful place," said Papagayo.

"I don't feel like it," said Popin, "but please ask me again in a few days."

Popin, Papagayo and Herbert admired the sun's reflection on the sea. That's when they saw that the nine palm thieves had built a raft and wanted to leave the island, but when faced with the might of the waves, the crabs failed miserably.

Soon, more parakeets joined the three friends while the dodos started their morning exercise and 'flew' around the island.

Not even three months had passed since the birds had left Earth. In retrospect, the bird migration turned out to be a wise decision as Mauritius was being overrun by ducks right now. The mallards were European tourists who took all the beach spots away from the dodos.

On Imleria, the *Year of the Mean Ducks* had ended much earlier than expected. Since midnight, the dodos and parrots were living according to Hookbeak's calendar.

It was the *Year of the Lucky Bird*.

It was pitch black when he awoke. He could barely breathe, not even gasp for air. And he was trapped.

This can't be the end, he thought.

He was completely covered in soil. He tried to move but only bumped his head on a large stone. He cursed in his mind. Then he pecked his beak into the soil until he ran out of his last oxygen. With the last of his strength, he pushed his head out of the ground.

Fresh air rushed through his lungs as he gazed at a beautiful gravestone. His gravestone.

He had no time to mourn himself because eight hallucinating dodos ran past him as a swarm. They didn't even stir the air with their wild wing beats.

"Hey, stop right there!" shouted Dirk, who was still up to his neck in his grave. "Which joker buried me?!"

He was as alive as a dodo could be.

And One Last Tweet…

In a vegetable field, a blue boy was playing with his new bird, which he had found stunned in a well.

"Come on, Wilbur," said the boy, "I'll throw a little stick in the air, and you'll catch it!"

"I still doubt that my name is *Wilbur*," said the bird in disgust. "But I can't be sure." He had lost his memory.

"I can call you something else," said the boy. "You have a hooked beak like the cockatoos. Maybe I'll call you Hookbeak. The cockatoos work in a shopping centre in space. Have you ever been to space?"

"Cockatoos in space? Ha ha," said the bird. "Wait a minute. Why do I know what a cockatoo looks like? And why do I know what a *Hookbeak* looks like?"

"I don't know, Wilbur," said the boy. "There are no cockatoos here. They live on the royal space station."

"Ah… yes! I've been there before," recalled the bird. "And my name is the second half of a word or animal name. Perhaps 'bat' from 'fruit bat'? Or 'cow' from 'sea cow'? No. Something more like 'boy' from 'glamour boy'? No. Yes. Oh, I'm so close to solving the mystery!"

"Mum's waving us into the house," said the boy. "Come, we're having lunch by the fireplace."

The bird suddenly beamed with joy.

"My home is where the hearth is," said Jay and perched on the boy's shoulder.

No squirrels were harmed in the making of this book.
(Page 87)

Printed in Great Britain
by Amazon